C000088478

HEADING HOME TO LAVENDER COTTAGE

ALISON SHERLOCK

Boldwood

First published in Great Britain in 2023 by Boldwood Books Ltd.

Copyright © Alison Sherlock, 2023

Cover Design by Alice Moore Design

Cover photography: Shutterstock

The moral right of Alison Sherlock to be identified as the author of this work has been asserted in accordance with the Copyright, Designs and Patents Act 1988.

All rights reserved. No part of this book may be reproduced in any form or by any electronic or mechanical means, including information storage and retrieval systems, without written permission from the author, except for the use of brief quotations in a book review.

This book is a work of fiction and, except in the case of historical fact, any resemblance to actual persons, living or dead, is purely coincidental.

Every effort has been made to obtain the necessary permissions with reference to copyright material, both illustrative and quoted. We apologise for any omissions in this respect and will be pleased to make the appropriate acknowledgements in any future edition.

A CIP catalogue record for this book is available from the British Library.

Paperback ISBN 978-1-80426-434-8

Large Print ISBN 978-1-80426-430-0

Hardback ISBN 978-1-80426-429-4

Ebook ISBN 978-1-80426-427-0

Kindle ISBN 978-1-80426-428-7

Audio CD ISBN 978-1-80426-435-5

MP3 CD ISBN 978-1-80426-432-4

Digital audio download ISBN 978-1-80426-426-3

Boldwood Books Ltd
23 Bowerdean Street
London SW6 3TN
www.boldwoodbooks.com

To Auntie Margaret. With much love x

According to the proverb, with age comes wisdom. Which left Harriet Colgan wondering why, at the age of thirty, she had forgotten to fill her car with petrol and was now sitting on a dark country lane in a broken-down vehicle.

She knew why she'd forgotten, of course. Having spent most of a frantic day packing up her car with nearly everything she owned, desperate to get to her aunt and uncle's cottage far away in Cranfield before nightfall, she had pushed on all the way from London without stopping. So, there she was, only two miles from her destination and stranded.

Well, not exactly stranded, she reminded herself. She had sent a text to Libby, one of her best friends who lived in Cranfield, asking her to come out and rescue her. The trouble was that the signal in the middle of the English countryside was decidedly hit and miss, and Libby hadn't replied yet.

Not to worry, thought Harriet, taking a calming breath. She would, as always, remain optimistic. A positive mental attitude meant everything to her. After all, although she was stuck, she was now able to look out at the beautiful starry March sky through her windscreen. She should be thankful that it was so clear and cold that night, thereby giving her a great view.

Actually, it was very cold, she realised with a shiver. She pulled a nearby sweatshirt over her head before checking her reflection in the mirror. She winced at the silhouette in the darkness. As anticipated, her long red hair was as wild and wavy as ever. No matter how many times she had tried to straighten it, her hair always kinked almost immediately afterwards, so she had given up trying. Although, the state of her hair was really the least of her worries right now.

Hoping for some kind of miracle by way of positive thinking, she turned the key in the ignition once more, but the engine merely gave her a pitiful sigh in response and refused to start up.

She rubbed her forehead where a headache threatened to come rushing in. Despite all of her determined positivity, it was a bad end to a spectacularly awful week.

The previous day, the beauty therapy salon in London that she had owned and managed had closed after three years. The exclusive address in Knightsbridge had provided droves of satisfied clientele, but it was the business figures that had let her down. The SW1 postcode came with way too high a rent for Harriet to cope with. She had tried to make the figures work in her favour by taking on even more customers over the past six months, working late into each and every evening, but it had been to no avail.

As the lease had been due to expire in the next few days, she had decided with a heavy heart to give up the business before she was saddled with ever-increasing amounts of debt. As it was, she had nothing but a bank balance in the red to show for all the long days of hard work tending to the whims of the demanding clientele she had catered for.

Harriet knew that her skills as a beauty therapist were good, but she should never have let her parents persuade her to set up a business in such an expensive area. If only she had been brave enough to say no at the very beginning and thus save herself all the current heartache. But, as always, Harriet had put on a brave front and found herself agreeing to run things their way, even though they were currently in the Caribbean setting up yet another law practice, this time in the tax haven of Bermuda. Her older siblings were in Paraguay and Australia, both also specialising in law with their own successful practices.

Harriet, born ten years after her brother and sister, was a red-headed anomaly in a family of high-achieving brunettes. She didn't excel at any kind of academic profession, even though she had tried many times over, every attempt ending in failure. Even her looks were different from the rest of the family. They all had straight, manageable hair and skin that tanned easily. Harriet had pale skin and freckles with wild, long, wavy hair.

Sent to an extremely expensive all-girls boarding school at the age of ten, she had continued to feel like an outsider, especially when frequently reminded by the teachers how her sister had excelled at most subjects when she had been there a decade previously. It hadn't helped Harriet's self-esteem that her dyslexia had been undiagnosed until she had been well into her teenage years, by which time any confidence in her academic abilities had completely disappeared.

However, whenever she had tried to tell her parents just how miserable she was feeling, they had dismissed her unhappiness as teenage grumbles. She always remembered the most brutal conversation of all with her mother, soon after her first term at senior school had begun.

'You'll find life very difficult if you're going to see the negativity in everything,' her mum had snapped, interrupting her daughter's moaning. 'For goodness sake, keep a stiff upper lip and carry on. Remember the family name. We have a reputation to uphold.'

So, Harriet did as she was told. She suppressed her unhappiness and, in turn, most of her emotions, instead putting on a brave face. The trouble was that she had continued to do so ever since, and now she wasn't sure she could be true even to herself any more.

Only in the tiny village of Cranfield had she ever felt as if she could behave truly like herself. With her parents abroad most of the time for work and her siblings already having left home to start studying for their law degrees, Harriet normally went to stay with her Aunt May and Uncle Fred for the school holidays. In complete contrast to her own parents, her aunt and uncle had never put any pressure on Harriet, merely giving her the love and support which she so desperately craved, having received almost no affection from her parents.

Uncle Fred had continued to encourage his niece to keep following her dreams, even when her business in London seemed doomed from the outset.

'So, your business might fail,' he had told Harriet only six months ago when she had confessed how worried she was about it. 'It happens, love. I know it's rubbish, but you'll be just fine. You've got a good heart, and that's all that matters. Just remember how much you're loved and always will be. That's the important thing.'

It had been the last conversation that they had ever had.

One day later, her uncle had passed away. The official reason had been listed as a heart attack, but Harriet knew it was a broken heart after the loss of his dear wife one year previously.

Equally broken-hearted six months on from that dreadful day, Harriet was still struggling without her beloved aunt and uncle in her life. But she was still carrying on, putting a brave face on her grief, even when her best friends pushed her to be open and honest with them.

Sitting in the darkness of her car, Harriet shook her head at herself. Why did she always have to put on a show and be so cheerful when really, she just wanted to wail and wallow that life was sometimes just too hard, too unfair? It was ridiculous.

But the positive attitude she had tried to live by since her childhood had saved her from much heartache, and it was a hard habit to break.

Libby and Flora mocked her gently for it. Her best friends had tried over and over to encourage her to be honest and lose the protective shell she had worn for so long. But it had gotten her this far, hadn't it?

At least their bond of friendship was unbreakable. There, in the tiny village where there weren't too many other children of a similar age, she had bonded quickly with Flora and Libby during the school holidays, both of whom had grown up in Cranfield.

Twenty years on, they were still as close a group of friends as ever, despite Harriet trying and failing to make her beauty salon business a success far away in London and Libby often absent with her job as a flight attendant. Only Flora, struggling to take care of the family farm, had remained in Cranfield full-time.

Harriet missed her friends terribly, although they tried to meet up as often as possible whenever she returned to Cranfield during the holidays. She would have loved to have lived closer, but glamorous beauty salons were hard to come by in the middle of the quiet English countryside. And business was the most important thing in life, as her father constantly reminded her.

She had yet to work up the courage to tell her parents of her decision to close down the beauty salon. She had last seen them at Uncle Fred's funeral, a sad, blustery, autumnal day six months ago. They had swiftly returned to the warmth of the Caribbean soon afterwards, leaving her to fend for herself once more.

She glanced over at the passenger seat, piled high with bags of clothes and shoes. On the back seat and in the car boot was everything else. She had kept most of her beauty therapy items but had

had to leave all the larger technical equipment behind in a small storage unit, intending to put them up for sale at a later date.

Harriet had told her friends that she was fine about the failure of the business, but she really wasn't. It had felt like the final straw after the loss of her aunt and uncle, and she was struggling to find any positivity at all these days.

Suddenly overcome with grief, she felt the tears begin to roll down her cheeks. She had managed to keep them mostly at bay for six months, but now she couldn't stop crying. Returning to Cranfield to sell up her aunt and uncle's cottage was hard enough. After all, if she hadn't been saddled with the business debts, she wouldn't have to sell Lavender Cottage but could live there permanently, as had been her dream for so long. But she had no savings to pay off the debts, so the cottage would have to be sold.

The worst part was knowing that her aunt and uncle wouldn't both be waiting for her on the doorstep when she arrived.

She shook her head and willed them to go away, but the tears continued to fall.

She grabbed her mobile from the passenger seat, turned it over, and stared at the back cover. There, pressed inside the clear case, was a sprig of lavender. She instantly felt a little calmer and began to feel comforted. Lavender had always had that effect on her.

During her many stays in Cranfield, the view out of her bedroom window had always been the same. At the end of the back garden was the old railway line, which hadn't been in use for many years. Across from the line, there was a long path that led to the nearby village of Cranbridge.

On either side of the path were fields. The ones to the right belonged to her best friend Flora's family farm. But on the other side, there were two fields full of the lavender plants that Uncle Fred had planted many years ago. The fields had long been left to run wild by the owner, but Uncle Fred had been a keen conservationist and had wanted to draw more bees and butterflies into the area. So, each summer, Harriet's days had been spent amongst the gloriously vivid purple flowers, enjoying the incredible display. They were her happiest memories of her times in Cranfield.

She could still remember her aunt giving her a sprig of lavender to place underneath her pillow when she returned to the dreaded boarding school each term. The sweet smell, as she lay there at night in the darkness, had been the only thing she had held onto when it had all gotten too much. The lavender reminded her of her aunt and uncle and that she was loved.

She looked down at the phone in her hand and brushed her thumb across the lavender imprinted on the case, lost in bittersweet memories. Suddenly, the phone lit up in the darkness with a text. It was from Libby.

No petrol? What are you like?! On my way! x

Harriet's mood immediately lifted. There it was, that spark of hope that had supported her through her unhappy childhood. It all came from the love and help she had always received from her friends and family in Cranfield.

She checked her face on her phone and wiped away the streaked mascara that her tears had caused. Libby mustn't know that she had been upset; she didn't want to worry her friend.

Harriet suddenly remembered a conversation she had had years ago when she had come home from boarding school upset and deflated after yet more failed exams. 'Keep fighting, love,' Uncle Fred had told her. 'Life is short, so you've got to make the best of it.'

'He's right,' Aunt May had added, drawing her into a warm hug. 'You need to dance in the rain as often as you can because the sun will always come out again the next day anyway.'

Harriet smiled to herself as she sat in the darkness and tapped the Music app on her phone. Scrolling through the songs, she spotted the Abba song 'Dancing Queen'.

'I couldn't agree more, Aunt May,' announced Harriet out loud with a grin to herself as she glanced at the starry heavens above.

So, she switched up the volume on her phone and held onto it as she climbed out of the car and began to dance in the middle of the lane.

The hazard lights flicking on and off almost matched the beat of the song blaring out, she realised with a laugh as she carried on dancing. Her woes lifted, she felt ready to face anything once more.

Headlights appeared in the distance, and she felt even more cheered up. Libby would understand about her needing to dance in the road. Or rather, Libby would laugh and shake that long pale blonde hair of hers in ironic despair over her friend's constant positivity that she always moaned about. Harriet would shrug her shoulders in response and might even persuade her friend to dance for a while with her. At least it was a way of keeping them both warm on that chilly night.

The car drew nearer, and in the glare of the bright headlights, Harriet gave the driver a cheerful wave and turned around to wiggle her bottom in an exaggerated manner, all the while laughing.

But as she turned back, she realised that it wasn't Libby's face behind the driver's wheel after all. Instead, it was a man, a complete stranger, who was staring in stunned amazement at her.

2

Joe Randall was lost and also somewhat bewildered.

Was there a rave nearby that he didn't know about? Because the woman dancing in front of his car was either high or a bit crazy. Why else would she be dancing in the middle of a country lane on a cold, dark night?

He hesitated before finally deciding to roll down the window. How did you approach someone of dubious mental health? Gently and politely, he decided.

'Good evening. Nice, er, night for it,' he said with a smile, raising his voice to be heard over the loud music coming from the woman's phone.

'Isn't it?' said the redhead, crashing to a halt right next to his car door. 'The stars are so beautiful tonight.'

Joe nodded in agreement, even though he'd been so busy thinking about work on the long journey that he hadn't noticed them.

The music blared on from the phone in the woman's hand. Realising that it was Abba, he had a sudden recollection of his younger sister dancing in the lounge to the soundtrack to her favourite movie, *Mamma Mia*. How old would Charlotte have been then? Twelve? Thirteen?

Joe's throat instantly felt thick with emotion, his mind taken back to much happier days in the past. Happiness that he hadn't known for such a long time, it felt at that moment.

Thankfully, the woman fiddled with her phone, and the music suddenly switched off, leaving the silence of the countryside around them.

She sighed in what appeared to be contentment and shook out her long hair, which had got caught in the collar of her sweatshirt. Wild was his first thought as he stared at the lustrous red waves swinging around her shoulders. Free was his second. Something he knew nothing about.

Everything about Joe was the opposite of wild and free. From his short black hair, gelled into place, to the smart suit and tie, still buttoned up even at that late hour, that he wore every business day. Of course, these days, business extended into the weekend as well.

'So, er, do you need any help?' he asked, still guessing at the reason why this attractive and seemingly coherent woman had been dancing around on her own in the darkness.

She gave him a wide smile that lit up her green eyes. She was more than attractive, he decided. She was actually very pretty indeed.

'No, I'm fine, thanks,' she replied. 'I'm sure you must think that I'm a little bit crazy! But, you see, my car broke down, and I was getting cold whilst waiting for my friend to pick me up, so I figured I'd better keep moving to prevent frostbite.' She laughed before adding, 'You could always join me in a dance whilst I wait?'

She carried on laughing, and Joe could feel his pulse beat a little faster at her flirtation. Despite the strange circumstances, for a brief second, he was seriously tempted.

But then he realised that she had asked him for a dance, and he instantly shut down once more.

'I don't think so,' he replied, trying not to wince as he heard the snappish tone in his voice.

It wasn't her fault, of course, but he had decided a long time ago that he would never dance again, not since losing his sister. He just couldn't face the heartache of the memories.

The woman's smile faded quickly at his response. 'No, I suppose not,' she said, looking a little embarrassed.

She didn't know, he thought. How could she? But even here in the darkness, fifteen years on, he could feel the warmth of Charlotte's hand taking his to drag him up from the sofa to dance with him. His sister had always loved to dance. She had even talked about becoming a professional ballroom dancer before the car accident had robbed her of any future at all.

A pair of headlights flashed in his rear-view mirror, and the woman looked down the lane with what appeared to be a sigh of relief.

'I guess that's my friend coming,' she told him, peering into the darkness at the rapidly approaching car. 'The rescue mission.'

'Right,' said Joe, nodding. 'Well, if you're sure you don't need any help?'

'None at all,' she replied, fixing another smile on her face. 'But thank you. It was very kind of you to stop and offer.'

Joe got the impression that she was faking her relaxed attitude, but she seemed to be in control of the situation, certainly more than he was, in any case.

So, he gave a nod and wished her goodnight, putting the car into gear.

He drove off slowly, however, just to make sure that it was the person she had been expecting in the other car. He watched in his rear-view mirror as a blonde woman jumped out and gave the redhead a hug.

Reassured that she was safe, he pressed his foot down on the accelerator and carried on down the lane until he came across the sign for Cranfield. Well, at least he wasn't lost any more, he thought. But Cranfield was his job for tomorrow.

Still, he slowed the car as he drove through the tiny village, which appeared remarkably quiet. Of course, it was early evening during the working week, but a lot of the places he looked at for business were lifeless these days. Some of the more vibrant villages had received a surge of newcomers in the past couple of years, all wanting a change of pace and to work from home. But the smaller places, without shops or even a pub at their heart, had begun to fade away into a steep decline. Cranfield appeared to be yet another failed village.

Joe knew nothing about villages. He had grown up in a large town over fifty miles away. It had been a happy childhood until the car accident that had taken his sister away from them all. Then everything had rapidly changed. Despite the accident not being his fault, his dad had been at the wheel and had blamed himself for the loss of his vibrant, beautiful daughter. Joe had watched his dad retreat into his grief-stricken shell, seemingly only able to concentrate on business, which left his mum to continue to shower Joe with the love and affection that he had always known.

It was his mum who had supported her son's desire to head to university. There Joe had met his best friend, Matt, in the halls of residence, both taking a Business Studies degree. They had swiftly bonded and had become lifelong friends. But whereas Matt was now an agricultural land agent who seemed to spend the majority of his time in wellington boots on windy, rainswept farms, enjoying his rural life immensely, Joe's career since university had been vastly different.

His skills in organisation and business had enabled him to quickly climb the corporate ladder and become a project manager for the oil and gas industries. Able to bring each project in on time and, more importantly, within budget meant that he was soon in demand with the biggest worldwide companies. His salary had been considerable, and he was able to live very comfortably, with a brand-new Range Rover every year and a luxury penthouse flat in London.

At first, he hadn't cared too much about the type of companies that he dealt with, but as the talk about climate change grew more urgent year by year, he had begun to ponder whether a change of direction might be worthwhile.

But that had all come to a crashing halt when his mother passed away from cancer two years ago. Joe had returned to help his dad run the family business when his mother had become seriously ill. Once home, he had realised that the business was near to financial ruin, as his dad had once more begun to retreat into his grief.

Joe had made a promise to his mum that he would take care of his dad and so had helped with the business whilst his father grieved. The trouble was that Joe had not been able to leave ever since, as his dad had never recovered from the loss.

His father had started the company, negotiating land purchases on behalf of wealthy clients, thirty years ago. The business had grown, and now it was Joe's responsibility to ensure it didn't fail. He wasn't sure that his father could bear it.

His father appeared to be all right, and yet nothing was the same. There were no easy conversations any more. They weren't even allowed to mention his mother. It was just business, business, and more business. Joe was exhausted, and in all of his thirty-one years, he didn't think he had ever felt so trapped. But he just couldn't bear to burden his father with any more bad news and admit that he wanted to leave and restart his own career. So, he remained at the helm of the family business, unhappily stuck in limbo with no exit route.

He drove out of Cranfield and quickly made the short journey to the larger village of Cranbridge. This at least seemed more prosperous and buzzing than Cranfield. When he had tried to find a hotel room, his online search had concluded that The Black Swan Inn was the only decent place to stay within a reasonable distance of Cranfield.

As it happened, the inn had been recently renovated and was remarkably stylish but with all the home comforts. The owners, Belle and Pete, were welcoming but also, thankfully, seemed to respect his privacy as they offered him dinner.

He sat alone at the table in the restaurant downstairs. He had found himself becoming more and more used to his own company these days. He just wasn't sure whether he enjoyed it or not.

After a delicious meal, Joe headed up to his room. It was a comfortable, well-appointed double bedroom with an en suite. At least the decent bed would aid a good night's sleep, he thought as he sank down onto the thick mattress.

If only his mind would rest, he realised, tossing and turning over an hour later. Perhaps he was just fed-up, really tired of being continually on the road.

It had been a job that he had enjoyed for a while. On behalf of his dad, he negotiated deals on unused land for major corporations to build warehouses and factories. The thrill of the chase of the signed contract had been all-encompassing at first. It had been all about the money and making sure that the company didn't go under. Good for the wallet. Not so great for the soul, perhaps, he was beginning to realise.

His dad became more and more obsessed with the work and kept pushing Joe on and on to each new deal, but Joe knew that it was for his sake, not his son's. They were both exhausted. Sometimes, Joe felt the need just to stop and be still for a while, but his dad wouldn't give in and couldn't give up the work. Stopping would mean time to think, which would mean the grief would rush in once more.

In the beginning, Joe's escape from the unhappiness in his work had been the enjoyment he had felt at travelling around the country, and even Europe, staying in various hotels. But even the thrill of a new city or hotel to discover had begun to pall in recent months. The hotels were very nice but mostly bland, where he would eat alone in the restaurant or in his room, feeling even more estranged from the outside world than ever. He had noticed that evening that quite a few locals in the bar downstairs all knew each other. To his surprise, Joe found himself wanting that same familiarity and friendship.

Of course, that might happen if he only stayed in the same place for more than a few days or even a week at a time. He owned a flat in London that he only ever went to at the weekends. Even then, with time so short, he still hadn't unpacked boxes from when he had bought it a few years ago. It was an empty shell, but he had no desire to put his own mark on the place. What he was craving was a home, but nowhere had felt like that since his mother had passed away, and with his father pushing him on and on, he wasn't sure anywhere ever would. Not that he even had the time to look anyway.

If they both slowed down, then perhaps his dad would finally face up to what had happened. In a way, Joe hoped that he could, and then they could both begin to move on.

In any case, he was tired of running away from his emotions. These days, he felt almost robotic. No time to live, certainly no time to love. When was the last time he went out on a date? He couldn't remember. Parties, celebrations, nights of conversation, and laughter had all passed him by, and he could feel himself withdrawing from a fuller life day by day.

His mum and sister had been the complete opposite, so full of life and laughter. There had always been music playing in the house, always the radio on. Now, whenever he went to his dad's house, it was silent, and Joe had found himself emulating the same thing. He didn't even play music in the car any more.

But when they had been happy and complete as a family, his sister and mum would drag Joe to dance with them on and on until they had all collapsed, exhausted. He hadn't danced since. The couple of times that he had attempted to dance, the memories had been too overwhelming for him to bear.

He sighed and turned over, but his mind kept going back to the woman dancing in the middle of the country lane. His mum would have wholeheartedly approved of her spirit, and his sister would have loved to dance along with her, despite the random location.

Joe closed his eyes, and when he finally fell asleep hours later, he dreamt of long red hair flying around in the dark night air.

3

'I can't believe you asked a complete stranger to dance with you,' said Libby, rolling her eyes before placing one of Harriet's bags in the boot of her car. 'He could have been a lunatic.'

Harriet shook her head. 'I told you already. He was perfectly polite and absolutely normal.'

And handsome, she added to herself, thinking about the dark-haired stranger. Not that it mattered as she wouldn't see him again. But still, it had been so long since she had had a mild flirt with anyone, let alone a full-blown relationship.

She had always been bad at relationships, according to her ex-boyfriends. Too closed off, they told her. But how did they expect her to trust anyone and not be hurt? She had spent her whole life hiding her innermost emotions; perhaps it was too late to start now.

'Normal?' muttered Libby in a disbelieving tone. 'You and your positive mental attitude are going to get you into trouble one of these days.'

'It hasn't so far,' said Harriet with a winning smile. 'Come on. You've got to see the funny side of it.'

'You know I love you and all that rubbish,' said Libby, slamming down the lid of the car boot, which was now full of Harriet's belongings. 'But I'm still on Hong Kong time, and my body clock is craving sleep right now, not night-time flits to pick up stranded best friends.'

'I'd have texted Flora instead, but she's always up so early on the farm,' said Harriet sheepishly. 'Sorry. You must be shattered.'

'Yeah, but I love you anyway.' Libby laughed, and Harriet suddenly found herself swept into an enormous bear hug.

Despite her petite stature and figure, Libby did everything on a grand scale. From her emotions and her dreams to her long pale blonde hair, which was almost to her waist, her natural beauty radiated out from within despite the jet lag. Libby didn't hide anything from anyone.

'It's so good to see you,' said Harriet as she took a step backwards.

'And for a bit longer this time, right?' said Libby as they got inside her car. 'Flora and I have big plans for you now that you can stay for a few weeks. Or months, hopefully!'

Harriet smiled to herself as they set off. Libby was impetuous and seemed to spend most of her time in a perpetual dreamlike state. She never thought about worrying things like business debts. That was left to Harriet to fret about, although she hadn't let her friends know how bad a financial situation she was in.

The journey to Cranfield didn't take very long and was taken up by Libby chatting away about her most recent trip for her work as a flight attendant.

'I tell you,' she said as she drew the car to a stop on Railway Lane. 'If I didn't know for certain that he had an A-list girlfriend back home waiting for him, I totally would have taken him up on his offer.'

Harriet heard her friend's laughter but was too busy looking out of the window at the row of cottages in front of them. She was home again, she thought. At last.

She looked around, but it was pretty quiet, not surprising, thanks to the late hour. Along Railway Lane, the windows and doors were all closed as everyone hunkered down away from the cold spring night. There were only a few other small streets that made up the whole village. In the soft light of a couple of street-lamps, she could see the daffodils and crocuses dotted all along either side of the narrow lane, bobbing their heads in greeting under the steady drizzle that had just commenced.

The warm feeling deep inside was the familiarity of Harriet's second home growing up. A place to relax and be herself without any expectations from her high-achieving parents and siblings. She had tried her best to live up to their stellar reputations, yet there was always someone at a party whom she could overhear asking, 'And Harriet? Such a shame she hasn't inherited your brains.'

But here in Cranfield, she had been loved by her aunt and uncle. Aunt May was soft and warm, a stark contrast to Harriet's mother, who had been strict and cold. Aunt May filled the cottage with homemade soft furnishings, music, and the aroma of baked cakes. Uncle Fred was as different from his brother, Harriet's father, as she was from her own siblings. Whereas her dad was uptight, perma-nently looking at his laptop or his phone, Uncle Fred relished the fresh air and was always to be found pottering outside. Whatever the weather, he was either in his garden or across the railway line in the lavender fields. The cherished memory of them both squeezed Harriet's heart tight until she allowed herself a steadying breath.

Of course, Libby was right. With the closure of her business, Harriet could stay for a couple of weeks whilst she readied the cottage to be put up for sale. She had put off that heartbreaking job long enough, but now that the will had been processed and all the legal documents were sorted, there was no need for any further delay.

But what Harriet really wanted most of all was a permanent home. Her parents were always chasing the next high-profile assignment as they had travelled to every corner of the earth to defend the innocent. Harriet just wanted somewhere to stop and belong. The cottage in front of her had been the only real place where she had ever felt anything close to that feeling, and it was going to have to be sold to pay off her debts.

In the dark, she could still see the small sign outside the front door that Aunt May had made a long time ago. No. 1 Railway Lane had been renamed Lavender Cottage for as long as Harriet could remember.

There were five railway cottages in the row, each built in the sandy-coloured brick that all the houses in the tiny village were made of. Their roofs were tiled, and nearly all the chimneys had smoke rising from them. All except Lavender Cottage.

At the far end of the row of cottages was Cranfield station, the last stop on a short branch line. It too was built in the same honey-coloured brick. In the early days, Harriet had often travelled on the train with her aunt and uncle to Aldwych, the nearest town.

She could still remember as a child being so excited as she stood in the back garden watching the train as it slowly exited the station, past the garden fence, before beginning its short journey to Aldwych at the other end of the line, ten miles away. She and her uncle would stand in the garden, waving to all the passengers, most of whom they knew as the village was such a tight-knit community back then. But that was twenty years ago, and the branch line had long since closed.

Without the station, the village had slowly begun to shut down. The small shop had closed, and without any commuters, people and families had started to drift away. Perhaps with the advent of working from home, people might be tempted to return to Cranfield, she thought. After all, the village might be tiny, but the much larger Cranbridge village was within walking distance.

Cranfield had become quieter as people left to follow jobs and their careers, but some remained, such as Libby, who had never lived anywhere else, and Flora, who had taken over the running of the farm, which had been in her family for generations.

Harriet could just see Flora's farmhouse now, beyond the station on the other side of the railway track. The upstairs bedroom lights were on as Flora and her grandmother settled down for an early start working on the land.

Harriet drew the front door key out of her handbag and headed down the short path. She had only been back a handful of times in the past six months since the funeral to check on the place, but it was still strange not to have her aunt and uncle here waiting for her with enormous hugs.

She put the key in the lock and pushed the door open. She hesitated, blinking away the tears at the dark empty cottage before heading back outside to help Libby clear the bags out of her car. She would pick up the remaining boxes when her car was filled with petrol the following day.

'I've switched on the fridge and put some milk and bread in there,' said Libby, suppressing a yawn as they stood in the narrow hallway.

'Come on, it's time you got some sleep,' Harriet told her, flicking on the overhead light so that she could see what she was doing.

'Will you be all right here on your own?' asked Libby, checking her face anxiously.

Harriet nodded. 'I'll be fine,' she replied.

'Not that you would tell me anyway,' said Libby, rolling her eyes. 'Flora and I have sorted out our diaries, and we're going to have a gin night tomorrow evening to welcome you back properly. We've invited ourselves over, so it's tough if you have other plans.'

'Sounds great,' Harriet told her.

With another hug from Libby, they wished each other good-night before Harriet finally closed the front door and was left to wander around the cottage on her own.

There was a tiny hallway where all her bags were now piled up. Harriet left them there whilst she headed into the front room and switched on the corner light. It was a small but cosy room with its real fireplace and bookshelves lined up along one wall. A door led to the kitchen and dining area, which just about had space for a table for two and chairs.

The kitchen still had its original range and butler sink, which was under a sash window looking out onto the long back. The only thing that was missing was a freshly baked cake cooling on the side, Harriet's favourite Victoria sponge. But that hadn't been there for a few years now.

In fact, without her uncle and aunt here, Harriet wasn't sure it even felt like the home that she had known and loved so much.

She sighed heavily as she looked out of the window, hating the peace and emptiness of the cottage. However, at that moment, Harriet saw a shooting star streaking across the clear night sky. She immediately sent up her heartfelt wish that everything could just stay the same from now on.

Please don't let me have to sell Lavender Cottage, she wished. *No more changes.* She didn't think she could cope with any more. However, she knew that the only way that would happen would be with a miracle.

She knew it was pointless and that, deep down, she would have to leave behind the lovely village that had brought her such comfort over the years. But at least Cranfield would never ever change.

4

In the crisp morning air, Joe looked down the lane at the heart of Cranfield and said, 'The whole place needs to change,' into the voice memo app on his phone. He took a few more paces from where he had parked his car before adding, 'Regeneration is key to local prosperity. This is number one on the list of potential sites. Access is good. The local searches flagged up zero protected species on the land. The land has no owner according to land registry.'

He put down his phone for a moment and took a sip of the takeaway coffee that he'd brought with him from Cranbridge Stores, the corner shop opposite the inn where he had stayed. It was good coffee, and he certainly needed the caffeine hit after a fitful night's sleep. He held his golf umbrella in his other hand in deference to the heavy drizzle that was coming down and creating a mist over the landscape.

There was a small gate on the side of the field that he was looking at, but it appeared to have a heavy lock keeping it shut. The gate on the far side of the field seemed to have swung wide open, so he went to investigate how to approach it from the other side of the railway track.

He headed down Railway Lane, past a small row of cottages, before finding the old station he had been looking for on his route. Then he turned and headed through a narrow corridor between two buildings before reaching the platform.

There was something special about an old railway station, he thought. Although neglected, there was still an air of old-world charm about the place, from the wooden benches that would once have held passengers to the old clock still hanging from the eaves and even the posters for trips taken many years ago. The sign for Cranfield station was even still there, although faded and cracked these days.

It had obviously been a busy station at some point, serving both Cranfield and Cranbridge beyond, but that was a long time ago. There was grass and weeds now growing across the railway tracks, unused for almost twenty years, as far as his records had shown.

The large station building was still there, although the ticket office and waiting rooms had an abandoned air about them as Joe peered in. They looked almost frozen in time, full of boxes and rubbish. When he stepped back to look up at the first floor, however, he could see one of the windows was ajar and framed with modern curtains, so presumably, someone still lived up there.

He looked back at the platform. All it needed to come alive once more were the trains bustling back and forth. And people too, he realised.

The nearby village of Cranbridge that morning had been thriving when he had headed outside. There were a couple of shops, the pub had also been busy, and there was also a new tearoom. But the people slowly ebbed away as he had driven the five minutes towards Cranfield. Whatever magic had ensured the survival of Cranbridge, it certainly hadn't headed this far out.

He spotted the narrow pedestrian bridge at the end of the platform, which would take him over to the gate and fields that he wanted to look at, so he began to walk towards it. The bridge was rusty but thankfully felt sturdy despite the obvious wear and tear from being so old. Even so, he was relieved when he made it over to the other side.

The station not being in use would actually help his cause, he thought, putting his business head back on. With no other businesses to be bothered by the industrial company that wanted to build their large storage facility there, it wouldn't kick up too much of a fuss locally. After all, it appeared as if hardly anyone was even living in Cranfield these days.

At the bottom of the bridge, a path opened up into a long track that stretched out into the distance. He spotted a church spire and looked on the map on his phone, where he realised that Cranbridge village was at the end of the path.

But it was the two fields fenced off to the left of the path that interested him the most. They held many rows of what he had been led to believe were lavender plants, although they looked grey and straggly. In any case, there was no official owner of the land to object to his enquiries to buy the fields, so at least that obstacle was out of the way.

The fields stretched all the way to some trees on the horizon and beyond, where it was hard to tell where they stopped and the grassy hills surrounding the village began.

Joe walked along the path, noting the decent size of the fields. It was a good space, he thought. Despite the locked gate on the other side, access from the lane would be preferable and easier.

Deep in thought, he turned to look across at the fields on the other side of the path and was surprised to see two women standing next to the fence, watching him in the drizzle with quizzical looks.

To his amazement, he recognised the redhead whom he had almost run over the previous evening when she had been dancing in the middle of the lane.

'Hello again,' she said, leaning against the other side of the fence and giving him a broad smile.

'Hi,' he replied, feeling a little pleased to see her again.

'Bit overdressed for a ramble, aren't you?' said the other woman, a brunette who was wearing a flat cap and waxed jacket.

Joe couldn't remember the last time he hadn't worn a suit during the working week. His whole time was spent in meetings, so he always dressed smart these days.

The women were dressed in jeans and wellington boots, which seemed a bit more appropriate for the setting.

'And I forgot my wellies,' he said, glancing down at the pair of smart black shoes he was wearing, which were now a little caked in mud.

'But at least you remembered your umbrella,' said the pretty redhead, smiling at him.

He found himself smiling back, staring into the pair of startling green eyes as he did so.

The brunette turned to look at her friend. 'Aren't you going to introduce me?' she asked in a pointed tone.

'This is the gentlemen who stopped last night to offer help when I broke down,' said the redhead.

'Oh.' The woman turned to study him with an appraising look. 'So, did you leave your golf trolley behind last night, or are you completely lost?'

He could understand why she was intent on finding out why someone in a business suit was standing next to an overgrown field.

'Just trying to get my bearings,' he replied.

'Not too difficult,' said the redhead. 'This is Cranfield. At the end of this path in the distance is Cranbridge, if you were looking for a bit more life in your, er, life.'

He smiled. 'Actually, I'm right where I need to be.'

'In that case, you're on the opposite side to my farm,' the brunette told him with a small frown.

'I see,' he replied. 'Good to know.'

Joe's phone rang at that moment. Glancing at the screen, he realised it was his dad.

'Excuse me. I need to take this call,' he told them before saying his goodbyes and walking away. He could hear the women talking in a hushed undertone as he went.

'How's it going?' asked his dad straight away.

'It's okay,' said Joe, heading up the stairs and over the railway bridge. 'I've been scoping out the site in Cranfield.'

'Do you think it's a suitable proposition?'

Joe sighed to himself. Did they ever have a conversation these days that wasn't about business? Not even at Christmas, he realised.

'I think it will suit the purposes of the client,' replied Joe. 'The fields look abandoned, certainly unused for many years.'

'Good,' said his dad. 'That'll make things go a lot quicker. Our clients are in a rush, as you know. And what about local resistance to our plans?'

Joe reached the other side of the bridge, and as he walked along the platform, he glanced over the railway track to where he could see the two women walking back across the field. Even that far away, the red hair shone out in the mist of the light drizzle.

'No, I don't think we'll run across any local opposition,' he replied before turning away to head out of the station.

5

Harriet walked back with Flora across the fields to the farmhouse. The drizzle didn't seem to be letting up at all.

'Are you coming in to see Grams?' asked Flora. 'She should be back from ploughing the top field by now.'

'Of course,' said Harriet. 'I can't wait to see her.'

Flora's grandmother was a strong, independent woman whose advanced age didn't seem to get in the way of helping her granddaughter complete the many chores required on the farm each and every day.

Grams was fierce in nature with almost everyone but Flora and her two childhood friends, Harriet and Libby, whom she adored and had always treated lovingly. When she was little, Flora had been unable to say the word Grandma, so it had become Grams. The nickname had stuck, but Harriet and Libby were the only two other people in the world that could refer to her by that name. Everyone else knew her as Helen.

Harriet followed Flora through the gate and into the main yard outside the farmhouse. It was a large L-shaped house in the same sandy-coloured brick as the rest of the village. They headed around to the back door, which was permanently unlocked.

They took off their muddy wellington boots before opening the back door. It led straight into the heart of the farmhouse – the large kitchen. It was somewhat messy but clean, as if the two women living there kept on top of their chores but had no other time to sort through anything. It did, however, smell the same as always, full of herbs and home cooking, with the warmth of the nearby range.

Flora flung off her cap onto the kitchen table before shrugging off her coat to hang it up on the nearby hat stand, which was filled with assorted outerwear.

'Let's get the kettle on,' she said, heading over to the sink.

'Best idea you've had all morning, girl.'

Harriet spun around and smiled as Grams came into the kitchen. She went straight over to give the grey-haired old lady a gentle hug.

Grams seemed even shorter than before, barely coming up to Harriet's shoulder level. But when she pulled back to study Harriet's face, Grams' blue eyes were as sharp as ever.

'You look tired, young Harriet,' said Grams. 'Has someone been keeping you awake all night?'

'Grams!' said Harriet, blushing furiously.

Flora laughed as she placed a plate of biscuits on the table. 'I think you'll find Harriet's love life is as non-existent as mine is.'

Grams shook her head as she sat down at the head of the large oak table. 'You young girls need to get your priorities straight.' She picked up a chocolate biscuit. 'By the time I was your age, I'd married your grandfather.'

Flora and Harriet had heard this before. 'Yes, but, Grams, you and Grandpa both grew up in the village. You'd sat next to him throughout school. It was easier back then.'

'So, find someone in the village!' Grams told her, laughing.

Harriet rolled her eyes. 'There are no single men in the village.'

'Except Eddie, of course,' said Grams with a wink.

Flora laughed as she placed three steaming mugs of coffee on the table. 'He's even older than you, Grams.'

Grams pretended to look offended. 'Age is just a number, my darling,' she told them. 'Even a number as high as mine.'

'The only single man I've seen around here for weeks is the one that we met on the path this morning, who said he was lost,' said Flora, looking at Harriet questioningly. 'The one that Harriet had already met last night.'

Grams followed her granddaughter's look with raised eyebrows. 'Well, this sounds promising. Was he handsome?'

Flora nodded.

'Excellent!' said Grams, with a wide smile.

'I told you already,' said Harriet, shuffling in her chair under their scrutiny, 'he just stopped to offer assistance when I broke down last night.'

'And did you accept?' asked Grams, her eyes gleaming. 'Was that all he offered? Did he offer mouth-to-mouth, for example?'

Flora burst out laughing.

'Of course not,' replied Harriet, also giggling. 'Anyway, he was just passing through. That was all.'

But it had been nice to see him again, she thought.

'I didn't think anyone ever just passed through Cranfield,' said Flora with a slight frown.

'Well, you both need to get a wiggle on whoever he was,' said Grams. 'I mean, at least Libby goes out on dates.'

'Yes, but none of them last longer than the second week,' remarked Flora, rolling her eyes.

Grams nodded thoughtfully. 'Well, she's still rebelling against her father, of course. Not sure how that's ever going to change, mind you.'

It was true. Since her mother had walked out early into her teenage years, Libby's father had become stricter and stricter with each passing year. Not that Libby ever seemed to either listen or care about his rules. She had been rebelling ever since, and it was only the fact he had suffered a small stroke that had stopped her from leaving altogether.

'So how are you finding being back?' asked Grams, giving Harriet one of her piercing looks.

Harriet immediately smiled. 'You know I love being back in Cranfield with you all.'

Grams didn't return the smile. 'But it must be hard for you to be here without May and Fred. I miss my dear friends terribly, as must you.'

Harriet's smile faded. 'Well, it's a bit, er, you know, strange to be staying in the cottage without them being there,' she finally replied.

In fact, she had barely slept. Lavender Cottage was too quiet, missing the ever-comforting presence of her aunt and uncle.

'If you ever need to talk,' said Grams gently.

'Thanks,' said Harriet quickly, as usual, dismissing the need to talk about her true feelings.

'Grief is the price we pay for love,' noted Grams, reaching out to touch her engagement and wedding rings with calloused fingers.

Her husband of fifty years had passed away in recent years, the catalyst to Flora returning to the farm permanently to help out.

'And how are things around here?' asked Harriet.

As she reached out to grab a biscuit, she heard Flora and Grams exchange a soft sigh.

'It was a soggy winter, so the crops didn't fare too well,' said Flora with a grimace.

'But I've just finished planting up the wheat and barley,' added Grams. 'We'll need a pretty good summer crop to make up for all the profits we've lost. If the weather behaves itself, of course.'

Harriet knew that the farm had been struggling for a few years and wondered just how bad things had got financially for them both.

'I'm around for a couple of weeks if you need any help,' she said, ever ready to help out her loved ones.

Grams gave her a wry smile. 'Thanks, love. Although I'm not sure about your tractor skills if you can't even fill your own car up with petrol.'

Harriet laughed. 'I was just in a rush to get here and see you all,' she said. 'Although, I'm not sure how good I'd be driving a tractor.'

'Let's hope we never need to find out,' remarked Flora with a wink. 'Anyway, after this tea break, I'll drop you down there with a jerry can of fuel.'

'Thanks. Then I'd better begin to get the house ready to be put on the market,' said Harriet, her heart dropping as she thought about someone else living there.

'Such a shame,' said Grams, shaking her head. 'So many places seem to be going up for sale in the village at the moment. Now that Mr Baggins in number 5 Railway Lane has passed away, that's two out of the five cottages that are lying empty. The village seems to be getting quieter and quieter.' She looked sad for a moment before appearing to brighten up deliberately. 'Still, with you three young ladies back together, there won't be too much peace, eh?'

Harriet and Flora smiled at each other.

'Especially if that handsome stranger returns again,' carried on Grams, with a gleam in her eye. 'To be lost in Cranfield twice is odd, but if he does it a third time, then it must be a sign!'

Harriet shook off the gentle teasing but still couldn't help thinking to herself that she really would like to bump into the man again, whatever his reasons would be to keep returning to Cranfield.

6

After Flora had helped fill up the car with petrol later that morning, Harriet was finally able to park up in the front of the cottage and carry her remaining possessions inside.

The furniture in the flat above the shop had been included in the rent, so she had no large items with her, just lots of bags and boxes, which had filled her small car up to the roof.

She placed most of her stuff upstairs, anxious to clear the front room to make space for her friends who were coming around later. She piled up most of the bags in her aunt and uncle's bedroom – the only other room upstairs apart from the bathroom. It still felt strange and empty without them.

Back in her own bedroom, she sank down on the bed briefly and looked around the room. It had long been her sanctuary from the world, the faded flowers on the wallpaper a safe harbour from her tumultuous childhood.

Of course, it had never been intended to be her bedroom at all. Underneath the faded flowers were teddy bears. She had once picked at a curled-up corner of the wallpaper by her bed and had taken a peek. It was the nursery that had never been used. Harriet had only heard her aunt refer to their desire to have a child once. 'But it never happened for us,' had been her aunt's only explanation, which was why they had doted on Harriet like their own. She was sad that they never became parents because they were far better suited to family life than her own parents had ever been.

She got up from the bed and walked downstairs. There was still so much to do and clear out, but she was overwhelmed with having to face it all and, instead, opened up the back door and walked out into her uncle's beloved garden.

The rain had finally stopped, and the late March sun was trying to peek through the clouds. However, here and there, tulips were almost in bud, and the daffodils brought some cheer with their bright yellow colour.

Beyond the railway track, to the left of the path, were the two lavender fields that her uncle had planted. They had been flowering for as long as Harriet could remember. 'Everyone's got to have a hobby,' her uncle had told her many years ago with a soft smile.

The flowers had long since faded from the previous summer and were now a pale grey in the overcast day. They had all been sown in rows and formed large stripes as they stretched out almost to the horizon. In the summer, the fields had been a blur of purple stretching as far as Cranbridge in the distance. Uncle Fred had tended the flowers for years, although his arthritis had slowed him up the past couple of years.

In the middle of the larger field was an oak tree, perfectly silhouetted against the horizon as the field rose slightly towards the back. It already had buds waiting to be turned into leaves in the next month or so.

Beyond the larger field on the left was the slightly smaller field. In the corner was Uncle Fred's tiny shed, which housed some of his gardening tools, as well as a large wooden summer house, in which they had sat outside on many occasions, overlooking the fields.

On the far border, which ran alongside a no-through road, was another oak tree. This one had an even larger trunk, and Harriet noticed that it had broken the picket fence that ran along the border and was now spreading out onto the lane beyond.

It wasn't as perfect a specimen as the other oak tree, but this one was always far more special to Harriet. Early on in her childhood, her uncle had shown her two initials carved into its trunk – FC & MB. They had been carved there by Uncle Fred for Aunt May when he had proposed, which had always struck Harriet as amusing because her Uncle Fred, for all his loving nature, had never been a romantic. And yet they had been young once too.

Harriet always made sure she visited the tree whenever she came to Cranfield, rubbing the initials with her fingers across the rough bark and hoping that the magic of her aunt and uncle's happy marriage would bring her romance as well. But it was yet to happen. She'd enjoyed a few relationships, but they had all fizzled out.

As she looked out beyond the railway track at the edge of the garden, she thought she saw a blonde furry blur through the white picket fence at the bottom, but it soon disappeared, and besides, she needed to get dinner ready for that evening with her friends.

She smiled to herself, so grateful to be back in Cranfield at last, with steady Flora and lively Libby. They were her rocks and had been ever since Libby had invited her to play one hot day many summers ago. Flora had joined in, and they had quickly bonded. They had been best friends ever since.

* * *

A few hours later, the fire in the front room was roaring, and so was the gossip.

'So, I said to him,' Libby was saying, as she picked up a chocolate truffle from the box she had brought with her, 'I shall report you to the pilot if you touch my bottom again.'

'And what did he say?' asked Harriet, agog.

'He just laughed,' said Libby with a grimace. 'So, I "may" have laced his coffee with a laxative later on in the flight.' Her pretty face lit up into a wicked grin.

Harriet and Flora laughed.

'Well done,' said Flora once she had stopped laughing long enough to pick up her gin and tonic. 'I'd have given him a swift kick somewhere with my wellies if he'd come near me.'

'A stiletto works wonders,' said Libby.

'Maybe a cattle prong's better,' Flora went on with a grin.

It was good to hear her joking, thought Harriet. She knew how hard Flora was working to keep the farm going.

Hopefully, the coming weeks would give Harriet plenty of opportunity to catch up properly with her friends. Of course, that was time-dependent on the cottage being sold and her finding a new job. She had no idea where she could find employment as a beauty therapist in the quiet of the countryside, so she would have to go back to the city eventually. Otherwise, her only other option would be to use the one-way flight ticket her parents had offered her and live with them. But that really would be a last resort option that nobody wanted. Their last conversation had been about her aunt and uncle's will being finalised. There was no bitterness about the inheritance only going to Harriet. After all, she was the only one not to have a stellar career with high earnings in the family. In a way, it had only emphasised just how little the rest of the family thought of her work skills that she couldn't even support herself without help. They were just assuming that the sale of Lavender Cottage was all about the profit when it was anything but.

She was suddenly aware of Libby studying her. 'Are you okay?' she asked softly. 'That was a heavy sigh.'

'I'm fine,' said Harriet automatically before taking a sip of her drink.

She had tried to battle through the worst of her grief in the short time she had been in the cottage so far, but it was so full of memories for her. She could see a Christmas tree in the corner and her uncle falling asleep, still wearing the paper hat from his cracker. The smell of lavender in the summer and Aunt May's baking all year around. The crackle of the fire in the winter and the sound of birdsong, and even the train going past.

The majority of her childhood had been so miserable, especially the strict boarding school that her parents insisted she attended, that coming to Cranfield had always felt as if she were coming alive again. It was a place to relax, be herself, laugh. To feel as if she did have something to contribute, as her aunt and uncle paid her the attention she so desperately craved from her parents.

'You're allowed to be upset, you know,' said Flora, breaking into her memories.

'I'm fine,' replied Harriet. 'It's just all a bit strange being here without them.'

'We understand,' Libby told her gently.

There was a short silence as they all took a sip of their drink. Harriet wished she could open up to her friends more, but it was just too hard a habit to break after all these years.

'What time are you off tomorrow?' asked Harriet, eager to move the conversation onto happier subjects.

Libby grimaced. 'Four in the morning,' she said. 'But at least the early wake-up call means I'll be in the sunny Canaries for lunch.'

'Wow,' said Flora. 'Sounds wonderful. A beach and cocktails. My idea of heaven. Just wish I had the chance to go with you.'

'We've already got the cocktails right here,' remarked Harriet, holding up her glass.

'Not at the moment,' replied Libby, glancing down at her empty glass. 'Nor will I be able to have any more with my early start.'

'Me neither,' said Flora. 'My alarm is set even earlier than yours.'

'So, I'm drinking by myself?' joked Harriet. 'I'm sure I'll regret it in the morning.'

'I'll put the kettle on.' Libby got up from the pile of cushions that she'd been lounging on and headed into the kitchen.

Harriet looked at the fire for a while, relishing the warmth and the familiar comfort the crackling flames gave her.

'You know you don't have to put on a front with us,' said Flora softly as she studied her.

'Right back at you,' countered Harriet.

Flora gave a grunt of grim humour. 'Oh, there's no front here. The farm is in serious trouble if this year's harvest isn't one of the best ever.'

Harriet reached out and squeezed her friend's hand. 'Poor you.'

'It'll be nice to have you around, even for just a short time,' said Flora, squeezing her hand in return.

'It's going to break my heart when I finally have to leave Lavender Cottage for good,' Harriet admitted.

'Is the work around here really so bad?' asked Flora.

'What work?' asked Harriet with a smile. 'No work for failed beauty salon owners here.'

'Except you're not a failure,' said Flora gently.

'I wasn't exactly a sparkling success story either,' remarked Harriet, thinking of the business she now needed to pay off with the sale of the cottage. She had also inherited a small sum that would cover half the debts, but it still wasn't enough.

'What about your parents?' asked Libby, coming back into the room with a packet of chocolate biscuits and two teas for her and Flora. 'Can't your dad do something to get you a job?'

Harriet shook her head. 'I don't want them involved. Not that they ever ring to ask how I am anyway...' Her voice trailed off into the distance. She stared into the flames once more before placing a smile back on her face to hide her hurt. 'Maybe there's a forgotten chest of gold coins or something in the attic,' she said, laughing. 'Then everything can be saved!'

She knew it was probably a lost cause, but she crossed her fingers, just in case.

She would just have to enjoy Cranfield whilst she was there, she decided. For however long that was going to be.

7

The following morning, Harriet woke up late with a start.

After another restless night, she had finally fallen asleep sometime in the early hours. She got dressed, but despite flicking the kettle on, she quickly turned it off again and put on her coat instead.

The emptiness of the house felt overwhelming to her in that instant, and she needed the fresh air to clear her head.

She wandered along the lane towards the station, noting the mist rising on the fields on the other side of the railway track. She walked through the narrow passageway and onto the station platform as a cool breeze whipped around her. The promise of a long hot summer still felt a long way away that morning, even though it was the first day of April.

She had been back in Cranfield for a couple of days, yet this was her first visit to the station. She wondered whether Bob was around. He wasn't technically an uncle but had become an honorary one over the course of many visits and had been Uncle Fred's best friend. The last time she had seen him, he had made her promise to come and visit him as soon as she arrived in the village.

She knocked on the door to the station but found nobody at home. The downstairs of the building was still frozen in time, with its waiting room and ticket office still set up as if in use, albeit in an abandoned state, full of rubbish and mess. The living quarters where Bob, the old stationmaster, and his wife, Rachel, lived were upstairs. Harriet knew from infrequent visits over the years that the apartment was equally messy as neither Bob nor Rachel were particularly house proud. But Harriet couldn't hear a sound from upstairs either, so she assumed they were both out.

She walked back onto the platform and stood for a moment, relishing the peace and birdsong that came from the fields opposite. The apple blossom fluttered across from the nearby trees on Flora's farm, laying like confetti on the tarmac.

At the end of the platform were the barriers signalling the end of the line. Beyond was a huge workshop, which had been used to house the different trains when the railway had still been running. Outside the workshop were a couple of old railway carriages, looking somewhat neglected and battered by the elements over the past couple of decades.

Suddenly, Harriet heard some kind of metal clanging from the workshop and went to investigate, suspecting that she would find Bob there.

Bob was a lifelong enthusiast of the railway, so living at the station had been a lifelong dream come true. He loved trains and had loved being the stationmaster, in charge of overseeing all the trains coming and going. His wife, Rachel, however, had always been less enthusiastic about the railway, even more so after the closure of the line, and had always expressed a desire to move away.

Harriet walked down the narrow path alongside the end of the tracks and through the vast double doors at the front of the workshop.

'Hello!' she called out as she walked inside. 'Anyone home?'

But she came to an abrupt halt as she found herself face to face with an enormous steam engine directly in front of her.

'Wow!'

'Wow indeed,' said Bob, appearing around the corner. He was smothered in black grease, which made his wide grin appear even whiter. 'It's so good to see you, love.'

'And you too,' said Harriet.

Bob had the kind of cheerful face that you couldn't help but smile at. He was a congenial gentleman, a little quiet but always with a sunny disposition.

'I'd hug you, but I don't want to mess you up,' he told her, wiping his greasy hands on his overalls. 'Glad to see you back after so long.'

She nodded, giving him a sad little smile. 'Well, I've got a few spare weeks to sort out the cottage.' She gulped away the end of the sentence about having to put it on the market. Bob understood and nodded.

'Been a tough time for you, love,' he said.

'It has,' she replied with a sigh before looking up at the engine. 'I don't remember seeing the train before. It's always been covered in tarpaulin. It looks like the Hogwarts Express!'

Bob looked proud. 'Even better than that, I reckon! Well, the bodywork is slowly coming together, so it was time to reveal her beauty to the world. And we've started on the engine as well.'

'You really think you can get it going?' she asked, amazed, staring up at the old train.

It was an old steam engine from a bygone era that had remained abandoned in the workshop for decades. Since the station had closed, Bob had become consumed with the notion that he could get it up and running again. It was a labour of love that he had begun to bring back to life with the help of his father, Eddie, a fellow enthusiast who lived in one of the cottages on Railway Lane.

'Oh yes,' said Bob, nodding. 'I'll definitely get it going.'

'Hopefully, it'll run him over when it does,' drawled Rachel, suddenly appearing next to them. She gave Harriet a hug. 'Nice to see you again, dear.'

'You too.'

Rachel, as always, wore a disapproving look on her pinched face. She was a woman who never seemed happy, thought Harriet.

'That dog's back again,' snapped Rachel, looking at her husband.

Bob shook his head. 'I'd better call the rescue centre,' he replied in a dull tone.

'Well, I'll let you deal with him,' said Rachel with a shudder. 'I'm going into Aldwych. Meeting a friend. See you later, Harriet.'

She gave them both a nod before disappearing once more.

'What dog?' asked Harriet, turning to look at Bob.

'Come on,' he said, heading out of the workshop. 'I'll show you.'

They walked back along the track and onto the platform, where Harriet saw a scruffy, shaggy-looking golden retriever curled up beside one of the old benches. She suspected it had been the blonde blur she had seen on the platform the day before.

'He's lovely,' she said, reaching out to stroke him before hesitating. 'Is he friendly?'

'Oh yes,' said Bob. 'He's a good chap. Just a bit homesick, I reckon.'

Harriet looked at Bob, confused.

'He was George Baggins' dog,' he explained. 'You know, the old vet. Lived in the end cottage on Railway Lane, next to my dad. Chap always had dogs. Can't remember a time when he didn't. Seemed to prefer them to humans, to be honest. Certainly didn't speak to any of us apart from a nod hello some mornings when they were out for a walk. Anyway, George passed away a few months ago. He never married and had no family, so the dog was taken to the rescue centre. Trouble is, every time he gets a new foster home, he escapes and comes back here instead.'

'Poor thing,' said Harriet, crouching down to give the dog's slightly grubby fur a stroke.

'Homesick for Cranfield and his old master, I reckon,' said Bob. 'We'd take him in, but Rachel is allergic to fur.'

Harriet carried on stroking the dog. 'What's his name?' she asked.

'We never found out,' said Bob, shaking his head. 'Anyway, I'd better call the rescue centre again.'

But as he drew out his phone, a man appeared on the platform nearby.

'Hello, Bob,' he said with a nod. 'I was just looking for you.'

'Hi, Tom,' replied Bob. 'What are you doing over here?'

'Came to see if the rumours were correct,' replied Tom. He looked down at Harriet with a smile and a hello.

'This is Harriet,' said Bob by way of an introduction. 'She's a friend of the family, living in one of the cottages for a while. Harriet, this is Tom, the editor of *The Cranbridge Times*, the local newspaper. What rumours are we talking about?'

'I've got a source at the planning department for the local council,' Tom told them, looking grim. 'Says that a large industrial warehouse is likely to be approved on some of the land over here.'

'A warehouse?' Bob looked astonished. 'Where?'

He and Harriet exchanged horrified looks. Lovely Cranfield with an enormous, soulless warehouse stuck in the middle of it? It didn't bear thinking about.

'Got the plans right here.' Tom brought out his phone, and Harriet immediately stood up to join them both in looking at the screen. 'It's all under a company name,' carried on Tom. 'Randall Enterprises, according to my source. Ah, here we are.'

Harriet tried to figure out what she was looking at. She finally realised it was a map of Cranfield.

'The parts coloured in red is the area allocated for the ware-house,' explained Tom. 'It's disused land apparently and has no owner rights.'

'Looks like it's two of the fields over there,' said Bob, looking up from the phone.

Harriet took one more look at the map before following his shocked gaze across the railway line. The land that had been allo-cated were the lavender fields.

'But that's my Uncle Fred's fields,' she blurted out.

Tom looked at her. 'Can you prove that?' he asked. 'If so, we may be in with a shot of defeating the plans before they get up and running.'

Harriet looked at Bob. 'I don't really know the history of the fields. What do you think?' she asked.

Bob looked dismayed. 'Sorry, love, but the land was just lying there empty for many years. It was only Fred's idea to plant the lavender all those years ago, seeing as nobody else was doing anything else with them. Those fields haven't been planted or used for anything since I was born, I reckon.'

Harriet felt sick. It was too awful to contemplate. First, the loss of her aunt and uncle, and now the lavender fields. It was too much.

She closed her eyes in pain. There, in her mind, she could see herself as a child, walking in the fields with her uncle, her little hand cupped in his. Cranfield to her was picnics, swimming in the river, and collecting wildflowers, which she pressed into a book. And, she had to admit, it was the blur of purple each summer holiday when she would run up and down the rows of lavender plants playing hide-and-seek that were some of the few precious happy memories when she was growing up.

As the tears pricked her eyes, she knew it was going to be an uphill battle, but she had to try to save the lavender fields somehow.

She just had no idea how to go about it.

8

Joe stifled a yawn again as he looked blearily around the strange bedroom. Where was he again? Oh yes, The Black Swan Inn in Cranbridge. A small dot in the middle of nowhere.

Despite the comfortable bed and quiet inn he was staying in, he hadn't slept well. He had endured a lengthy meeting over dinner with someone from the local council. Joe had taken an instant dislike to the chap; his charm was too oily and his personality insincere.

Joe was reminded of the last time he had met up with his best friend, Matt.

'Don't tell me you actually like dealing with some of your clients,' Matt had questioned him with a look of distaste. 'I mean, some of them are literally destroying natural wildlife habitats, all for great sums of money. But who's really profiting?'

'Me!' quipped Joe. 'That's why I have an expensive flat and drive a brand-new hybrid Range Rover, and your battered old Land Rover is currently in the garage being fixed for the umpteenth time.'

Matt had rolled his eyes. 'But that's just money. What about heart? What about soul?'

'I'm pretty sure I can buy both of those, if necessary,' Joe had told him with a grin.

At the time, they had carried on their usual banter, but afterwards, Joe had been left a little uncomfortable. Was his best friend right? Had his business ethics slipped somewhere along the way, so much so that he had to deal with the likes of the councillor the previous evening?

But business was business, after all, so Joe had laughed at the lame jokes and nodded understandingly in the right places. As far as he was concerned, the purchase and development of the fields was going to go very smoothly. Then he could move onto the next project and forget all about Cranfield.

* * *

After breakfast and having settled up his bill, Joe was determined to leave Cranbridge and head straight for the main road out of the area.

And yet, as if it had a mind of its own, he suddenly found himself parked up in the no-through lane in Cranfield next to the second lavender field. The previous day's drizzle had disappeared, and the sun was shining once more. On the opposite side of the road, the apple trees had burst into blossom, their pink and white flowers bobbing in a gentle breeze. It really was a glorious spring day outside.

To his surprise, Joe couldn't seem to stop himself from getting out of the car. Just for a moment, he promised himself. That was all. A last breath of fresh air before heading back to the smog-filled city.

It was certainly more peaceful than where he was living in the middle of London. Noisy, dirty, and busy, it was in stark contrast to the peace of Cranfield. Maybe that was it, he thought. The peace. He hadn't felt that for a long time.

He squeezed past a gap in the fence next to a large oak tree. The trunk was so large it was spilling out onto the lane.

Joe looked up and down the first row of lavender plants. They had obviously been there for many years, although the land wasn't registered in any name, which was why the sale would go through so smoothly. Someone had taken time and care over these plants at one time. He wondered who it had been and why the lavender had been planted.

He ventured further into the field. He had been abroad quite a bit over the winter months, so it was nice to be back in the English countryside for the spring. The sound of the birdsong filled the air. He couldn't hear anything else other than the breeze rustling through the deadheads of the lavender. He touched one of the flower heads before bringing it up to his fingers, the faint but familiar aroma of lavender staying on his fingers even months after finishing their summer display.

He just straightened up when he saw someone walking towards him between two rows of lavender plants. It was the dancing redhead.

'You again?' she said as she drew nearer. She looked surprised but also pleased to see him.

He found himself smiling in response. 'Like a bad penny,' he replied. 'Although, I wasn't expecting to find anyone here this morning.'

'Well, you're standing in the middle of my family's lavender fields,' said the redhead with a sad smile.

'*Your* family's?' said Joe, a little stunned.

'My uncle planted all of this,' she replied, gesturing around the field before looking back at him with a frown. 'Sorry, I don't think we've been introduced. I'm Harriet Colgan.'

Joe sighed, suddenly feeling uneasy. 'I'm Joe Randall,' he told her, holding out his hand for her to shake.

Harriet had begun to move her hand towards his when she appeared to register his words. 'As in Randall Enterprises?' she said, instantly snatching back her hand and glaring at him with her green eyes. 'The company that wants to destroy all of this?'

'Not destroy,' said Joe quickly. 'However, the land has been designated as being one of the ideal sites for a large warehouse for a major distribution company.'

'A warehouse?' repeated Harriet, making a face. 'Sounds horrible.'

'Well, perhaps at first impression,' said Joe, who had come across this kind of reaction before, albeit not quite as vehemently as the lady in front of him. 'But it would certainly bring some economic regeneration into an area that certainly needs it, from my research.'

'And what else did your research tell you?' asked Harriet, sounding annoyed. 'Did it tell you that our cottage has a beautiful view which your warehouse would destroy? Let alone my neighbours' views. And then there's my friend's farm over there. I'm sure she certainly wouldn't want a vast warehouse next to it, destroying the ecosystem. The biodiversity of these fields is something to cherish and nurture, not concrete over.'

She stopped to take a deep breath. Her temper was obviously as hot as her hair colour.

'Listen, I understand your initial objections,' he began.

But she wasn't going to let him get many words in; such was the apparent anger that she had. 'Worst of all is the fact that you will be destroying all of my uncle's hard work on these fields,' she carried on. 'Uncle Fred was responsible for every one of these lavender plants, and you're just going to mow down all of it without a second thought? Is that what Randall Enterprises does?' she asked with a sneer. 'Tears apart people's hopes and dreams?'

'Well, that's not quite what we say in our advertising campaign,' he drawled before realising now really wasn't the time for humour. She was glaring at him even more. 'Listen, we're not the bad guys here. We act on behalf of corporations seeking space to expand their operations.'

'So, you're just the middleman for the bad guys, is that it?' she said, putting her hands on her hips.

'Perhaps any views should be taken up with the local council,' he told her smoothly. 'But without ownership papers, I don't see how you can be paid any compensation, I'm afraid.'

'It's not about the money,' snapped Harriet, rolling her eyes. 'It might be to someone like you, but to me, this,' she said, gesturing wildly about with her arm, 'is more precious than monetary value. These are – were my uncle's fields. He took care of them for years. The lavender is glorious. To destroy it is to destroy his legacy and everything he cared and stood for!'

Joe watched in horror as she began to blink away tears that had formed in her eyes. His research obviously had some glaring holes in it. Someone had been taking care of the fields. Harriet's uncle, it appeared. He also understood from her words that her uncle had passed away, possibly recently, he guessed.

To Joe, it had always been about the business. It had never felt personal. Until now.

He stood there for a moment in silence, but as he did so, he noticed Harriet squeezing her fingers in and out of tight balls on either side of her body, a gesture of underlying stress.

Joe sighed heavily and suddenly felt every one of his thirty-one years. 'I'm sorry,' he found himself blurting out. 'I understand that this must be hard for you.'

Harriet caught the pity in his eyes and instantly brought up her chin. 'We'll think of something. There's no way this development is going ahead,' she told him in a lofty tone, spinning around and marching away from him.

For a moment, Joe found himself vehemently hoping that she succeeded before shaking his head in surprise at himself.

It was just business, he reminded himself as he got into his car and started the engine, just like all the other times and other deals that he had made.

So why did he suddenly feel so guilty?

9

Harriet felt extremely upset after bumping into Joe Randall.

Her first impression of him had obviously been way off the mark. She had thought him a knight in shining armour when he had stopped on that country lane. In reality, he was a suited destroyer of all the good things in life.

What worried her most was the plans for the lavender fields. Companies seeking to expand their operations. What on earth did that even mean? The thought of massive warehouses being built over Uncle Fred's precious lavender was too awful to contemplate, as too was what was going to happen to her beloved Cranfield and her uncle's legacy. She had to put a stop to this now, but how? Business had always been a bewildering subject to her. She needed an expert.

The thought suddenly came to her. She would have to do the unthinkable, but there was no time to waste.

With a grimace, she steeled herself and tentatively rang her father.

'Harriet?' asked her dad. She could hear his surprised tone of voice all the way from the Caribbean. 'We haven't forgotten your birthday, have we?'

'Not yet,' she murmured but made it so quiet that he couldn't hear. 'No, Dad. But I need help. I'm in Cranfield.'

'You are?' he asked. 'Are you taking a day off? What about the business? You can't just take time off when you want if you want to succeed.'

'Oh, er, well, it didn't succeed anyway, I'm afraid,' she told him, her voice holding a tremor as she spoke. 'You see, I had to close the salon down last week.' Her words came out in a rush from nervousness.

'You've closed the salon?' he said, sounding shocked. 'For good?'

'Yes. The debts were too high. Anyway, that's not why I'm calling.' For once, Harriet found she didn't care about her father's view on her lack of business acumen; this was way more important, so she carried on. 'I've come to Cranfield to tidy up the cottage ready for sale.'

The silence down the line spoke volumes, and she forced herself to continue.

'Actually, it's legal help I need from you, Dad,' she said, rushing on. 'It's regarding the lavender fields.'

'The what?' he asked.

'You know, the lavender fields in Cranfield that Uncle Fred planted. Well, they want to flatten the whole thing and turn it into some awful industrial warehouse or something. So, obviously, it needs to be stopped, but I'm not sure where to start.'

'Who owns the land?' he asked, all business as usual.

'I don't know,' she told him. 'Apparently, nobody does. It was unused for decades until Uncle Fred planted the lavender.'

'Then who is authorising the sale?' he asked.

'The council,' she replied.

'Right,' he said, sounding distracted. 'It doesn't sound as if there's too much of an appeal for you to mount in that case.'

'But there must be something,' she urged him.

There was a short silence before her dad spoke again. 'I'd forgotten.' To Harriet's surprise, her dad sounded almost wistful. 'My father planted some of the original lavender, you know. I remember playing in the lavender field, running up and down the long rows to hide from Fred. I think that's where he got his love for the lavender from...' His voice trailed off into silence.

'That's nice,' said Harriet, somewhat amazed as her father never mentioned his childhood or his older brother if he could help it. She had trouble reconciling the serious lawyer as a young boy running amongst the purple flowers, just as she had done decades later.

'Of course, that was a long time ago now,' snapped her dad, sounding more like his usual self. 'Right, so which company is dealing with the purchase?'

'It's someone called Randall Enterprises,' she said, thinking back to Joe with the nice face, whom she had completely misread.

'Randall Enterprises?' Her dad sounded surprised. 'They're a pretty impressive set-up for such a small firm. I dealt with them last year.'

Harriet rolled her eyes down the phone at her dad's typical reaction, which was to be impressed by such a horrible company. 'So, what should I do?' she asked.

'My suggestion would be to get the cottage on the market as quickly as you can before the price of houses plummets in the area,' he replied. 'After all, your aunt and uncle left you that cottage in good faith. You need to make as much money as you can to set yourself up with the right amount of capital for your next business and property.'

Harriet felt exasperated, but her dad continued to rave about how great Randall Enterprises were and the cost of houses until she couldn't bear it any longer and told him she had to go.

'Of course,' said her dad. 'We'll speak soon.'

Harriet finished the call and sighed. As expected, her parents weren't going to help. When she had been growing up and had called them in tears from the boarding school, they had told her to keep a stiff upper lip.

So, what could she do now but follow the same advice?

But nothing was more important than saving her uncle's legacy.

The fight against the lavender fields started at that very moment.

10

The will to fight against the destruction of the lavender fields was strong inside Harriet when she woke up the following morning.

Harriet decided what she needed was help and where better to start than her best friends. So, she texted the girls to come over for an emergency coffee, briefly describing the horrible news about the planned warehouse in the middle of Cranfield.

Libby lived in one of the railway cottages, so hadn't far to come.

'Flora's joining us in a while,' said Libby over her shoulder, rushing inside as soon as Harriet opened the front door. 'She's busy with wheat, I think? Maybe it was the chickens. I honestly can't remember, but she said to have a large coffee waiting for her.'

Flora had always been the quiet, thoughtful one in the friendship of three, Libby the artistic wild one, and Harriet the peacekeeper and cheer-up committee. It had worked for almost twenty years, and they never lost their tempers with each other despite being so different in personalities.

'How's your dad?' asked Harriet.

Libby made a face. 'I told him about the plan for the lavender fields, but he doesn't seem to get worked up about anything these days.'

Mr Matthews had always been strong-willed, but the stroke he had suffered appeared to have weakened a lot of the fighting spirit that Libby had rebelled against for so long. They continued to live together in an uneasy truce.

When Flora arrived, they discussed the plans for the destruction of the fields.

'That council are so rotten!' said Libby, rolling her eyes. 'We should kick up a big stink about this.'

'The trouble is that if it's legal, what can we do?' asked Flora, looking worried. 'What's Grams going to say?'

Harriet sighed as she looked out of the kitchen window. 'It's such a shame. I mean, the fields aren't at their best right now. If only they were in full bloom, then maybe these cold-hearted developers would think differently about them.'

She immediately thought of Joe, who had seemed so kind when he had stopped to see if she needed help when she had broken down. Appearances could most definitely be deceiving.

'I don't know what's going to happen to the farm if this enormous thing gets built,' said Flora, looking tearful. 'As if things weren't bad enough.'

Harriet rushed across to give her a hug. 'We'll think of something,' she told her friend, although even Harriet was finding it hard to give this terrible news a positive spin.

'Absolutely,' said Libby, adding her arms to the group hug.

'We'll have to think fast,' remarked Harriet as she stepped away. 'Especially as I might not be here very long once the cottage goes up for sale.'

'Stay for the summer,' said Libby with a shrug. 'Take some time off from the rat race.'

Harriet frowned. 'I need to look for another job. Again.' For a second, she allowed herself to wallow in self-pity. Then she drew herself up straight once more. 'Maybe my business failing was a good thing so that I can be here to fight against this thing. Anyway, a change is a good as a rest and all that.'

Libby rolled her eyes. 'Your positive mantra is sickening, and I've missed it terribly,' she added, coming over to give her friend a quick hug.

With no ideas about what could be done, her friends had left, and Harriet was still pondering on the lavender fields. She thought about a protest to get the village community behind her, but what community? She'd barely seen anyone since coming to Cranfield, apart from Bob and Rachel at the station. And, she realised, that was the problem. There would be strength in numbers, but she was just one person. She needed a community. In the end, she fired up Aunt May's ancient printer and managed to print out a flyer to be put through each letter box of the fifty or so homes in Cranfield.

She just hoped they wouldn't be binned along with the normal junk mail that got delivered. To ensure they wouldn't, she highlighted the words STOP! and FIGHT! in fluorescent green.

The rest of the afternoon was spent delivering the flyers around the village.

As usual, it was quiet, which didn't make her feel much more positive about the outcome of the fight. The few people that she bumped into were worried about the planned development, but what could they do?

'When do the little people ever win against these big companies?' said one man.

Harriet realised he was right and that flyers alone weren't going to be enough. What she needed was a better plan. A bigger and better one, with more of a splash than a whimper for the headlines, but what that could be was a complete loss to Harriet, no matter how much she wracked her brains.

Late in the afternoon, she wandered into the kitchen and flicked on the kettle to make a cup of tea. As she stood at the sink, she stared out of the window down the garden and out to the fields beyond. She could just make out the rows of old lavender plants, still somewhat amazed that her dad had mentioned playing in there as a child. She spent a happy minute imagining the two brothers as small children running and laughing through the rows of lavender. She still couldn't imagine her father growing up in a place like Cranfield. He had never spoken about it before.

She had to think of something, she told herself. She brought out her phone, thinking back to an idea about protests. Once she had made her cup of tea, she sat down at the kitchen table to flick through Google Images to see if anything could spark an idea.

Protests might work if Cranfield wasn't so quiet. Was a protest actually a protest if there was no one around to see it?

She carried on googling and came across an image of the brave women of the suffragettes movement holding up their placards for Votes for Women. Harriet sat back in her chair, thinking back to a conversation she had had with Grams years ago about how her own grandmother had been a suffragette. She idly continued to scroll further down the page before coming across a few images of suffragettes chained to railings.

The cup of tea stopped halfway to Harriet's mouth as she began to smile and nod to herself with an idea forming. Of course! She didn't know why she hadn't thought of it before! It was absolutely perfect!

She put down the mug and quickly called Flora.

'Hi,' she said to her friend when she picked up. 'You don't happen to have a large chain I can borrow, do you?'

11

'I'm not sure this is a good idea,' said Flora as she turned the key in the padlock. 'What if something happens and you need to escape?'

'What's going to happen?' asked Harriet, laughing as she wriggled her back against the rough bark of the large oak tree in the middle of the lavender field. She glanced down at the heavy and somewhat rusty chain, which was now across her torso and around the tree, holding her firmly in place. 'I don't think there's any wild animals around here.'

'Don't joke,' said Flora, frowning. 'But are you really agreeing that it's sensible to do this for twenty-four hours?'

'What other choice do I have?' said Harriet, shrugging her shoulders. She was trying to stay positive but was having serious doubts about whether a mad plan like this would actually work. 'Look, Tom from the local newspaper is coming, and I need to generate a buzz to start some sort of protest campaign. This will look great in a photo!'

'What about the leaflets?' asked Flora.

'Well, I've put one through every door,' Harriet reminded her, 'but I need something more.'

'This is most definitely more,' said Flora with a grimace. 'I'd stay and support you, but I've got a couple of sick hens I need to keep an eye on for a couple of hours, and Grams is a bit tired tonight. Although, she wanted me to tell you that she loves you and thinks that this is a "grand idea".'

'Glad to hear it,' said Harriet. 'Anyway, this is a fight, not a social event, and I intend to win.'

'That's the spirit,' said Flora, giving her a hug. 'And you'll need that attitude when the rain comes in overnight.'

'Oh.' Harriet made a face. 'I didn't check the forecast.'

'Hope you've got a waterproof in there,' said Flora, nodding at the bag on the floor, which contained some water, a flask of hot tea, and some sandwiches.

Harriet nodded. 'I'm sure it'll be okay.'

But soon after Flora had left, the breeze whipped up, and Harriet had to shrug on her coat whilst still trying to stay inside the chain. She glanced around, hoping nobody had seen her break her self-inflicted prison. It was all about the story, she reckoned. Hopefully, Tom wouldn't be too late, she thought.

Being next to the tree in the middle of the field meant she was quite conspicuous, which she hoped would look good for any news story in *The Cranbridge Times*. She shivered. She hoped it wouldn't be too long before Tom got here.

She glanced over at the other oak tree further away and blew a kiss at the initials she knew were carved into the bark. Her aunt and uncle would be with her in spirit, she decided.

However, pretty soon, the light began to fade, and Harriet was left wondering if she was completely mad to be doing this. If only it had been a warm summer's evening, she thought. Instead, it was a somewhat chilly April night, but needs must, and time was of the essence with this fight.

Then her phone rang out with a text.

'Sorry, I'm caught up on another story,' said the text from Tom, the editor of *The Cranbridge Times*. 'I'll be there first thing tomorrow. Keep fighting!'

Harriet grimaced at the thought of being there alone all night. Then she thought back to what she had read about the suffragettes and their sacrifices. This really wasn't so bad, was it?

In the fading light, she saw someone crossing the pedestrian bridge across the railway line and prayed it was Flora, who had finished earlier than hoped and had come to keep her company. But, as the person grew nearer, she realised, to her horror, it wasn't Flora at all.

It was Joe Randall. The enemy.

Harriet drew herself up straighter and held her head up high as he walked towards her.

'Good evening,' he said as he came closer.

The fact that he was in his smart business coat over his suit, and she was in her jeans and an old jacket, didn't help her awkwardness. But then she remembered that he was in the wrong here, not her.

'Good evening,' she replied in a light tone as if there were absolutely nothing unusual in the situation whatsoever.

'How are you?' he asked, coming to stand in front of her.

'Fine, thank you,' she told him. 'What are you doing here? Shouldn't you be concreting over some national park somewhere?'

'Well, that was my plan for tonight, but here's the funny thing,' he said, putting his hand into his pockets. 'I received a phone call from Tom Addison of *The Cranbridge Times* asking for a comment on the protest that was taking place here.'

'Really?' she said, smiling. That was good, wasn't it? It meant that perhaps it was an even bigger story than she had anticipated.

'So, I thought I'd better see what was going on.'

'Well, here I am, and as you can see, I'm here for the long haul,' she told him, jutting out her chin as she held her head even higher.

He raised an eyebrow at her, and there was something akin to humour twinkling in his eyes. 'Your hands have gone blue,' he told her.

'They're a little cold, yes,' she replied, her winning smile fading somewhat.

'Perhaps we could discuss this matter over dinner somewhere in the warm,' he suggested.

Harriet shook her head. 'Oh, no. No way. I'm not leaving.'

'Trust me,' he told her with a sigh. 'This is not going to help your cause.'

'I'm not so sure,' she told him. 'Once word gets out of your ghastly plans, then I'll have the weight of the community behind me.'

'So where are they?' he asked, glancing around the empty field.

'On their way,' she lied.

He leant against the large tree trunk and looked at her, growing more serious. 'So, tell me,' he said gently. 'What is it that's so special about a couple of abandoned fields?'

'It's not just the fields,' she told him. 'It's about Cranfield as well. Your plans would ruin it.'

'Ruin what?' he said, laughing. 'There's nothing here.'

'Well, that's just where you're wrong,' she told him, suddenly cross at his careless attitude. 'For some of us, it's not just a quiet village. It's a refuge. Somewhere to escape to. At the lowest moments of my life, this place has held me close and kept me safe and loved. That's what's so special, and there's no way I'm letting it change!'

She stopped, aghast, as she realised that she had gone way too far in revealing her pain.

But he didn't laugh at her as she expected. Instead, she was surprised to see worry in his eyes, even a small amount of pity.

Finally, he nodded thoughtfully. 'Well, don't give up hope yet,' he told her, straightening up from leaning against the tree. 'You may still win this battle.'

Harriet was shocked at his words. 'Really?' she said.

'Perhaps,' he told her.

'Record yourself on my phone saying that there is still hope,' she urged him. 'Go on.'

He laughed. 'You have trust issues.'

'So would you if you'd had my upbringing,' she replied.

His laughter faded. 'Look, I appreciate how much this place means to you, but maybe I'm not the bad guy. Do you think that you can believe that?'

She hesitated, surprised to find herself thinking that she could.

He sighed and brought out a pair of gloves from his pockets and held them out for her to take. 'A peace offering,' he said.

Harriet looked at them and up into his face. For a long time, they held their gaze before she finally looked down. 'Only because I don't want to catch a chill and get a cold. I must be strong to fight this,' she told him.

A smile played on his lips as she finally took the gloves.

'Thank you,' she told him softly.

He nodded. 'I'll see you in the morning.'

'You will?' she asked, a little surprised.

'Once I've got up from my lovely, warm, comfortable bed at the inn, of course,' he told her, breaking into a wicked grin before he turned away.

Harriet was left in the darkening field, thinking how much better he looked when he smiled.

12

Flora returned to join Harriet for the night-time protest, and Harriet was grateful for her friend's company on such a chilly night.

'You could have picked a nice summer evening,' grumbled Flora, snuggling down deeper into one of the two sleeping bags she had brought with her.

'We might not have until summer,' said Harriet, with a sigh, clutching the cup of hot soup that Flora had brought with her in a flask.

Flora looked across at her friend sitting next to her, still tied up beside the tree trunk. 'Is that what he said? That Joe, when he came to see you earlier?'

Harriet shrugged her shoulders. 'They're not going to hang around, are they?' she muttered. 'These places go up in a flash, overnight sometimes.'

Although she couldn't help but think on his words about him not being the bad guy, was that true? She glanced down at the gloves he had given her, which were too big but were definitely keeping her hands much warmer.

Certainly, his statement about her having trust issues was right.

Harriet had been let down on so many occasions by her parents not turning up at concerts or parents' evenings. She was their last concern, way behind her much more intelligent siblings and their own stellar careers. But she didn't care. Or at least that's what she had continued to tell herself.

That was why Cranfield was so important to her. It was her safe place, her happy place. Somewhere she felt as if she finally belonged. She had found herself blabbing that to Joe as well. He seemed to bring out the very worst in her and also the most honest side of her as well. For some reason, she didn't have a filter with him, which made her feel very uncomfortable to be that exposed emotionally.

'Maybe he's not so bad,' said Flora, breaking into Harriet's reverie and guessing what she was thinking about.

'Humph,' said Harriet, with a toss of her head, nearly banging it against the tree bark at the same time. 'I'm pretty sure that he is, actually. I mean, look at his job. What kind of person, other than a cold-hearted one, would choose a job where the fundamental principle is to destroy fields and villages?'

'Not everyone has a choice over their job,' said Flora softly.

Harriet looked across at her friend in sympathy. Flora had been interested in crafting growing up. She had even gone on to study Art at college, but following her education, she had returned to Cranfield to take care of her elderly grandparents. They had been her steady rock during a tumultuous childhood when her parents had divorced, and her father had kept trying to find a happy marriage. He was currently on wife number four. At the farm, her grandfather had been unable to perform the heavy work as his illness took its toll, and so Flora had begun to take over, forgoing her passion for duty. She had been there ever since, trying to keep the farm going, but Harriet and Libby knew just how much of a struggle it was.

'Are you doing okay?' asked Harriet softly.

Flora smiled gently. 'I'm fine,' she said. 'After all, I'm not the one chained to a tree.'

Harriet giggled and snuggled deeper into the sleeping bag as the temperature dropped. They spent the night chatting and dozing.

* * *

In the early light of dawn, Flora unzipped her sleeping bag and wrapped it around Harriet for extra warmth.

'Thankfully, the rain never came, so I've got to get back and get on with the ploughing whilst the weather stays dry,' she said. 'Will you be all right for a while?'

Harriet nodded. 'I've got a flask of coffee and some biscuits somewhere. That'll keep me going until the newspaper guy arrives.'

'Good luck!' said Flora as she headed off.

Unfortunately, the coffee had grown cold, and the biscuits were smashed to pieces at the bottom of Harriet's bag. She hadn't prepared quite as well as she had hoped.

She shivered and longed for the warmth of the sun to bring some feelings back to her cold bones, but the day looked as overcast as the previous one.

She gazed out across the field as dawn slowly brought daylight and birdsong to the place. It was truly magical, she thought, despite how cold she was feeling. However, it had been a long, dark, cold night, and she was hoping that Tom might not be too late that morning.

She saw someone coming over the pedestrian bridge of the railway and squinted at the figure in the soft light of dawn, hoping it wasn't Joe Randall again. Thankfully, it wasn't him, she thought with a grateful sigh. And it wasn't Flora or Libby either. It was one of her next-door neighbours from the cottages on Railway Lane.

She only knew of Maggie from her Aunt May. She was a widow who had lived in the cottages for a few years, but she kept herself to herself. Harriet remembered Grams saying that Maggie was never seen out and about. And yet, here she was at the crack of dawn, heading towards Harriet.

'Good morning,' said Maggie, with a soft smile. She was an attractive lady of around sixty years of age but had an air of shyness about her.

'Good morning,' replied Harriet, struggling to a standing position, if only to bring some life back to her bones, which were sore after sitting on the ground all night.

'I saw you out of my bedroom window first thing,' said Maggie. 'And I wondered if you needed a warm drink?' She held out a small flask for Harriet to take.

'Oh, that's so kind of you,' said Harriet, opening up the lid to see the steam rising from the hot drink.

'And there's a pastry in here as well, if you'd like,' added Maggie, holding out a bag for Harriet to take in her other hand.

'Thank you so much,' said Harriet.

'I saw your pamphlet, by the way, and put two and two together when I saw you here last night. I think it's smashing what you're doing,' carried on Maggie. 'I've often looked out of my window these past few years. Gave me a bit of peace to watch the changing of the seasons on this old oak tree.'

'It is lovely,' said Harriet in between mouthfuls of the delicious pastry. 'Wow! This is amazing. Did you make this?' she mumbled, her mouth still full of buttery pastry.

Maggie shrugged her shoulders. 'It's easy when you know how.'

'I think you'll find it's not,' said Harriet, laughing. 'Not if you've seen my many failed attempts at baking.'

Maggie smiled at her. 'It's freezing out here. Do you need a break?'

'I'm actually desperate for a hot shower,' admitted Harriet with a rueful smile. 'But I daren't leave in case the editor from the newspaper comes. If nobody's here, then there'll be no protest, and we'll probably lose the case.'

Maggie thought for a moment. 'Then you head home quickly, and I'll take over for a while,' she said.

Harriet was stunned. 'You will?'

'Of course,' replied Maggie, nodding. 'And if that chap comes, I'll keep him here until you return. Give me your mobile number, and I'll call you if anyone turns up.'

So, they swapped places.

'I'd knock on Bob's door at the station when you're over there,' said Maggie. 'I can't have been the only person to have noticed you out here this morning. It might look better with a crowd if the press is coming.'

'Okay.' But before leaving, Harriet hesitated. 'Are you sure you're okay doing this?'

Maggie looked down at the chain wrapped around her before grinning. 'First bit of excitement in my life for many years,' she said. 'Who knew protesting would bring a bit of life into my life.'

Harriet laughed and rushed off, grateful for kind neighbours and even more determined that the field needed to be saved, not just for her but for everyone else in the village.

13

Joe was both exasperated and impressed with the press campaign that had been so swiftly organised regarding the sale of the lavender field in Cranfield.

Of course, it had meant a last-minute alteration to his full diary of meetings and an extra, unexpected night's stay at the Black Swan Inn. But once he had returned to the inn from the somewhat out-of-the-ordinary sight of Harriet tied to a large oak tree with a heavy chain, it had played on his mind all night.

Protests weren't anything new, of course. He had come across quite a bit of opposition in his time, but this felt personal, and he wasn't sure why.

Harriet was fiercely protective of the land, and she had let slip the previous evening that she had obviously found it a safe place during her childhood. He found himself wanting to know more about the redhead whose passion for the lavender fields matched the colour of her hair.

Feeling at a bit of a loss as to how to approach the situation, he called his dad as he drove away from the inn.

'Hey,' he said when the call was picked up.

'What's the story?' said his dad almost immediately. 'You've spent too much time down in Cranfield already.'

'There's a problem,' Joe told him. 'The press have got wind of the development, and now there's some kind of protest going on.'

'So?' said his dad brusquely. 'That's nothing new.'

'I know,' began Joe. 'But this time it's a bit more extreme. A local woman has tied herself to an oak tree.' He found himself laughing in amusement. 'It's quite a sight.'

But his dad didn't laugh along with him. He never laughed these days, Joe realised.

'Look, this is business,' his dad told him. 'You're going to get weirdos and hippies protesting at anything these days. Just get the deal signed off. I've got other projects for you already lined up.'

Joe sighed. 'Actually, Dad, I'm feeling a bit run-down, to be honest.'

There was a small pause down the line. 'What are you talking about?' asked his dad, suddenly sounding worried. 'Are you ill?'

'No. I just need a break,' Joe found himself confessing. 'I haven't had a weekend off for months, let alone a holiday.'

'A holiday?' His dad sounded shocked.

'I am entitled to some breaks throughout the working year, like any other normal employee,' said Joe fiercely.

There was a silence down the line. 'I suppose,' his dad agreed eventually. 'Although, I won't be taking any days off.'

'You wouldn't go back to Portugal?' asked Joe tentatively.

His parents had enjoyed many trips to Portugal over the years before his mum became unwell.

'No,' said his dad bluntly. 'And I don't understand how you can think about taking time off when things are so busy.'

'It's always busy,' replied Joe. 'It never stops. You never stop...' His voice trailed off.

They both knew why his dad was such a workaholic these days, but Joe was getting tired. He thought back to Harriet's passion for the lavender field. His conversations with her had brought up many unexpected feelings. Most of all, guilt. Which was ridiculous because in all the years he had been working, he had never once felt guilty. Or had he just remained deliberately blinded to the plight of the people whose land he was buying? What had happened to the communities afterwards? He had never considered it until now.

'Do you ever worry that we're seen as the bad guys?' he found himself asking.

'What are you talking about?' asked his dad.

'I mean, we come in and take the land wherever it may be, and we never stop to think about the impact afterwards,' replied Joe. 'Do you ever go back to any of the places where you've made a deal to see what happens in the aftermath of the new industrial estate or whatever going up?'

'Of course not,' replied his dad, sounding astonished. 'Besides, if we didn't do it, someone else would. So why don't we profit from it instead of them?'

'That doesn't mean it's always the right choice for the place,' countered Joe.

There was another short silence down the line.

'I can sign this deal off if you're losing your nerve,' said his dad finally.

Joe sagged. 'No,' he answered with a heavy sigh. 'That's okay. I'll keep you posted.'

'Good,' said his dad. 'The family business needs you, son.'

'Yeah, I know,' replied Joe before saying goodbye.

He parked the car in front of the cottages and sighed again. He knew his dad wasn't right, but he was carrying so much hurt already that Joe couldn't add any more to his burden.

With a heavy heart, he got out of the car to walk to the station to see what was happening over in the lavender field. He had been expecting to see all signs of the protest having been wound down with the dawn of the new day, but to his surprise, this wasn't the case at all. As he went down the steps on the other side of the bridge over the railway line, he could see there were about a dozen people standing next to the oak tree.

As he drew nearer, he could see Harriet standing there, a triumphant look on her face. He did notice, however, that she was wearing a different outfit, which made him somewhat suspicious.

'There he is,' Joe heard her announce as he drew nearer. 'That's the representative from Randall Enterprises.'

The group spun around, and he realised they were a wide range of ages.

'You don't frighten us, young man,' said one lady, who appeared to be wearing a flowery apron underneath her heavy coat.

'That was never my intention,' said Joe softly.

As he stood in front of them, a man of a similar age to himself stepped forward.

'Tom Addison of *The Cranbridge Times*,' he said, holding out his phone, obviously recording the conversation. 'There is significant local opposition gathering online and here in person to the plans to sell up the lavender fields. Would you care to give your reasons why you feel a large warehouse would fit into this beautiful landscape?'

Joe smiled congenially and began the speech that he usually rolled out for such developments. 'First of all, it will bring significant economic and social regeneration to the area.'

'No, it won't,' came a shout from nearby. 'Where are the roads? Access to all the lorries thundering up and down our lanes?'

'I agree,' said another woman. 'Social regeneration? You sound like a politician!'

Joe dragged a hand through his hair. When had he become the bad guy? And why hadn't he seen this before?

'The local council can, of course, be contacted for their take on all this,' he began to say.

But another woman stepped forward. 'My grandmother was a suffragette, dear,' she told him with glaring blue eyes. 'You don't frighten me.'

'I don't want to,' he said, somewhat non-plussed.

But every time he tried to tell the journalist his point of view, he was shouted down. In the end, he gave up.

He noticed that Harriet had temporarily slipped out of her chains to hold out his gloves.

'Here,' she said. 'You could always hold them up to your ears to block out all the insults.'

Her green eyes twinkled with amusement as he took the gloves from her.

'Thank you,' she added more softly for him to hear. 'But I can't say I'm not sorry that you couldn't get your point across.'

'There'll be other times,' he said, staring at a long lock of red hair that was trailing across her cheek.

As he walked away, he wondered about the protests and whether Harriet and the other protestors were actually right. But what could he do about it? He had always been certain of where he stood, that he was doing the right thing by regenerating sites and areas with the industrial properties that were built on the land that he helped to sell.

The trouble was, he wasn't so sure he was on the right side any more.

14

Harriet completed her interview with Tom from *The Cranbridge Times* with a rallying call to everyone nearby to protest. They all cheered and waved as the footage was filmed. She urged them to carry on and confirmed that they would keep protesting until the council changed their minds.

'So, what happens now?' she asked when Tom had finally stopped filming.

'We'll try to generate enough noise to get it into the national papers,' he replied. 'That always helps.'

'That's great,' she said, relieved.

'I think you're doing a great thing here,' he told her. 'Well done.'

'Thanks,' she muttered, blushing.

But Tom wasn't the only one who appeared to be impressed at Harriet's small stand against the destruction of the lavender fields.

Libby turned up later that morning, having just come in on an overnight flight.

'I go away for one day and come back to find you've become a rebel overnight!' she said, laughing.

'I'm not a rebel,' Harriet told her.

'Of course you're a rebel. You're chained to a tree!' said Libby, still laughing. 'I'm so proud of you! Now, shove over, will you? It looks like there's room for another one.'

In fact, there was quite a queue of people who wanted to be chained to the tree throughout the day, so when someone arrived from the council to try to speak, he got shouted down. Then Bob's father, Eddie, chained himself to the councillor's car by looping a chain through his Mercedes badge.

'Find him a chair and a large gin!' shouted Libby once the councillor had finally freed his car from the elderly pensioner and sped off.

'Three cheers for Eddie!' announced Flora as she led the hero of the hour across the field.

'Where's that gin?' asked Eddie, sinking gratefully into a camping chair that someone had brought along.

'Here you go,' said Grams, drawing out a hip flask. 'A nice strong gin and tonic is what you need.'

Therefore, there was a mix of gin-induced merriment, as well as heady excitement, as a couple of journalists from the national press arrived late in the afternoon.

Harriet explained their cause, but the journalists were more interested in getting photographs of the chained-up pensioners who by now were singing the protest suffragette song from Mary Poppins, led by Grams.

'Emily Pankhurst would be proud,' murmured Flora into Harriet's ear.

Harriet grinned. 'I hope she would.'

'So, are we here for the night?' Libby asked.

Harriet shrugged her shoulders. 'I guess we need to show willing just in case Joe Randall shows up again.'

Libby shrugged. 'Oh, well, you've already ruined my morning, so why not my evening as well.'

'Why?' asked Flora. 'Did you have a hot date planned?'

Libby grimaced. 'I should be so lucky. I was going to do my washing.'

'I guess this is more glamorous,' Harriet told her.

'If a little chillier,' said Flora, shivering in the rapidly cooling temperature.

But someone had brought along a little terracotta chiminea which gave off a little cheery glow and some warmth as the night drew in.

Ten or so hardy souls stayed overnight, doing the bathroom run in shifts so that someone was always tied up against the tree.

The next morning brought about a beautiful sunrise, which Harriet found herself realising she would never have seen had the protest not taken such a hold on the village.

However, the morning light also lit up the neglected lavender plants. She chatted to Bob as they sat next to each other at the base of the oak tree.

'I wish you could have seen it in all its glory,' Bob told her. 'It really was something. Fred just planted them for the sheer pleasure of their beauty. That and all those insects that it encouraged.'

'I remember,' said Harriet, nodding. It had been a field of purple up and over the horizon. Very beautiful. 'But they've not been like that for a few years now.'

'Your uncle always pruned them in the autumn each year,' said Grams from the other side of the tree. 'Apart from last autumn when he was too ill.'

'Pruning,' said Bob, nodding wisely. 'That's the magic trick. Keeps the flowers and the colour at their best.'

'Then maybe I should give that a go,' said Harriet.

Bob immediately cheered up. 'That's the spirit,' he replied with a smile. 'It should be done at the end of the summer, really, but I don't see how it can do any harm now if you get it finished soon.

You just need to cut the tops off and don't touch the woody bit, or you'll kill the plant. You'll get the hang of it.'

Harriet smiled and nodded whilst seriously worried by her lack of knowledge of all things gardening. It would be too awful if she ruined the plants altogether.

'It's just a matter of giving it a haircut,' explained Grams, obviously sensing Harriet's doubt. 'And it would be lovely to see them bloom one last time.'

'I agree,' said Harriet, nodding, her words catching in her throat at the thought that it might be the last summer of lavender in Cranfield.

As breakfast was shared and more people began to gather in the light of day, a buzz ran around the group. It turned out that the photographs, both in *The Cranbridge Times* and the national press, were gathering momentum, as well as on social media.

'Everyone's talking about it,' said Flora, sounding excited. 'It's like David versus Goliath. Us the little people against a massive corporate baddie.'

'Great,' said Harriet. 'But is there any chance of us winning?'

Surely all the cold nights would be worth it, she hoped.

'Wait!' called out Libby, looking at her phone. 'There's breaking news on *The Cranbridge Times* website! It seems as if the decision has now been delayed for a few months! That's what the council is saying, at any case.'

A huge cheer went up around the small group.

'We've done it!' shouted Flora, grabbing Harriet and giving her a hug.

Harriet nodded in disbelief. So, it turned out that the protest had done wonders and a couple of chilly nights spent outside was worth it. If only a reprieve for now.

'Well done,' said everyone as they began to leave with a spring in their step.

But Harriet was still frowning as they headed back over the bridge and onto the station platform.

'So, you can relax for a bit now,' Flora told her. 'After the longest bath in history, that is.'

'You're kidding,' replied Harriet. 'The decision has only been temporarily delayed. I've been thinking that I need to prune the whole field to get the colour as best as possible this summer. If it looks as wonderful as it's ever been, then maybe we've still got a chance.' She sighed. 'Relaxing is for other people.'

'What about a love life?' said Libby, giving her a nudge. 'Is that for other people too?'

'Shurrup,' muttered Harriet as they turned towards the short passageway leading out into Railway Lane.

'There's always Joe Randall,' Libby carried on as she went first down the narrow gap. 'You know the old saying. Keep your friends close and your enemies closer.'

'I don't think so. I'd rather date a tarantula than Joe Randall,' replied Harriet as she came to the end of the passageway and almost ran into the back of Libby, who had abruptly stopped.

To her horror, she found Joe standing just around the corner, seemingly having heard every word.

'I suppose it's whether the tarantula would ask you out in the first place,' he said, raising a sardonic eyebrow.

Harriet blushed. 'What are you doing here?' she asked.

'I came to congratulate you on a job well done,' he told her. 'The delay gives you a bit of time to decide what you can do with the fields.'

'I'm not going to do anything with the fields but give them a good pruning,' said Harriet. 'Then, when it's flowering in the summer, we'll get the press back and show you that you can't possibly concrete over the place.'

Joe nodded thoughtfully. 'Well then, I wish you good luck. And for your date with the tarantula as well,' he added before giving her a wink and walking away.

Libby burst out laughing. 'Well, at least he's got a sense of humour,' she said. 'Are you sure you don't want to date him?'

'Of course not,' snapped Harriet.

Although the thought of sitting opposite Joe at a dinner table and having an hour or two to stare into those brown eyes wasn't exactly filling her with dread, she found.

But he was the enemy, she reminded herself. Wasn't he?

15

So, the protest had sort of worked, Harriet decided. A few more villagers had rallied to the cause, and the council had given them an official deferral until the autumn, which gave them the whole summer to enjoy the lavender fields. If they bloomed, of course. And mother nature most definitely needed a hand.

'Are you sure you know what you're doing?' asked Libby a couple of days later.

'I'm doing exactly what Bob and Grams told me to do, as well as a man on YouTube last night,' Harriet told her, pointing the phone camera down so that Libby could see the first lavender plant that Harriet had pruned that morning. 'I've taken five centimetres off the top as instructed.'

'Great,' said Libby. 'But, for the record, I haven't a clue what I'm looking at.'

'Not sure I have either,' admitted Harriet with a sigh. 'I'm just hoping that it works. So, how's the ocean looking over there?'

'Smashing,' said Libby. 'I can just about see it from the airport runway.' She was currently in the Canary Islands, about to step back on board the plane.

'Sounds very relaxing,' replied Harriet dryly.

'I spent this morning on a sun lounger by the hotel pool. You should try it sometime,' countered Libby.

Chance would be a fine thing for her, thought Harriet after finishing the call.

She had originally planned to have a few emotional weeks to clear the final pieces in the cottage before putting it on the market. Then there was the small matter of her business debts, so she needed a job fast. But she had barely begun to sort anything out and had spent her days organising protests and being tied to a tree instead. Now she was venturing into horticulture, and the cottage remained untouched, still filled with all of her boxed possessions and those of her aunt and uncle. Not that she minded, she found. It was comforting, in a way, to have the cottage feel the same way as it had always done.

Harriet slid her phone into the baggy pocket of her jacket and stared around the expanse of the field as she stood in one corner of it. The trouble was there were at least five thousand or so plants to prune. It would take days, if not weeks, with just her doing all the work.

But at least it wasn't raining, she decided, looking up at the clear blue sky. The temperature was a bit chilly that afternoon, though.

Harriet wasn't looking forward to pruning both fields, but it had to be done. After all, the plants hadn't been pruned for a whole year, and the colour had to return the strongest it had ever been. Otherwise, it would all have been for nothing because a field full of dead lavender wasn't going to win over people's hearts. Nothing short of perfection would do.

An hour later, she grimaced and stretched her back. She had only pruned fifty plants and was already aching. It really was going to take her forever. In fact, the chances were that she would be nowhere near finished by the time her self-imposed deadline of the end of the month came, and that was only a couple of weeks away. But she had to keep going before May arrived. Otherwise, it would be too late for the flowers to bloom in time.

Having pruned the next plant along, she straightened up once more, wincing as her back twinged. It was an old problem that had been exacerbated by her work in the beauty salon.

As she looked across the field, just over the brow of the hill, she could see Cranbridge, the spire of the tiny church just peeping over the trees. Cranbridge had done really well over the past couple of years, she had heard. But then it had a shop and pub. What could be done about Cranfield when its heart was the station that was no longer in use?

It was a heavenly setting. The hills surrounding the village were green and lush. The buildings were all the same pretty sandy-coloured stone, and yet, it felt empty somehow. Idyllic, yet in need of help.

Harriet carried on, forcing herself to continue even though she was beginning to feel a bit rubbish. Her back was aching, her nose had begun to stream, and she couldn't stop sneezing. Had she caught a cold? A couple of nights sleeping on the hard ground hadn't helped, but it had helped the cause. Or had it? Just because the decision was being delayed didn't mean that the council still wouldn't rule against them.

But still, she continued to prune plant after plant, hour after hour, trying to stay positive with the thought that all the hard work would be worth it come the summertime. Even though now, she was on her own. After a day of excitement, everyone had gone back into their houses. After all, what else was there to do?

Libby was on another trip, Flora was busy trying to keep the farm afloat, and everyone else in the village? Well, Harriet supposed that they had just gone back to their lives. There had been quite a hubbub the previous day when everyone had come out to protest for the national press. But without the protest, there was nothing else to connect them in Cranfield. There was no corner shop or gathering point, so people remained lonely if they didn't have friends. She couldn't imagine not having Flora and Libby to talk to or share her thoughts and experiences with. Although she wished she had her friends with her now to help with the pruning.

By the end of the day, it was beginning to turn dark, and she was just reaching the end of the second row. She groaned. She wasn't even halfway through the first field yet!

She shivered once more. If she could just get a few more plants pruned, then perhaps tomorrow she could take a break. Lie in bed all day. It sounded absolute bliss, but she knew the sense of failure hanging over her would be complete if she didn't make every effort to save the lavender fields.

She had just reached the plant nearest the pedestrian bridge and was bending down to prune it, and end the day's hard work, when something went twang in her back. She took a sharp intake of breath and cried out, 'Ow!' near to tears. The pain was excruciating.

Harriet glanced at the pedestrian bridge, but it might as well have been Mount Everest. There was no way she could walk over that at the moment to head home.

Not knowing what else to do, she lay down on the flat but cold ground to stretch out her back. Okay, that helped a little, she thought.

Realising that she couldn't lie there all night, she scrabbled around in her pockets for her phone but was shocked to find it wasn't there. She must have dropped it somewhere along the long row of plants!

She groaned and felt the tears come to her eyes, both from pain and the sense of failure hanging over her. She had tried to stay positive, but maybe her parents were right after all. Maybe she was pretty useless, all being said and done.

She was just tired, she told herself. It had been a crazy few days. She needed a good night's sleep. Then she would find her positivity once more. Maybe it was hidden next to her phone, she thought, rolling her eyes to herself.

She was just about to move when something loomed out of the semi-darkness nearby.

Harriet gave a short scream of shock before she realised that it was the runaway golden retriever.

She clutched her chest and tried to calm her racing pulse. 'You gave me such a fright,' she told the dog.

The dog didn't seem at all concerned and merely came over to give her cheek a small lick as if to check that she was okay. Perhaps he wasn't used to coming across people lying down in the middle of the fields, thought Harriet.

'Well, that was very nice of you,' she said to the dog. 'Maybe you have hidden search and rescue skills that I didn't know about. Come on. Let's go home.'

She thought she'd better attempt to get up and go home. But when she tried to move, she found she couldn't do so without her back giving her terrible pain. To her horror, she was stuck on the ground until someone came to find her. Libby's flight had been delayed, so she wasn't home yet, but surely Flora would text her and become worried when there wasn't an answer? What if she had to stay here all night? There was no sleeping bag this time around, no nice, friendly chat around the warmth of the campfire.

The dog seemed to sense that she wasn't going anywhere, so he settled down alongside her, his doggy warmth giving her a tiny amount of comfort. Two lost souls together, thought Harriet. He had obviously escaped from his new foster home again.

She reached out to stroke his soft fur, thinking that he definitely needed a bath at some point. But despite the comfort that he brought her, Harriet still felt like crying. She and the dog were lying on the freezing cold ground. Surely someone would find them both and help.

16

Joe had spent most of the last few days in intense meetings and was feeling fairly drained as he left the hotel in Manchester.

As he started up his car, he realised that he had missed a call from Matt, so Joe rang him back as he began the long drive home down the motorway.

However, when Joe told him about the protests in Cranfield, Matt laughed and asked if he could join in.

'Glad you've come up against some decent opposition at last,' said Matt before growing more serious. 'It's like I told you before, perhaps it's time to consider the people affected by your dad's business and rethink your plans.'

After the conversation ended, Joe carried on towards London, but his flat didn't hold much appeal to him. He had no feelings about it. It was another bed, albeit somewhere which wasn't a hotel, that was all.

He couldn't stop his thoughts from straying towards Cranfield. The heartfelt protests had weighed heavily on his mind over the past few days despite being away from the village. It wasn't just Harriet and her passion for saving the lavender fields. It had been the group of people all gathering together at the protest. It had been a community full of warmth, cheer and friendship, and he couldn't stop himself from yearning to be a part of it, to be on their side for a change.

But his time in Cranfield was done for now. There was no need to go there for a couple of months until the next council decision was due. After all, what else could he do?

However, the car seemed to have a mind of its own, and he soon found himself leaving the motorway to arrive in Cranfield soon after dusk.

His mind was in such a muddle. Perhaps just a bit of peace and quiet might help quieten down his thoughts. It was ironic that he thought of Cranfield as peaceful when his every intention had been to disturb that very peace, according to Harriet's protest.

He parked up in the lane and walked through the narrow passageway and onto the empty railway platform. It had been a busy station at one time, according to his notes. But these days, the track was overgrown, and time had stood still since it had shut down over twenty years ago.

He found himself walking up the steps to gaze across the lavender fields, even though it was getting dark. He glanced across to the row of cottages. The last one, which he knew to be Harriet's, remained in darkness. He wondered if she was out, perhaps even on a date somewhere. Then he wondered what on earth he was doing out there on a cold, dark evening, thinking about a woman he barely knew.

He leant against the peeling paint of the iron bridge, staring out across to the hills in the distance. It was certainly very peaceful. He had spent his first few years growing up in a village much like this one, but his father's ambitions had led the family to move to the larger town. His mother had never liked the urban sprawl and had taken refuge in her garden, building a green oasis to take sanctuary in. Perhaps she had been trying to recreate the countryside in her own back garden, thought Joe.

He missed her. Not as much as his father did, of course, that heartbreak was obvious for everyone to see, apart from his dad himself. It was just one of the many reasons why he felt he needed to step aside from it all. But how to break the news to his dad that he needed respite from the travelling and business? That he desperately needed a change. And when change had already been inflicted on his dad so much already without any of it being his own making, Joe was reluctant to speak up and cause him more pain. The trouble was that Joe was unhappy, and unless something changed, he was likely to remain so.

Joe slowly turned direction to look out to the large oak tree in the middle of the field, outlined like a shadow in the dusk. He smiled to himself at the thought of Harriet chained up against it. He dug deep into the pockets of his coat and pulled out his gloves. For some reason he couldn't fathom, he drew them up to his nose and could just make out the faint aroma of her flowery perfume.

He shook his head. He must be more tired than he had first imagined.

He had just decided that this whole detour was nonsensical and that he really ought to head home when he thought he saw something on the ground in the lavender fields. He squinted in the darkness. Was it a wounded animal?

He hesitated but found himself drawn to the other side of the bridge and headed down the steps.

He thought he could hear someone talking as he grew nearer. Was his mind playing games on him?

But just when he was about to call out, the words suddenly became clearer to his ears, and he recognised Harriet's voice.

'I can't do this,' she said, with what sounded like a sob. 'I can't do all the pruning. My back won't take it. What am I going to do?'

Joe peered into the darkness to work out who she was talking to.

'How am I going to save the lavender fields now?' She definitely sounded upset. 'Oh, Aunty and Uncle! I so wish you were here right now. I miss you both so much.'

Joe took in a swift breath. The grief in her voice he recognised instantly. That much they had in common. He felt and shared the heartache with Harriet.

However, there was still no response from whomever she was conversing with, so Joe took another step forward. Suddenly, there amongst the row of plants nearby, he saw the head of a large dog slowly rise up as if sensing his arrival, staring at him with dark eyes. But where was Harriet? Then as the clouds parted briefly and a shaft of moonlight lit up the field, he could just about make out a cloud of long red wavy hair lying on the ground next to the dog. He took a deep breath in shock before rushing forwards.

'Hello? Who's there?' called out a teary voice. 'Flora? Is that you?'

'No,' he said, rushing up to stand next to her. 'It's me. Joe.'

'Oh.' She was lying on the ground, looking somewhat wretched but, as always, trying to put a brave face on everything.

He looked at the golden retriever lying alongside her. He didn't even know that she owned a dog. He certainly hadn't seen it before.

'What are you doing here?' she asked. 'Shouldn't you be brokering your next Wall Street deal or something?'

He shook his head. 'Not tonight,' he replied, still staring down at her. 'Are you okay?' he asked, glancing over her as if to check for broken bones.

'I'm fine,' she said quickly. 'We just fancied doing some stargazing, that's all.'

'I see.' Except all he could see was that she was lying. She wasn't even wearing a coat. 'Aren't you cold?' he asked.

'A bit,' she conceded with a gulp. 'But the dog didn't seem to mind too much. The joy of having a fur coat, I suppose.'

'Why don't you head inside for a while to warm up?' he suggested.

'In a while,' she began before her voice trailed off faintly.

Joe crouched down next to her. 'Harriet,' he said softly, 'what's going on?'

Suddenly, her fake bonhomie evaporated, and her face creased up in pain. 'I can't do this,' she said with a sob. 'I can't lie to you, no matter how much I want to. I've lost my phone somewhere.' Then she began to cry.

'Don't cry,' he told her, reaching out to take her hand. It was freezing cold. 'How long have you been lying here?' he asked, now seriously worried about her.

'I don't know,' she groaned. 'Hours. It was still just about light. I suppose you think I'm even more crazy now.'

Joe found himself thinking that she was one of the bravest people that he had ever met. And astonishing. And beautiful too, her cheeks pink in the cold.

'Come on,' he told her. 'You're just exhausted, that's all. Tomorrow will seem better. Get some sleep. A new day will make you feel much better.'

But Harriet was still crying. 'I can't move! My back hurts. It just went suddenly. I can't even go home,' she told him. 'It aches so much when I try to move.'

She looked and sounded utterly and completely exhausted.

Joe made a swift decision there and then. 'Put your hands behind my neck,' he told Harriet, moving in front of her.

She hesitated before reaching out her arms with a groan of pain and wrapping her hands around the back of his neck.

She moaned as he moved his arms around her and tried to lift her off the cold ground as gently as he could.

'Sorry,' he muttered, 'but you can't lay there all night.'

'Not as sorry as I am,' she replied. 'And it's not your fault. This one's all on me.'

He looked down and found that the dog had also risen, intent on coming back with them. Joe began to walk back to the bridge, holding Harriet in his arms and feeling just how chilled she was. The moon was bright and full, but it meant that the temperature had plummeted.

He tried to ignore how she felt in his arms. Soft. How her hair tickled his chin. The feel of her hands on the back of his neck. Her faint perfume making his senses reel.

'You don't need to do this,' she began but didn't finish. Joe realised that she was too exhausted even to protest.

Once they had reached the front door of Lavender Cottage, he waited for her to bring out the key from her pocket with another wince.

'Where are your friends?' he asked.

'Libby's away, and Flora's at the farm,' she told him.

'Is the dog coming in as well?' he asked, glancing down at their furry companion.

'Why not?' she said, sounding exhausted.

Joe took her inside the warm, cosy cottage, found the light switch, and began to carry her up the staircase. It was a lot steeper than he had imagined, so it was a bit of a struggle, but eventually, they were upstairs.

'Which way?' he asked.

'In there,' she told him, nodding her head.

'There' turned out to be a bedroom with a large double bed in its centre. Joe gently laid her down on the covers. She groaned and bit her lip in pain as he did so.

'Do you want me to call someone? A doctor or something?' he asked.

'No,' she said, closing her eyes. 'I'll be fine once I've rested.'

Harriet was so exhausted that she was beginning to fall asleep in front of his eyes, so Joe picked up the edges of the duvet and blankets she was lying on and drew them over her so that she was cocooned, nice and warm.

'Thank you,' she murmured. 'That's lovely.'

She had a leaf caught in a strand of her long red hair, which was splayed across the pillow. He found his hand went out automatically to pull the leaf out, but he stopped just short and let his hand drop to his side once more.

The dog turned a few times in a circle before settling down on the floor next to the bed and closing his eyes as well.

Joe watched Harriet for a moment, but she was peaceful, so he turned to leave.

Both Harriet and the dog were already asleep before he had even left the room.

17

The following morning, Harriet woke up in a tangle of duvet and covers, wondering why on earth she ached so much. And then she remembered what had happened the night before in the lavender field.

'Oh no!' she groaned out loud.

'And a good morning to you too,' said a voice nearby.

She turned her head to see Flora standing at the bottom of the bed holding a steaming mug of what Harriet very much hoped to be coffee.

'What are you doing here?' asked Harriet, wondering if the whole world had turned upside down whilst Joe Randall, of all people, had carried her up to bed.

She whimpered in mortification as she shuffled up in the bed and felt her back ache as she moved.

'Joe came to the farm last night to let me know what had happened to you,' said Flora, frowning. 'So, I spent the night on the sofa in case you needed me. And, by the way, I wasn't alone.'

Harriet followed Flora's gaze and, to her surprise, saw the

runaway golden retriever sitting up next to her bed, panting and smiling at her.

Flora sank down on the other side of the bed gently and placed the mug on the bedside table. 'Why didn't you call me?' she asked.

'Because I lost my phone!' groaned Harriet, leaning back against the pillows. 'So, it was real? I didn't dream any of that?'

'Do you often dream about Joe Randall?' asked Flora with a grin.

Harriet ignored the jibe. 'How embarrassing,' she whined. 'I mean, I was stuck on the ground at the side of the field, for goodness sake!'

'Well, I'm just glad he found you,' said Flora, looking more serious. 'You could have caught pneumonia out there.'

Harriet found herself thinking that Joe was a hero, but she didn't want to think of him that way. She certainly didn't want to owe him anything. He was cold and unfeeling and wanted to take away the lavender fields, didn't he? It was all such a muddle.

'Ooof! My back aches so much,' said Harriet, pulling off one of the many blankets that were covering her, realising that she was still dressed in her old jeans and top.

Flora caught her surprised look and smiled. 'So, he didn't undress you first. Shame.'

'No, it's not,' said Harriet, her cheeks flaming red in embarrassment. 'It's the first decent thing he's ever done. Other than carry me all the way from the lavender field up here,' she added with a heavy sigh.

Flora burst into laughter. 'He must be pretty strong.'

'Yes, very funny,' replied Harriet, sticking her tongue out. 'I'd laugh if I didn't want to cry.'

Flora looked at her. 'Your back will mend if you give it enough time,' she told Harriet. 'You just need to rest a little, but you also need to move around as well.'

'Since when were you a medical expert?' asked Harriet.

'Since I googled it this morning,' said Flora with a smile. 'Since when were you ever embarrassed about a bit of male attention?'

'That wasn't attention. That was pity, and it's just awful,' snapped Harriet, the pain making her cranky. She reached out to take the mug of coffee and took a sip. The coffee was hot and sweet, and she sank back against the pillows gratefully. 'Thanks,' she muttered. 'Sorry. I don't mean to snap at you. This has just come at the worst possible time.'

'You need to try to relax,' Flora told her softly.

'I've got a couple of massive lavender fields to prune, remember?' said Harriet.

She felt so disheartened. She had promised to keep the lavender fields alive for her aunt and uncle in thanks for all they had given her. And now what? It felt as if the fight had come to a dead end.

But, to her surprise, Flora continued to smile. 'I don't think things are as bad as you think they are,' she said. 'After all, help can come from the most surprising of places sometimes.'

Harriet was confused. Who on earth could be helping?

After struggling to get up and head into the bathroom for a much-needed shower, she glanced out of the window and stopped in amazement. A figure looking very much like Joe Randall was in the middle of the first lavender field, working along each plant.

'What's he doing?' asked Harriet, looking around at Flora in disbelief.

'He's pruning,' Flora told her with a smile. 'Yes, I was a bit surprised as well. And he's not going to be the only one. Word's got out that you need help. Have a shower, and then we'll take a very gentle walk over there so you can see for yourself.'

Harriet was still feeling confused. Joe wanted to tear out the heart of Cranfield, so why was he bothering to help her now?

'I'll fix you both some breakfast,' said Flora, looking down at the dog, who wagged his tail in anticipation and followed her out of the room.

He obviously knew that food was imminent, thought Harriet with a smile. But the dog had been a good listener when he had come across her the previous evening.

She had a sudden vision of being in Joe's arms and headed into the bathroom to try to dismiss it as quickly as possible.

Once Harriet was showered and dressed, she carefully made her way downstairs. Flora had made her a bacon sandwich whilst the dog enjoyed a few of the extra scraps. Then they all headed out onto Railway Lane.

Harriet's back was still aching, but it felt a little better to be moving. She could feel the stiffness easing as she went.

Flora held on to her as they made their careful way along the station platform and up and over the bridge. Harriet took her time with the steps and thought back to Joe carrying her over the bridge. He certainly was very fit to carry her all this way, she thought.

'Maybe he goes to the gym,' said Flora, guessing her thoughts.

'Humph,' muttered Harriet, still embarrassed and wondering what on earth she was going to say to Joe when she saw him.

But that would have to wait as she realised that there were now at least half a dozen people pruning each lavender plant in the field. She recognised Grams, Bob, Eddie and Maggie as well as a couple of other people from the village.

'What are you all doing here?' she asked in astonishment.

'I was out on my tractor and saw this gentleman standing in the middle of the lavender field earlier,' said Grams, pointing at Joe. 'I wondered what on earth he was doing, so I came over to investigate.'

'She then came and knocked on my door,' said Maggie.

'Mine too,' added Bob. 'We figured you'd done such a grand job with the protest that the least we could do was take a couple of hours out to help you.'

His father, Eddie, nodded his agreement. 'Absolutely,' he added.

'Morning all,' said a voice nearby. 'Heard you needed a hand.'

Harriet looked around to see a skinny man with dark hair walking towards them.

'Hi, Del,' said Flora with a smile.

As he greeted everyone with a hearty handshake, Harriet looked at Flora with raised eyebrows. 'As in Dodgy Del?' she murmured.

Flora nodded. 'The one and only,' she whispered back.

Harriet had heard the rumours about Bob's infamous nephew. He was the local coach driver and apparently a nice enough guy, always trying to be helpful around the local villages and area. It was just that his way of dreaming up dubious ideas to help the village and himself had earned him the nickname Dodgy Del a long time ago. Harriet had been told many times that Del's heart was generous, even if his methods were somewhat questionable.

'Now you must rest,' said Grams, gently moving Harriet towards a fold-up camping chair that someone had brought with them.

Harriet sank down gratefully onto the chair and looked around with tears in her eyes.

'I can't believe you all turned out to help,' she said. 'Thank you so much.'

They all smiled at her before moving away to continue their work on the lavender plants. That just left Joe, who had been standing to one side on his own.

He stepped forward, holding out something for her to take. She realised it was her phone.

'I found it down one of the rows about an hour ago,' he told her.

'Thank you,' she said, taking it from him. She noticed in his

other hand was an ancient pair of secateurs. 'What I don't understand is what are you doing here?' she asked.

'I'm not so sure myself,' he told her with a sheepish smile that lit
up his handsome face. 'But it seemed the right thing to do after last
night, so I rearranged my diary to make some time. You're
passionate about the place, and that's not something I come across
very often. Normally, it's about cold hard cash and how much the
vendor can get for it, but this is different.' He cocked his head to one
side. 'Better, actually. More life-affirming.'

'Well, don't be so sure,' said Harriet, still not wanting to get her
hopes up. 'Maybe you'll still win the fight.'

'Perhaps I don't want to win any more,' he told her. 'Perhaps
some things are worth more than money and profits.'

He went to speak on, but they were interrupted by Maggie
offering them both a piece of lemon drizzle cake.

Joe thanked her and took the cake with him as he headed back
along the row to carry on his work.

Harriet watched Joe as he walked away. He had proven himself
to be cold and unfeeling regarding the business deal to get rid of
the lavender fields. And yet he was something of a hero as well, the
way he had saved her the previous evening. There had been tenderness when he had taken her in his arms.

She groaned under her breath. She had let down her guard,
which had kept her safe for so many years, and the worst possible
person had seen her at her most miserable. She was just hoping he
hadn't heard anything else when he had arrived to save her.

As she ate her own delicious slice of cake, Harriet was left
mulling over his words. He was a contradiction, and she didn't
know what to think. Was it true? Had Joe really changed his mind?
And what did that mean for the future of the lavender fields if
he had?

18

The pruning of the lavender fields by a number of villagers continued that afternoon under Harriet's watchful eye whilst she was ordered to rest her back by Flora and Grams.

Harriet wriggled in her camping chair as she watched everyone hard at work, uncomfortable with merely overseeing them, but as her back gave a prophetic twinge at the motion, she knew she couldn't push it any further or else she would have a total setback. And the last time she had done that, she had ended up being in Joe's arms as he carried her back home.

She blushed, even as nobody was looking at her or guessed her thoughts.

She glanced over at him in the far distance, hard at work, along with everyone else. He was wearing casual clothes, for once, and out of his suit, he seemed less stiff, less aloof.

Had he truly changed his mind over the clearing of the field to make way for an industrial site? She wasn't sure. But perhaps there was a chink in that hard armour he wore, and he had realised how much it meant to everyone in the village.

Harriet was certainly beginning to understand what her protest had achieved. Everyone was chatting about the newspaper headlines and photographs in the local news.

In the end, she felt too guilty just to sit there and do nothing and slowly stood up to wander up the first row. Everyone who was helping was dragging bin liners full to the brim of the faded flower heads from the previous summer. She touched one of the flower heads but could barely smell any of the lavender aroma she loved so much.

'What on earth are we going to do with all the cuttings?' she asked Grams as she paused at the end of the row with yet another bag.

'Shame for it to go onto the compost heap, but it's no use to anyone if it's not been dried properly,' Grams told her.

'Dried properly?' asked Harriet, confused.

'When the flowers still have their colour and scent at the end of the summer,' said Grams, 'then they can be dried out and used for all manner of things. But these flowers have been out over a damp, cold winter and haven't any use left.'

As Grams wandered away, Harriet felt a little sad. A whole summer of flowers, possibly the last summer of flowers if the lavender fields weren't saved, had gone to waste. It was heartbreaking.

She slowly bent down to pick up a small branch that had fallen out of one of the bags and was lying on the ground.

'Hold it,' said a voice nearby, and she straightened back up once more. 'Let me get that for you.'

It was Joe.

'I can manage,' she told him, still not wanting to appear weak in front of him. She held out the stray branch. 'See?'

'Yes, I'm sure you can cope,' he replied with a faint smile. 'However, last time you told me that you could, I ended up carrying you home.'

'I haven't had a chance to thank you for that,' she told him, blushing.

'It's fine,' he replied brusquely. 'Anyone else would have done the same.'

Harriet wasn't so sure and was about to tell him so when she caught his eye and found that she couldn't look away. There was a breathless moment when she wasn't even aware of a soft breeze wafting over the brow of the hill. Nor that Libby had apparently come to join them until she began to speak.

'Hey,' said Libby, giving Harriet a gentle hug. 'Have you really hurt yourself? Are you okay?'

'I'm fine,' Harriet told her.

Libby rolled her eyes. 'As if you'd tell us otherwise anyway.' She turned to look at Joe with narrowed eyes. 'Joe Randall, isn't it? Surprised to see you here again. Shouldn't you be destroying the Amazon rainforest or something?'

Harriet was surprised when Joe burst into laughter. At least he had a good sense of humour, she thought.

Libby raised an eyebrow as she looked from Harriet to Joe and then back again. 'So, what is he doing here?'

'I'm actually not sure,' said Harriet, turning to look at Joe questioningly.

'I came back to find your phone,' he said, looking almost embarrassed. 'Then I got strong-armed into helping out with the pruning by Flora's grandmother.'

'Glad to hear it,' said Libby, stepping in to talk for both of them. 'So, does that mean the pressure is off? We can all put our feet up and stop breaking our backs out here?'

'You've only just arrived,' murmured Harriet.

Libby shot her a grin.

Joe shook his head. 'Just because the judgement by the council is delayed doesn't mean you're out of danger. You still need to prove that the fields are necessary to the village. So, you need to see if it makes some sort of business sense to keep it here.'

Harriet felt sick to the stomach once more. The pressure was most definitely still on to find a solution.

'It's just a couple of lavender fields,' said Libby, looking worried. 'I don't know what else we can do about it.'

'We'll think of something,' said Joe.

'I hope so,' replied Libby, giving Harriet a concerned look before walking away and leaving them alone once more.

'So, you're on our side now?' asked Harriet, her mind racing.

Joe nodded. 'Yes.'

'What changed your mind?' she asked before she could stop herself.

'You.'

'Oh.' Somewhat stunned, she shuffled from foot to foot, trying to take it all in.

Joe carried on, 'I figured that if it meant enough for you to keep pruning even when it was causing you actual bodily harm, then maybe I should rethink my priorities.'

'Well, the pain was worth it if that's the case,' she told him, pleased that he was finally on their side. 'We need all the help we can get.'

'I'm not sure of the welcome I'll receive from everyone else,' he said, frowning.

They both looked over to where the other villagers were throwing scowls in his direction.

'There's plans to have a drink and a slice of cake on the station platform later,' Harriet told him. 'Why don't you join us? The villagers will soon come around and welcome you.'

'Yes, but what with?' he joked, obviously still somewhat worried about their reaction to him.

They shared a smile before Harriet continued her walk up and down the row to check on progress. But despite the sweet smell in the air and the beautiful view, her mind was filled only with Joe. She wondered what had truly changed his mind.

Whatever the reason, she was pleased and maybe even hopeful that perhaps he would be spending more time in Cranfield if he had decided to help them.

19

Later on that afternoon, Joe sat down on one of the dilapidated benches on the old station platform, slightly apart from the small gathering of villagers celebrating a day of hard work pruning the lavender.

He was somewhat bemused by the turn of events. He had only decided on his last-minute detour to Cranfield the previous evening on a whim. Twenty-four hours later and he was discovering that he had hidden gardening skills, to his and everyone else's surprise.

With the help of many hands, the lavender plants in the first field were all clipped and pruned, hopefully yielding the impressive summer display that Harriet so desperately wanted. Although who on earth was going to see it was another matter, but he kept that view to himself.

He glanced down at the homemade cake that had been given to him. He couldn't even remember the last time he had eaten cake. Probably a birthday celebration with his family a long time ago. But, as Harriet had predicted, the villagers of Cranfield had been grateful for his help, so he kept getting given wedges of admittedly delicious cake placed into his hands.

'Well, that's the first field done,' he said, looking at Harriet, who had just sat down next to him.

'Thank you for your help,' she said. 'I don't know how much I'd have accomplished without everyone chipping in.'

She winced and then shuffled a little on the bench, and he was conscious that she was still in pain. Not that she would admit it. Harriet was one of those people who most definitely put on a positive front, he was beginning to realise. She had let her defences down with him the previous evening, and he wondered how he could broach the subject without upsetting her.

At that moment, something brushed against his leg, and he jumped as he looked down at a pair of big brown eyes staring up at him through tangled, golden fur. It was the large, scruffy-looking golden retriever.

The dog leant his head on Joe's knee and left a dribble of drool across his jeans.

Joe tried to move his knee away, but the dog merely followed his movement with his head, continuing to lean against his legs.

'Seems like someone's made a friend,' said Harriet, with a soft laugh.

'I think he's only interested in the cake, to be honest,' replied Joe, breaking a piece of the vanilla sponge off and giving it to the dog. 'Is he yours?'

She shook her head. 'He's a runaway,' she told him, reaching out to stroke the dog's head. 'His owner lived here, but he passed away. The dog keeps running away from his foster homes and returning here. Breaks your heart, doesn't it?'

Joe suddenly found he didn't mind the drool quite so much and shared the remaining cake between them. He wasn't going to go as far as stroking the filthy fur as Harriet was doing, but he did feel sorry for the dog. 'That's pretty sad,' he said.

Harriet nodded in agreement.

'You seem in a good mood today despite everything,' he told her. 'You must still be in considerable pain.'

'I'm fine,' she replied in an overly bright tone.

Joe knew she was lying and thought back to her conversation with the dog when she had thought nobody else was listening. 'Well, I'm here if you ever want someone to chat to about any problems,' he told her.

She frowned as if trying to work out the meaning of his words.

He was unsure whether to press on further, but he wanted to help her. He needed to persuade Harriet that he was on the right side. Her side.

'I've heard dogs make very good listeners, though, if you were thinking of taking one on as a pet,' said Joe. 'You know, when people feel they have nobody else to talk to, they find the companionship pretty comforting.'

The silence stretched out until recognition appeared to dawn on Harriet's face as her eyes grew wider.

'You heard all that?' she asked, her voice almost a whisper. 'What I was saying to the dog last night, I mean? When I was stuck on the ground?'

He nodded. 'I did. I'm sorry. I know it was personal to you.'

She gulped and looked away across the lavender fields.

For a moment, she was silent.

'You see, they took care of me,' she began, still looking across at the fields. 'My aunt and uncle, I mean. I got so much love from them when I received precious little from my own parents. I was never ambitious like them. Nor academically gifted, like my sister and brother. But Aunt May and Uncle Fred loved me as if I were their own child, and each holiday I would rush back from that horrible boarding school, and suddenly I was wanted and loved. It was as if I became whole again when I returned to Cranfield to stay with them.' She sighed and finally looked at Joe. 'But Aunt May died a couple of years ago and then Uncle Fred six months ago. And it feels like if I lose the lavender fields as well, then I've lost everything.' She hung her head, obviously fighting back tears.

Joe struggled to think of something to say. Other than his best friend, nobody else really discussed their emotions or confided in him. Most of the time, talking was about business and profits. He didn't normally do feelings. Or, at least, he hadn't done for a very long time.

'You were very lucky to have them,' he finally told her.

'I know,' said Harriet with a nod. 'I'm so grateful for their love. That's why I must keep fighting. To say thank you and repay the love they gave to me.'

'I understand,' he said. 'And I'm truly sorry for the loss of your aunt and uncle.' He hesitated before he found himself carrying on. 'I know how difficult and heartbreaking grief can be.'

She turned to look at him, studying him with her green eyes. 'You've lost someone dear to you?' she asked.

He nodded. 'Two people, actually.' He sighed. 'My younger sister Charlotte died a long time ago, and my mum a couple of years ago.'

'I'm sorry,' she told him. 'That must be tough for you.'

'My dad was never the same after we lost my sister in the car crash,' he found himself saying. 'I survived. My sister didn't.'

'At least you had your parents' love and support,' said Harriet. 'I'm just a disappointment to my parents.'

Joe was shocked. 'I'm sure you're not,' he started to say.

But Harriet shook her head. 'I hear the disappointment in their voices all the time. Couldn't make the right grades at school. Can't make a business last. No discernible talent.'

'Everyone has a talent for something,' Joe told her, anxious to reassure her. 'Anyway, if you're talking disappointment in children, I think I pick up the winner's medal for that.' He stopped and thought. 'Although perhaps it's the other way around. I'm disappointed in my dad.'

Harriet looked at him, surprised. 'Why?' she asked.

'It's my dad's company, you see,' he told her. 'Randall Enterprises. Since we lost Mum, I had to help him out with the business, but he's driving it on and on. I've tried to get him to slow down. To tell him that I want a break, but he doesn't listen. He doesn't want to, I think.'

'Perhaps if he keeps busy, then he doesn't have time to think about your mum and miss her,' said Harriet.

Joe nodded. 'That's definitely it,' he said. 'Well, you know how all-encompassing grief can be.'

'Yes,' she replied, looking sad. 'I do.'

'At least you have your friends to talk to,' he told her.

But, to his surprise, Harriet shook her head. 'They've got their own problems to deal with. I won't burden anyone with mine. Besides, my parents told me to keep a stiff upper lip at all times. It's always better to face everything with a smile.'

To prove her point, she gave him a dazzling smile that made his senses reel for a moment, and he almost lost his train of thought.

'But truth has a way of coming out,' he told her. 'Maybe it's better to be honest.'

'But from what you've said, you haven't been honest with your dad, have you?' she replied.

Joe was lost for words as he realised what she was saying was true.

'You see?' She shot him another smile. 'It's not as easy as you think.'

'Good point,' he said, laughing.

Her smile faded a little. 'So now you know why your plan to get rid of the lavender fields can't succeed.'

'If you're trying to make me feel guilty, then well done,' he told her with a grin. 'You've succeeded.'

Her face lit up. 'Well, if you're capable of feeling guilt, then maybe there's hope for you yet!' she joked.

But Joe couldn't laugh. He felt as if he had been struck by lightning. Was there really hope for him? He had been living on autopilot for so long that he wasn't sure he was capable of feeling anything.

And yet, he most definitely had feelings for this astonishing woman sitting next to him. It was admiration and, yes, a little desire too. But, most of all, it was awe of the way she had battled so hard throughout her life and kept fighting. He suddenly knew that he wanted to save the lavender fields for Harriet.

The dog settled down on Joe's feet and put his head on his paw as if to fall asleep. It was a heavy feeling but quite comforting in a way, he thought.

'Could he stay with you for a while?' asked Joe, looking down at the dog.

Harriet sighed heavily. 'I'd say yes, but my purpose of coming back here was to tidy up my aunt and uncle's cottage and then put it up for sale. I also need to find a new job. I'm not sure what I would do with a dog in London with a busy job.'

Joe looked back at the dog. 'Seems a shame when it sounds like you both want to stay in Cranfield that neither of you can find a solution.'

She looked across to the lavender fields. 'I really wish I could stay.'

'So why don't you?' he asked softly.

She smiled at him. 'Aren't you leaving soon too?'

With a start, he realised that he was.

As Harriet reached out to stroke the dog's head, Joe knew he would be sad to leave. And found himself hoping that he would have an opportunity to come back as well. Sooner rather than later.

20

Joe sat with Harriet for a while longer on the bench. His excuse was that the dog was sitting on his feet and that he didn't want to disturb him. But the reality was that he was enjoying her company and didn't want to break the moment.

'How's the back?' he asked.

'Definitely easing, thanks,' she replied. 'And it's a big relief that so many people helped out today.'

It was the community spirit that he had heard all about over the years but had never come across before. They were certainly a friendly bunch of people, thought Joe. Considering that it had only been a short while ago that Harriet had branded him the enemy, now they were offering him cake and a hot drink from a couple of thermos flasks.

He found the attention somewhat overwhelming, having spent so long on his own. He was almost out of touch with small talk that didn't involve business, and yet he could feel himself beginning to respond and warm to the feeling of being a part of something.

'What are you going to do with all of this?' he asked, gesturing at the large amount of sacks now piled up on the station platform that were holding the discarded flower heads from the day's pruning.

'They're going on Flora's compost heap,' Harriet told him.

She really was very pretty, he thought. Those green eyes were such a deep shade of emerald that he had to force himself to look away.

'Shame, really.' She gave a short laugh. 'I was hoping they might magically turn into bags of gold instead, and I could bribe those councillors to change their minds.'

Joe frowned. 'We just need to think up some kind of business plan, that's all,' he said.

'That's all, he says,' she laughed. 'I don't think there's much money in herbs, to be honest.'

'We'll think of something,' he told her.

'We will?' she asked, looking at him surprised.

He pushed on, thinking quickly as he did so. 'You need to show people what's so special about Cranfield and the lavender fields,' he told her. 'Make them take notice of what's here rather than what they can replace it with.'

It suddenly felt important to him that Cranfield won this battle, regardless of his dad losing business because of it. Perhaps some things really were more important, he wondered, turning to Harriet.

Once more, he found himself staring at her, and he couldn't look away until they were interrupted by Eddie, the elderly gentleman who lived at the station, along with his son Bob.

Eddie sat down in the seat vacated by Harriet as she got up to talk to a group of ladies nearby.

'It's a great view,' said Joe, making conversation.

'The best,' replied Eddie, nodding as he looked across the countryside. The rolling green hills surrounded the village, framing the natural outlook. All around, there was evidence that spring had arrived, from the birds swooping back and forth from trees to hedgerows, to the new green leaves beginning to appear and covering all the bare branches.

Eddie turned to look at the station. 'You should have seen it here in its heyday. I mean, the steam train era long before all those electric ones. It was a sight to see, make no mistake. The hiss of the steam. The puff of the smoke rising in the air.' He looked downcast. 'Seems when the trains stopped, the life stopped in Cranfield as well. Folks left so they could commute from easier places and without having to negotiate all those narrow lanes in their big cars.'

'I heard your son mention that you're both renovating a steam train,' said Joe.

Eddie immediately cheered up. 'You must come and see it,' he replied, quickly standing up. 'It's going to be wonderful. It's so important, you see, to keep the magic of steam alive and all the heritage that goes with it. Let me show you our progress.'

Joe followed Eddie down the platform, along the short path and into the large workshop at the end of the track. Joe was amazed by the sheer amount of leftover parts and carriages from when the railway had closed. It was a train enthusiast's heaven, he decided.

He was equally amazed by the large steam engine that Eddie showed him, despite the fact that there appeared to be many pieces missing.

'Built in 1927, train no 42007,' said Eddie proudly. 'We looked it up. She used to haul express trains to and from Scotland. The old girl wants to get going once more, I reckon,' he added, patting her on one of the side panels. 'She's a grand old lady, and they need admiration.'

After his brief tour of the steam train, Joe wandered back outside again with Eddie.

'I'd love to see the steam train work someday,' said Joe.

Eddie smiled at him. 'Stick around, lad, and you might just be lucky enough to see it,' he replied.

Joe found himself hoping that was true because he really did want to stay there.

He looked across the tracks. Nearby, there were a couple of abandoned train carriages, but beyond that, there was nothing but fields. 'Were there ever any other businesses in Cranfield?' he asked.

'There was the shop, of course,' said Eddie, creasing up his eyes as he tried to remember. 'It was a tiny post office, but it did the trick. That closed soon afterwards. The station brought in quite a few folks, and the farm always employed a few extra people in harvest time.'

Joe looked across at the other fields next to the lavender field. 'Seems like this year's crop might be a good one,' he said, without any kind of knowledge.

'I'm afraid you're way off base with that one, lad,' said Eddie, shaking his head sadly. 'Flora was telling me yesterday that they're way behind where the crops should be due to all that flooding last autumn and winter. They're just rotting away, not much yield there to be had. The weather's changing year on year, and the winter's only getting wetter, unfortunately. Doesn't do the crops any favours at all. Just end up with a soggy, mouldy mess instead.'

Joe felt sorry for Flora and her grandmother. 'I see.'

Diversification, he thought to himself. That was a word he had heard Matt use quite a bit over the past couple of years. People in rural businesses were getting more desperate, especially farmers, but how could they diversify? He wondered whether he should have a word with Flora but didn't want to appear pushy. Besides, Matt probably had more knowledge regarding that kind of thing than he did.

It gave him a thought. 'Are there many farms in the area?' he asked. 'Or other small businesses?'

'Oh yes,' said Eddie, nodding. 'Think they're more or less in the same amount of trouble finance wise, unfortunately.'

Joe's phone suddenly rang, and he glanced down to see it was his dad calling.

'Excuse me,' he said to Eddie and walked towards the platform. 'Hey, Dad,' he said when he was on his own.

'Are you all finished up?' asked his dad. 'I need you to head off to Slovenia for a while.'

'Slovenia?' Joe suddenly realised he didn't want to leave. 'How long is a while?'

'I'm not sure,' replied his dad. 'As long as it takes. There's a castle over there that our client wants to convert into a luxury spa, but the old lady who owns it is holding tight. Normal rubbish about heritage and all that. You work your charm, son, and there'll be quite a large payday for this one.'

Joe ran a hand through his hair, trying to work out what to say. 'Dad,' he began after a short silence. 'Do you ever feel like we don't build anything any more?'

'What are you talking about?'

Joe hesitated before speaking. 'I mean, we just seem to knock everything down or take it over. What about the heritage of the place? Maybe it's more important than you think it is.'

'It's just bricks and mortar,' replied his dad brusquely.

Joe shook his head. 'No, I don't think it is to some people.' He turned to look down the platform to where the small group was chatting and laughing. 'This is where people live. Some of these places are the heart of the community as well. It might not be a very prosperous one, but they matter all the same.'

There was a pause down the line. 'Look, can we talk about this later? I need to shore up this deal.'

'Why? How much more money do you need to make?' snapped Joe.

'Listen, if you don't want to do this,' said his dad, sounding cross, 'I'll find someone else that can.'

'There is no one else,' said Joe in a dull tone. 'So, you'd better email me the details.'

After hanging up, he felt utterly miserable. He knew that he was the best person for the job. He just didn't like it particularly well at that moment and found himself wishing he could stay in Cranfield for a while longer.

He looked over at Harriet. Perhaps she was right. Perhaps they both finally needed to start being honest with the people they loved, however hard that would be.

21

The pruning of the final lavender field had only taken two days, thanks to the number of volunteers that had turned out to help.

However, Harriet continued to feel guilty about her lack of input. Even though her back pain had almost eased, nobody would let her do any of the work.

But once the final bags of discarded flower heads had been placed onto the trailer connected to Flora's tractor and driven away, the pruning was done. There was no more to be done but wait for the summer and see if they flowered.

So, what now? She had been so consumed with saving the lavender fields that she had almost forgotten about having to put up Lavender Cottage for sale until her bank statement arrived via email a week later.

Without a job and income, she needed to put her finances in order. The thought of selling Lavender Cottage was almost too awful to contemplate, but until the lavender flowers hopefully bloomed, there was nothing more to be done with regards to the fields. It was time to face the worst of the jobs she had been putting off and sort through all the cupboards and drawers in the cottage.

She spent a week clearing the upstairs rooms, taking all the clothes for charity and getting rid of the perishables in the bathroom. Even the attic held many memories with the boxes of much-loved Christmas decorations. It was time-consuming and sometimes terribly upsetting, but eventually, the upstairs had been cleared of everything but the personal items that she wanted to keep, such as her aunt's jewellery and favourite Christmas ornaments. The front room took another couple of days, and gradually the place began to empty out.

But standing in the kitchen, it felt just as hard as when she had begun. Harriet had given the dresser a good clean and intended to pack up the cups, bowls and plates that had always been placed on the shelves. However, she found she just couldn't do it. So, having washed and dried each item, she carefully put them back into their usual place.

She knew it was ridiculous and that she was only putting off the inevitable, but for now, it gave her comfort to still have her aunt and uncle's things around her.

May had heralded in some much-needed warm sun, and with the back door wide open, she could see the stray dog sprawled out on the patio. After a discussion with the dog's foster home, it turned out that they were going on holiday, so Harriet had offered, somewhat reluctantly, to let the dog stay with her for a couple of weeks. He seemed to want to be in Cranfield, so they continued their unplanned partnership. Harriet found it was nice having someone else in the cottage with her.

Next to the dresser was the huge larder, which went all the way back to underneath the stairs. She switched on the light switch just outside the door and went in, relishing the cool air, perfect for preserving the many tins and jars of food that had once filled the floor-to-ceiling shelves.

At the far end of the larder, she had to crouch down to stop her head from bumping against the underneath of the stairs. It was darker back there, so she was amazed to find hidden behind a couple of bags of material, twenty or so large plastic boxes.

She picked up one of the boxes and carried it out to see better. At first, she wondered whether it was more food carefully packed away, but when she placed the box on the kitchen table, she saw the label. Carefully written in Uncle Fred's writing were the words *Lavender Harvest*.

Harriet took in a large, shaky breath. With trembling fingers, she carefully broke the seal on the lid and lifted it up. Instantly, she was enveloped in the sweet aroma of lavender. She lifted the tissue paper that lay on the top, and there it was, the last harvest of flowers that her uncle had been able to gather. She looked down at the flowers, slightly faded in colour but, apart from that, perfect in every way.

Harriet sank down onto a nearby chair as the tears rolled down her cheeks. She sat for a long time, breathing in the heady smell of the lavender flowers, lost in the many happy memories spent with her aunt and uncle.

She wasn't sure how long she sat there crying until the dog suddenly placed his head on her knee and made her jump.

'Oh!' she said with a start. 'Sorry. I'd forgotten you were here.'

The dog seemed to sense that she was upset and left his head on her lap for her to stroke his soft silky ears.

Harriet glanced up at the kitchen clock and realised that it had now gone six o'clock. She leapt up from her chair. 'Oh my goodness,' she said to the dog. 'We'd better get our skates on otherwise—'

But she was interrupted by a knock on the door. It was too late. She had invited Flora and Libby over for dinner and cocktails, and they had already arrived. A glance in the mirror over the fireplace confirmed that her eyes were as small and red as they felt.

For a moment, Harriet considered dashing upstairs with the excuse of the onset of hay fever, but then she remembered her discussion with Joe. Maybe it was time to be honest with her friends about her feelings.

So she took a deep breath and opened up the front door. Libby and Flora were standing on the front doorstep holding takeaway pizzas from Cranbridge stores.

Harriet watched as her friends' cheery smiles quickly faded into shock and worry.

'What on earth's the matter?' cried Libby as they both dashed forward.

'You'd better come and see,' Harriet told them, turning around to lead them into the kitchen and show them the box on the table. 'Look what I found this afternoon.'

Flora and Libby moved forward and stared at the contents before both looking up at her with sorrow and concern.

Harriet felt the tears come again but, for once, didn't try and hide them. She let them pour down her cheeks as her friends swept her into a group hug.

When they finally let go of each other, Libby looked at her. 'I think it's time for a gin, don't you?'

* * *

Soon afterwards, the three of them were settled in the front room with large glasses of gin and tonic, alongside the pizza and the large box of lavender that Harriet had brought in as well.

'Better now?' asked Flora gently, watching Harriet finish the slice of pizza that she had been eating.

Harriet nodded. 'Yes, thanks,' she replied. She sighed and shook her head. 'I've tried so hard to think positively,' she told them. 'But I'm scared. Scared of having to sell the cottage. Scared of losing the lavender fields.' She gave a little shrug of her shoulders. 'It just feels like I'm losing everything I ever loved.'

'First of all,' said Libby, 'you'll never lose us. Okay?'

Harriet gave her a teary nod in reply.

'Second,' added Flora. 'We know you're still grieving. We've known for ages. We're just surprised to hear you admit it.'

Harriet sighed. 'Maybe it was time to be honest,' she said.

'Well, we're glad you're opening up to us at last,' Flora told her with a soft smile.

'So where is this new Harriet coming from because I've never seen you like this?' asked Libby.

'I don't know,' Harriet told her quickly.

It was obviously too quick a reply as both of her friends broke into a grin.

'Shut up,' she muttered before picking up her drink.

They knew, of course. They all knew. It was down to Joe.

'Well, between the pizza and the lavender, it does smell amazing in here,' said Libby, nodding her approval.

'It certainly takes away the smell of dog too,' said Harriet in a pointed tone.

They all looked down at the golden retriever sprawled in the middle of the tiny front room, taking up most of the carpet. He had thoroughly enjoyed his slice of pizza and was now enjoying a post-dinner nap.

'At least he's made himself at home,' said Flora, laughing.

'Temporarily,' added Harriet quickly.

'And he looks better for a wash and cut,' said Libby.

Harriet had also taken the dog into Aldwych to find a groomers that could take away most of the matted fur. She had then bought a brush and lead, neither of which he was particularly keen on but seemed happy to put up with.

'Has he run away yet?' asked Libby.

Harriet shook her head. 'I think he just wants to live in the lane again,' she replied. 'And I guess the cottage feels very similar to his old home, so maybe that's why he's so relaxed.'

They both looked down at the dog, who gave a little snore and thumped his tail in his sleep, oblivious to anyone else.

'And your back's better?' asked Libby.

Harriet shrugged. 'A bit achy, but it's gradually easing. To be honest, I think walking the dog helps loosen it up.'

'You know, lavender's known for its health properties,' said Flora, reaching out to pick up a piece of the lavender before inhaling deeply. 'Maybe you could make some soaps or something. They might bring in some income.'

'I certainly need some money coming in soon,' said Harriet, thinking of her business debts still waiting to be paid off.

Her mind drifted back to what Joe had said about a business plan. About putting Cranfield on the map. She just didn't know how. She found herself wishing he was still here to talk to, but he had told her that he was going away for a while. She was already missing him, and he'd only been gone a couple of days. It was ridiculous. She didn't even know the guy.

'You need to get creative,' said Libby in a firm tone.

'I need to start making money,' replied Harriet.

'So, think about the beauty products,' said Flora. 'All the articles I read about are about farmers diversifying, what kind of things they can make. Organic and all that. It's a hot topic.'

'I've used these kinds of beauty products at the salon but never made my own,' said Harriet frowning. 'You really think I can make some kind of income from it?'

'You can't make any less than I am at the moment,' remarked Flora with a grimace.

Harriet and Libby exchanged a worried glance. 'Are things really that bad?' asked Libby gently.

Flora hesitated before nodding her head. 'Yes,' she said finally. 'Oh, look, let's move the conversation on. It's too depressing to talk about money.'

'Okay,' said Libby quickly. 'Let's talk about the crush that Harriet has on Joe Randall.'

Flora cheered up immediately. 'Oh, yes. Let's!'

'No, no, no,' said Harriet, shaking her head so strongly that some of her gin slopped out of her glass and onto the floor. 'He's the enemy, remember?'

Libby's eyes gleamed. 'Not sure about that, but he's certainly easy on the eye,' she said.

'No! He's not,' lied Harriet before sighing. 'Well, maybe just a little. Anyway, he's gone now. Back to his business. Probably got a tall, skinny girlfriend. Someone with dead straight hair and zero personality.'

Libby raised an eyebrow at her friend's heated tone. 'My, my,' she said, looking across to Flora, 'someone has got it bad.'

Flora nodded in agreement before taking a sip of her gin.

Harriet rolled her eyes. Why did every conversation keep coming back to Joe?

After her friends had left, she drew herself a hot bath to ease her aching back. It was certainly getting better day by day, but she still needed to be careful. At the last minute, she flung in some Epsom salts and then a handful of lavender leaves. To her amazement, her aching muscles were immediately enveloped, and she felt so much better. And it smelt wonderful with the lavender in there.

Herbal remedies. Was that a thing?

Her mind wandered as she lay in the heat of the bath.

Her high-end customers at the London salon had demanded the very best ingredients, whereas Harriet had always privately preferred organic. Maybe her friends were right. Maybe there was something to be said for investigating what was possible.

What could she make, if she could create anything? Soap, perhaps. Some kind of bath salts. How did you make hand cream? Could she look that up too? What harm could it do? And maybe she could come up with the much-needed business plan that Joe had suggested.

She lay in the steamy water and wondered why her mind kept drifting back to think about him as well. She tossed her head at herself and closed her eyes, trying to relax. But all she could see was Joe's face.

22

The following morning, Harriet was still pondering over Flora's idea of making beauty products with the many boxes of dried lavender she had found in the larder. The trouble was that she had no idea what to do. She decided to take a morning walk to try to see if the fresh air would inspire her.

Walking the dog gave her the perfect excuse. He was almost constantly at her side these days. Not that Harriet found it particularly irritating. He obviously wanted companionship, and in a funny way, so did she. She still found the cottage too quiet and empty, and the dog had helped fill the silence with his presence.

They both walked along Railway Lane before heading into the station, intending to walk over the bridge and along the long path towards Cranbridge. However, she found Rachel on the platform, watching Bob fill up one of the old pots with some summer bedding plants.

'It needs a bit of prettying up around here,' announced Bob, stepping back and admiring his handiwork after greeting Harriet.

'It needs flattening,' muttered Rachel, stepping backwards and giving the dog a glare and a wide berth.

Harriet ignored her barbed comment; Rachel had always been a bit spiky.

'Well, if this plan to build a warehouse goes through, you may just yet get your wish,' snapped Bob before turning to Harriet with a more congenial expression. 'So, what are you up to today, love?'

'Not sure,' said Harriet before going on to tell them both about all the dried lavender that she had found. 'Flora suggested making some soaps. Or something like that. Not that I have any idea at all how it's done.'

'There's a lady over at Willow Tree Hall who makes her own beauty stuff,' said Rachel. 'Eleanor's Apothecary, it's called. Once in a while, I treat myself to it. It's good stuff.'

'You don't need any lotions,' said Bob with a soft smile. 'You always look beautiful to me.'

But Rachel didn't return the smile. 'What's the point in dolling myself up anyway? We never go anywhere, and it's not like I can invite anyone over as the apartment is such a mess, thanks to your engine parts all over the place.'

She gave Harriet a nod before walking away and out of view.

There was an awkward silence before Harriet gave Bob a sympathetic smile. 'Things still not improved?' she asked.

'No, love.' Bob gave a heavy sigh. 'I don't know what to do any more to make things better, so I disappear into the shed most days.'

'How's the steam engine renovation going?' she asked.

His face immediately brightened up. 'I fixed one of the wheels yesterday,' he told her.

'That's great,' said Harriet.

'Only nine more to go, eh?' he replied with a short laugh. He looked across at the platform. 'Looking forward to seeing the lavender again, I must say. We all need a bit of cheering up.'

Harriet felt so sorry for him that she found herself stepping forward to give him a warm hug.

As she stepped backwards, Bob's elderly father came out of the gate from the back garden of his cottage, which led directly onto the station platform.

'Is there one of those for me as well?' he asked.

Harriet laughed and stepped forward to give him a hug. 'Of course,' she told him.

Bob and Eddie were like surrogate uncles to her, and she had a great fondness for them both.

'Saw you out here and was wondering what you're up to now,' he said, bending down to stroke the dog's head.

'I found the last lavender harvest that Uncle Fred had cut and dried and was wondering what to do with it all,' said Harriet. 'I don't want to waste it.'

Eddie nodded thoughtfully. 'The healing properties of lavender have long been known.'

Harriet smiled. 'Certainly, when I mixed some into my bath last night, they helped my back enormously.'

Eddie frowned, deep in thought, before speaking. 'You know, I always used to have a posset of lavender under my pillow when I slept growing up. I have terrible nightmares, you see. Always have done. The smell used to calm me down and stop me getting any bad dreams.'

'Aunt May used to do the same for me,' Harriet recalled. 'Would you like me to make you one? After all, there's plenty of lavender.'

His face lit up. 'Oh, that would be lovely.' He bent down once more to give the dog a stroke. 'Poor old fella,' he said before straightening back up. 'I think it's nice that you've given him a home. Now he just needs a name.'

'I'm not sure that's down to me,' said Harriet. 'It's only a temporary holiday for us both.'

She looked down at the dog with a sad smile, once more reminded that neither of them could stay in Cranfield forever.

'Well, he seems happy to be with you,' remarked Eddie. 'Anyway, I'd best see how that engine's coming along.'

He headed off in the direction of the train workshop, leaving Harriet deep in thought. Creating any lotions sounded quite complicated, but she could start off with the simple task of making possets of lavender for Eddie and Bob.

After her walk and with the dog sprawled out on the floor once more, she placed together some small bundles of the flowers before wondering what was going to go around the outside of the possets. In the bags of materials that she had found in the larder, there had been some organza. As the material was see-through and also in a soft lilac, she thought they would do very nicely, so Harriet placed as many leaves as she could before wrapping the material into a bag and tying it with a matching ribbon.

'Oh, how lovely,' said Eddie when Harriet presented one to him the following day. 'You know, I bet if you sold these on the internet they'd be ever so popular.'

It got Harriet thinking, so she began to look up the uses of lavender and was surprised to find there were so many, especially where lavender oil was concerned. As well as a sleep and anxiety remedy, it could also be used to heal and calm minor burns, bruises, insect stings and cuts.

She decided to experiment with some of the shea butter that she had left over from her beauty salon. She layered in some of the lavender petals to soak on the windowsill to make the oil whilst she read up about making soaps and bath bombs.

'Are you getting into baking?' asked Libby when she found Harriet going through the kitchen cupboards to find any old tins later that week.

'I'm making soaps,' said Harriet.

Libby looked surprised but pleased. 'Are you about to become a cottage industry?' she asked.

'Why not?' said Harriet, laughing. 'After all, I live in an actual cottage these days.'

'Well, go for it.' Libby looked out at the fields beyond the railway line. 'At least it keeps you busy. I'm so bored these days. Sick of flying here, there and everywhere. Maybe I should think about doing something different as well.'

'And do what?' asked Harriet, surprised. Libby had never confessed that she was unhappy with her choice of career before now.

'I've been thinking about chocolate,' said Libby, nodding thoughtfully.

'Aren't we always?' replied Harriet, laughing.

'No, not just to snack on,' said Libby. 'I mean to make. I went on a one-day workshop years ago and loved it. I've always wanted to dabble and create my own, but there never seems to be enough time with my flight schedule.'

For once, she looked a little less sure of herself, so Harriet quickly said, 'Well, I think that sounds amazing. I'll be first in the queue if you're making chocolate.'

'Okay,' said Libby, smiling once more. 'Maybe I will.'

Later on, Harriet began to wonder just how far the lavender fields might carry all of them towards achieving new dreams.

23

'Are you sure this is going to work?' asked Flora, looking at Harriet with a bemused expression. 'Because I'm pretty sure you failed science at school.'

They were standing under the eaves of the pergola in the back garden of Lavender Cottage on a warm but drizzly May day. Thankfully, the wisteria growing over the back was keeping her dry.

Harriet smiled at her friend. 'It's got to work,' she replied. 'Otherwise, I've got all those boxes of lavender and nothing to do with them. I don't want to waste them. They're too precious to have them fade and lose their scent.'

She looked down at the pile of old bakeware that she had discovered in the cottage. There were old saucepans, a few wooden spoons and some silicone muffin cases.

'I thought you needed some kind of chemical to make soap,' said Flora frowning.

'I googled it,' Harriet told her. 'It's called lye, but it's pretty toxic. Not exactly keeping with the one hundred per cent organic range that I was hoping to make, so I'll do without.'

'Okay.' Flora didn't sound convinced but didn't say any more about it. 'And what's all that?' she asked, pointing at some old bottles.

'They're for the hand creams and moisturisers,' Harriet replied.

'Sounds like we've both got a busy day ahead,' said Flora, looking out across the railway track to her fields beyond. 'I've got some accounts to sort out. Not that it will take very long if it's just profit margins.'

'You could always stay here and help,' suggested Harriet in a hopeful tone.

Flora shook her head, smiling. 'I'd love to, but the tax man won't wait, unfortunately for me. Good luck! Let me know how you get on!'

Flora gave her friend a hug before heading off.

Harriet had been hoping that Flora would stay and not only for moral support. The trouble was she hadn't done anything like this before, and there was so much riding on making some money from it that it suddenly felt a bit overwhelming. Whilst Flora hadn't any experience either, she was certainly a lot more practical than Harriet.

But for now, she was on her own.

The soaps needed to set in their moulds, so that was Harriet's first job. It was a bit tricky trying to melt the mixture of shea butter and lavender oil on top of the camping stove that she had found in her uncle's shed, but finally, she had a liquid to pour into the moulds. It didn't look great, she had to admit. There seemed to be a layer of grease floating on top of each soap mould, but perhaps that was normal.

She left the mixture to set whilst beginning to make up the hand cream, but that too, seemed to be too grainy once it was done. Plus, the handfuls of lavender she had mixed into the cream couldn't really be seen, apart from dark bits dotted about.

She was just contemplating adding some more when Dodgy

Del suddenly appeared over the back garden fence holding a broom.

'Hiya. Was just sweeping up the place for Aunty Rachel, thought I heard someone,' he said, looking at all the saucepans and baking tins surrounding Harriet. 'What's this? Practising for *Bake Off*?'

'Hi,' said Harriet, feeling a bit embarrassed about having an audience. 'No, I'm just trying to make some creams and stuff with the lavender.'

'Right,' said Dodgy Del, nodding thoughtfully. 'What's that then?'

Harriet followed his extended finger and replied, 'Soap.'

'I'm no expert, but is it supposed to have all that oil on top?' he asked before then adding, 'And that?'

'Lavender hand cream,' Harriet told him.

'Doesn't look like it,' said Del, wrinkling up his nose. 'Shouldn't it have more colour than that?'

'I'm not sure,' replied Harriet.

'Should be purple if it's lavender, shouldn't it? Tell you what,' said Del, 'I bet a touch of food colouring will make it look better. Aunty Rachel used to make all kinds of cakes. I'll go and ask her for some.'

Before Harriet could reply, he had headed away along the platform and disappeared out of view.

She shrugged her shoulders at the dog who was sitting nearby watching her. 'Well, boy,' she said. 'What do you think?'

The dog leant his head on his paws and closed his eyes.

'Thanks for the confidence boost,' she muttered.

Del returned quite quickly, bearing a bottle of purple food dye.

'Aunty Rachel wasn't home,' he told her. 'But I found this in the kitchen cupboard. That should do the trick, eh?'

Harriet reluctantly took it from him and opened the top to add a few drops of the mixture. After all, what harm could it do?

'It'll need a bit more than that,' said Del, urging her on so that Harriet tentatively added some more of the purple dye into the hand cream. 'That looks much better.'

Harriet used an old wooden spoon to mix it all together. It had turned quite a lurid shade of violet. Perhaps she had used too much.

'I think it looks smashing,' said Del, nodding his approval. 'I mean, you want it to look like lavender, don't you? Smells nice as well, I bet, if you put some on.'

Harriet nodded out of politeness as she rubbed some into her hands. She had to admit to herself that it certainly smelled lovely. It felt nice as well, she thought, smothering the cream so that it was absorbed into her skin.

But a few minutes later, she was beginning to panic. Should her hands have turned purple as well?

She rubbed at them furiously with the kitchen paper and towel she had brought with her, but to no avail.

She looked up at Del, who was staring down at her hands with wide eyes.

'Like I said, I'm no expert,' he remarked before adding, 'Gotta see a man about a thing.'

Then he quickly disappeared, leaving Harriet standing in the garden alone.

It was fine, she told herself. Absolutely fine. She just had purple hands, that was all.

To add insult to injury, the cream had separated as it had cooled and looked completely disgusting, let alone utterly unusable. The soaps wouldn't set and didn't even look as if they ever would, ever. In addition, they smelt bad. Really bad. It was hopeless.

Harriet let her shoulders sag under the failure. She'd told everyone what she was doing, and now they would all know it was useless, that she was useless. Just like she'd always known. She couldn't do it, and now she wouldn't make any money. The cottage would have to be sold, and the lavender fields would probably be lost forever. So would her dream of living in Cranfield full-time.

Thankful that she had brought a dustbin bag with her outside, she quickly dumped all the failed lotions and soaps inside and tidied it all away before anyone else came along.

Once all the evidence was hidden, she slumped onto a nearby chair on the patio, tears pricking her eyes. Why couldn't she do anything right? Why didn't she have any proper skills? Why was she useless Harriet, who hadn't inherited any of her parents' or siblings' talents?

She looked across at the fields. It had all been so promising a week or so ago. People had come out of their houses and joined in with both the protest and the pruning, but now they had all retreated back indoors once more. Still, at least there was nobody to see how badly she was getting on.

Her phone bleeped with a text message from Flora.

How's it going?

She asked.

I've failed, thought Harriet.

For a second, she contemplated telling her friend how badly it had gone. She remembered her conversation with Joe about how much better for everyone it would be if she could be truthful, and she had tried, she really had. But this time, she couldn't. Hard habits were even harder to break, it seemed.

Anyway, she had to stay positive, didn't she? It was better for everyone else if she did.

So, Harriet wiped away the tears from her cheeks with her purple-stained hand and replied, Great! Next stop Selfridges beauty counter!

But the tears kept coming, and eventually, she must have worried the dog so much that he walked over to lean against her legs and place his head on her knees.

She stroked his head before he gave her hand a lick, and she laughed despite the tears.

'At least it tastes nice, eh?' she told him.

He gave her another lick, and her eyes softened as she stroked him once more.

'You know, it's such a shame that we don't know your name,' she said. 'I bet you'd like one, even a temporary name.' Harriet leant back against the bench. 'Let me see. Well, all I really know about you is that you love the railway cottages, just like me. Should I call you Cranfield?' She shook her head. 'I don't think so.' Harriet looked down the garden to where it met the end of the station platform, deep in thought. 'Something to do with the railway, I reckon. I know!' She laughed. 'How about Paddington? After all, you're big, brown-ish and furry and like being at the station!'

The dog quickly stood up, his tail wagging.

'Well, that's decided that!' said Harriet, bending down to give him a hug, which made his tail wag even more. 'From now on, you'll be known as Paddington. You've got a name. Now we just need to find you a home.' She smiled at the dog. 'Something we both have in common, I guess.'

With that momentous decision made, Harriet packed up her things and headed back to the cottage with Paddington the dog alongside her.

24

Joe sat at the meeting table in a very smart hotel in Mayfair, but he wasn't really concentrating on the client's proposal.

Someone was haggling over a million pounds here and there and what kind of air-conditioning units could be installed, but all he could think about was that he didn't care any more. It was all so impersonal and money-orientated. Much like him, he suspected. Or at least how he had begun to consider himself.

He looked around the table at the other men and women earnestly discussing such important matters. Or so they believed. They were all immaculately turned out from head to foot, wearing expensive designer suits and all toned from many spare hours spent in the gym.

Matt had teased him often enough about it. Was it true? Was that what people saw when they looked at him? he wondered. He thought back to Harriet's initial hostility. Was there more to him than met the eye? He sincerely hoped so.

His eyes were drawn to the middle of the table, where large bottles of chilled water and heavy, expensive glasses had been placed. Presumably for show as nobody was taking any kind of refreshment, too busy discussing proposals and money.

Where was the humanity? The spirit of togetherness? Where, he found himself thinking to his amazement, was the lemon drizzle cake?

He missed Cranfield. He missed Harriet. He missed all of it. It hit him so quickly that he nearly reeled from the thought. He found himself itching to leave.

It had been over two weeks since he had last visited the lavender field, carried Harriet back to her cottage and ended up spending a very happy day helping to prune the crop. That had never been his intention, of course. But somehow, he had felt it necessary. As if to prove a point to Harriet and maybe even to himself as well.

Was he a better man for it? A changed one, certainly, because ever since that day, he had been dissatisfied with his daily routine. With his life, in fact. The meetings held no purpose. The outcomes of any sales just left him more wretched and wondering what would become of the place they were in the process of changing.

He managed to get through to the end of the meeting without walking out. Outside the hotel, he rang his father. 'The deal's done,' he said in a dull tone.

'Good.' There was a pause. 'Anything else?'

'No,' replied Joe.

What else was there to say? What else did he have in his life to offer? Maybe he was just a suit, after all.

'Listen, son,' said his dad, 'you seem a bit tired at the moment. You were talking about taking a break, maybe...'

'I'm fine,' said Joe automatically.

'Except you're not,' his dad continued. 'You know, we all lose the thrill of the deal eventually.'

'I don't think that's it,' replied Joe with a heavy sigh.

'So, what is it?' asked his dad.

'I'm not sure,' said Joe honestly. 'Anyway, don't worry about it. Like you said, I'm probably just tired.'

Although deep down, Joe knew there was much more to it than just weariness.

* * *

Later on that afternoon, Joe sat in front of his laptop. However, instead of the screen, he couldn't stop himself from looking out through the window at the sky peeping out between the city skyscrapers. As a small stream of smoke rose out of one of the nearby chimneys, he thought back to Eddie showing him the old steam train at Cranfield station. One of Joe's favourite toys growing up had been a model train set. He would have liked to have seen a real one in action.

He shook his head. He didn't know what was wrong with him at the moment, except he was lonely. Really lonely. He had nothing in his life but business, which made him feel depressed. He missed the community feel, the small talk and chat with the villagers of Cranfield. It was almost as if they cared when nobody else did.

With a sigh, he grabbed his laptop more purposely and flicked around various documents, but he couldn't settle his mind.

In the end, he gave up looking at the technical documents that his solicitors had provided to check on the latest contract and idly mooched around the internet instead. He even ended up on holiday websites, seeing if anything took his fancy, destination wise, but it didn't. Perhaps the places he used to enjoy were too mundane, he thought. A beach was boring. Another city was just more of the same of his daily routine.

He looked up adventure and touring holidays. A page on cycling through France didn't appeal. He was about to give up when he spotted a photograph at the bottom. Beyond the smiling cyclists next to their bicycles was a lavender field, and it was busy with people. Visitors who had obviously paid money to go there.

Joe sat bolt upright, his mind racing. He felt more excited than he had felt about any kind of business for a long time. A search on Instagram yielded quite a surprising result. Many people had gone to visit lavender fields the previous summer, not only to enjoy the beauty but also because they made such pleasing photographs. Was that it? Was that the money-generating idea that might just save the fields? Was it enough?

His mind still on the lavender fields, he gave a start as the phone rang. It was Matt.

'Hey,' said Matt, talking loudly to be heard above some form of whistling.

'Hey,' said Joe, having to speak up to be heard. 'Where are you? It sounds like you're in a wind tunnel.'

'Outer Hebrides,' Matt told him. 'It's beautiful up here despite the fact that it's blowing a hoolie today. Certainly blows the cobwebs away. You should try a little nature sometime. Get rid of that city smog out of your lungs.'

Joe found himself thinking wistfully of Cranfield. 'Maybe I will.'

Matt laughed. 'Yeah, right.'

His friend's sarcasm gave Joe another mental shake. 'Talk to me about lavender farms,' he found himself saying.

'Seriously?' Matt sounded stunned. 'Didn't think they came under the portfolio of the climate-wrecking business you normally bid for. But yeah, they're big business with regards to tourism. Good for the environment too.'

Joe nodded. 'That's what I thought.'

'Careful,' Matt told him. 'You sound almost like me.'

'But better looking, right?' quipped Joe.

Matt laughed. 'Ha! If you'd seen the date I was out with last weekend, you wouldn't sound so smug.'

Matt was a serial dater, always searching for the next Miss Right Now. Joe found his mind drifting to Harriet as his friend chatted. By the time they had finished the conversation, Joe was convinced about the idea of opening up the lavender fields to the public.

However, as soon as he had hung up on Matt, the phone rang once more.

'Hi,' said his dad. 'I've had some business come up in Germany. Thought you could combine it with a few days off if you wanted.'

'Actually, Dad, you're right,' Joe found himself saying, still staring at the photo of the lavender field on the screen. 'I think I will take some time off next weekend. But I was thinking about somewhere that doesn't involve airplanes.'

Soon after they had finished their conversation, he scrolled through his contacts list. He found Harriet's details, having exchanged numbers before he had left Cranfield.

She answered, sounding breathless but surprised. 'Hi,' she said. 'Long time no hear.'

He could feel her warm smile down the line and felt ridiculously pleased by her reaction.

'Hi,' he said. 'Yeah, it's been a bit busy. But I've got a proposition for you. I think I've found that business plan we were talking about.'

'You have?' She paused. 'Will it save the lavender fields?'

'It just might,' he told her. 'How about we talk it over face to face later this week? Can I come by and see you?'

'I'd love that,' she replied. 'When are you coming home? I mean, back to Cranfield?'

'I should be with you by late Friday afternoon,' he said before they said their goodbyes.

And, he realised, she was right. It felt as if he were coming home. At last.

25

Joe's phone call had cheered up Harriet more than she had realised, and she spent the rest of the week on a bit of an excited high. They had arranged to meet up on Friday evening, and she found that she was counting the hours until he arrived later that day.

'He's only coming for the weekend,' said Harriet, as she walked Paddington the dog with Libby. She was aware that her words were coming out in a bit of an animated rush. 'But it's good that he wants to help with the lavender fields, don't you think?'

She looked at Libby, but she was staring down at Harriet's hands with a bemused look on her face. 'Is it me, or are your hands a touch Violet Beauregarde?' she asked, raising an eyebrow at her best friend.

'Does that make you Augustus Gloop because you're covered in chocolate,' replied Harriet.

'Bet I taste good, though,' said Libby, drawing out her phone to check her reflection in the camera. She wiped the chocolate smear off her cheek as she carried on. 'I was trying out some of the recipes I found online. Anyway, you're changing the subject. What gives with the purple hands?'

Harriet had yet to confess how poorly her trials with the lavender had gone. 'It was just a slight error with the lavender oil. Why? Is it really noticeable?'

'Only in the daylight,' said Libby as she finished wiping her face. 'Perhaps it's a good thing that he's not showing up until tonight.'

'It doesn't matter anyway,' Harriet told her.

When she got home, she spent another hour scrubbing her hands so that they turned pinker from the effort. But at least that made a change from purple, she figured.

'Bloomin' Dodgy Del and his bright ideas,' she said, looking at Paddington as she studied her hands for any signs that her endeavours had worked. They were perhaps slightly better than before.

By the time the front doorbell went, she was in a state of giddy excitement, which was ridiculous. It was just Joe.

'Hello,' he said with a smile. He looked far more relaxed than she could remember him looking and was even dressed in cargo shorts and a T-shirt.

'Hi,' she said, trying not to look at his bare legs. 'Come on in.'

He followed her inside and greeted the dog with a tentative stroke of his head. Harriet watched as Paddington instantly slumped onto his back and bared his belly, then waited for it to be stroked.

'Paddington shows no loyalty whatsoever,' she muttered.

'I'm glad you've given him a name,' said Joe, bending down and stroking Paddington's stomach.

Once due attention had been given to the dog, they went into the kitchen.

Joe stopped and stared in surprise. 'Wow, you've been busy,' he said.

She followed his gaze to where the twenty large boxes of lavender were still piled up on one side.

'I found them when I was sorting out,' she told him. 'They're all full of dried lavender. It smells wonderful, so I was hoping to use some for my new venture of soaps and lotions.' She hoped that he didn't want to see any of the evidence of her failed attempts.

'Sounds promising,' he told her before looking out of the back door across the railway track to the fields on the other side.

She followed his look to where the new green growth on the top of the plants he had helped prune could be seen in the fading light.

'The lavender is coming along,' he said as they headed outside.

She brought out a tray of drinks before they sat down at the patio table.

'Isn't it?' replied Harriet. 'There was quite a lot of rain last week, which should bring on the new growth, apparently. Not that I know much about these things. We just need a really warm spring and summer now, so fingers crossed.'

She crossed the fingers of one hand in front of him, temporarily forgetting about their stained colour.

He nodded and smiled, although his smile faded a little as he stared down at her hands with a quizzical look on his face. She quickly shoved them onto her lap under the table.

'So how have you been?' he asked.

'Same old, same old,' she replied.

'You mean dancing in the middle of the road again, or have you tied yourself to another tree in recent weeks?' he asked with a smile.

She looked at him and laughed. 'I suppose it was a bit of a bizarre meeting, now I come to think of it. But, hey, we've all danced in the moment, haven't we?'

He didn't reply, merely looked away at the fields once more.

'The fields are looking great,' he said before turning to look at her. 'And so do you.'

Harriet blushed at the compliment. She wasn't so sure about that, despite wearing a pair of cut-offs and a pretty top that she had chosen especially for seeing Joe. She wasn't sure why she had dressed up, but she wanted to look nice for him, she had found to her surprise.

'I nearly didn't recognise you out of your suit,' she told him.

'It's a whole new me,' he replied, leaning back in his seat.

But there was still an air of almost weariness about him, so she couldn't help but ask, 'So how are you? Really?'

'Tired,' he told her.

'You're not sleeping?' she asked before wondering if that was too personal a question.

'Just a lot going on with my dad's business.' He paused before giving her a soft smile. 'I could do with a break, to be honest, so I thought I'd take a couple of days off and come back to make sure you weren't causing any more trouble.'

She went to make a joke but found she couldn't. Her throat felt thick, and the words wouldn't come all of a sudden. Why could she act in front of everyone else but this man?

'Oh, Joe,' she finally managed to say, her shoulders sagging.

'What's the matter?' His eyes searched her face, worry seared across his. 'Is it your friends? The cottage?'

'No. It's the dried lavender.' She sighed heavily. 'I daren't tell anyone, but I've had such a disaster with the products. I can't do it. All I have to show for my efforts is this...' She pulled her hands out from under the table and held them out in front of her.

'So, it's not the light making them look purple?' he asked with a soft smile. 'Or some strange health condition that I was too polite to ask about?'

She shook her head. 'Nope. I've tried to hide it but look at them!'

But instead, he was looking at her. 'Can I ask you something? Why do you keep so many things to yourself?'

She gave a shrug of her shoulders. 'It's ridiculous, I know, but when my parents sent me to this awful boarding school, I hated it. I was so unhappy. But my mum told me not to contact them unless I had something happy to share. So, I started trying to only think of positive things to tell them so I could ring them up. Ever since then, I guess I've kept putting on the same brave face.' She paused and gave a little sigh. 'And I've been doing it for so long that I'm not sure I know how to be any different.'

He reached out across the table and took her hand. His touch made her heart beat a little faster, but as she looked down, the contrast between his pink skin and her purple-stained one made her feel even worse.

'And now I'm failing again,' she told him.

Joe withdrew his hand and looked directly into her face. 'You haven't failed. And I've got some good news, actually. That's why I'm here.'

She felt a pang of disappointment that he was only here to talk about business but hid it as usual.

'Have you thought about opening up the lavender field to visitors for the summer?' he asked.

That was the last thing that Harriet had been expecting him to say.

'I hadn't,' she replied slowly. 'Although it's funny, Libby mentioned something about Instagram a couple of weeks ago.'

'She's right,' said Joe, suddenly all businesslike. He brought out his phone and began to show Harriet photos of lavender fields that he had screenshotted from various websites. She was amazed at how busy the places were.

'If the flower yields are high,' said Joe, 'then you should be able to charge quite a high-ticket price. The generation of income could be pretty substantial.'

'It could?' she asked, trying to keep up with the business wording.

'You could make quite a profit,' he told her. 'Enough to perhaps even prove that there's an ongoing business concern regarding the fields, which may help the council to decide in your favour.'

Tears unexpectedly stung Harriet's eyes. 'Oh!' she cried, frantically brushing them off her cheeks. 'You really think so?'

He nodded. 'I do.'

'You have no idea,' she found herself saying. 'To know that we might save the fields. It's so important to me. My aunt and uncle meant everything to me.'

He looked at her with deep understanding in his eyes. 'I know,' he told her softly.

'And now we might just have a chance?' She still couldn't believe it. 'Joe, that's amazing!'

To both of their surprise, she catapulted herself out of her seat and drew him into a huge, and not exactly unwelcome, hug.

She held him tight for a moment until she slowly realised she was sitting on his lap.

'Whoops,' she said, quickly getting up before sitting back down on her chair once more, blushing furiously. 'Sorry. It was just knowing that there may be a small ray of hope.'

'Don't apologise,' he told her with a grin. 'That's the most enjoyable business meeting I've had in years.'

She giggled, still blushing a little.

'Glad I could cheer you up,' he said before looking more serious once more. 'Listen, have you talked to anyone about your, er, interesting skin dye?'

She glanced down at her hands before shaking her head. 'I thought that I'd better keep my failures to myself. Sometimes it's easier to lie, don't you think?' she said.

'Better than facing the consequences, you mean,' he replied with a frown. 'I understand. More than you think.'

They were both quiet for a while before he spoke once more.

'But these people are your friends and family. Maybe they deserve to know the truth and could help you.'

'They'll certainly be pleased about opening up the fields to the public.' She looked at him. 'Do you really think it will work?'

'I think we have to give it our best shot, don't you?'

Harriet nodded, thinking how pleased she was to hear him say 'we', that she was so grateful that he had returned to help them out. She longed for him to stay on just a little bit longer as well. For now, though, she was happy to share a drink with him and even happier when he asked her out to dinner the following evening.

26

After her conversation the previous evening, Harriet knew that Joe was right. She had to tell everyone how badly the experiments with the lavender had gone. But it went against every strain of her personality. She had always tried to be so positive. At least she now had something to be positive about, she realised. Was Joe right? Was opening the lavender fields to the public going to save them? She didn't know, but she could only hope so.

'You seem on a bit of a high this morning,' said Libby as they walked down the lane towards the station, with Paddington alongside.

'It just feels like there's hope in the air this morning,' said Harriet. She actually couldn't stop smiling.

'As opposed to the usual despair?' drawled Libby. 'By the way, what *is* going on with your hands?'

Harriet quickly shoved them in the pockets of her shorts and was about to swiftly change the subject when Maggie opened the door as they walked past.

'Oh, hi!' said Harriet. 'How are you?'

'Good, thanks,' said Maggie, pulling the front door almost to a close behind her.

'Oh, do you have that sugar thermometer we were talking about?' asked Libby, coming to a stop. 'I can take it off your hands now if you like.'

'I'm not sure where it is,' began Maggie, looking away.

'It's just that I've got a chocolate recipe I'm dying to try out later, and I've got a free weekend, you see,' carried on Libby, heading up the front path.

'Erm,' said Maggie, shuffling from foot to foot. 'It's just that, er, it's in a very awkward place.'

'Oh, I can get it for you,' replied Libby. 'I may be tiny, but I'm very bendy! I put that on a dating website last month. You wouldn't believe the replies I got. They'd make your hair and toes curl, I tell you.'

She and Harriet waited expectantly, looking at Maggie. Harriet realised that she was looking very uncomfortable, as opposed to her usual cheerful but shy self.

'Is everything all right?' asked Harriet gently.

'It's fine,' said Maggie quickly. 'You both wait here. I'll get it for you.'

But as she went to head back inside, Libby followed her in, saying, 'If it's in an awkward place, I can help.'

However, the words died away as she and Harriet stepped into the front room. In fact, they had to step almost sideways because there really was no other space to move or barely turn around. There were piles of magazines, books and boxes piled up everywhere.

Maggie looked absolutely horrified, and it was then that Harriet realised that she had been hiding the mess away all this time, that this was the first time they had ever been inside the cottage.

'Well, er,' said Libby, obviously struggling for something to say. She looked across at Harriet with urgent eyes.

Think positive, Harriet told herself.

'On the plus side, at least you don't need to bother with any dusting,' she said finally.

Maggie immediately disintegrated into tears. 'I'm so ashamed,' she cried. 'This was all my husband's stuff, and I just can't summon up the will to get rid of it.'

Harriet and Libby led her into the kitchen, which wasn't much better space wise, but at least there was a small dining room table with a chair. Libby moved the boxes that were on piled on top of the table, and they sat Maggie down whilst Harriet found the kettle.

'So, your husband was a little messy,' began Libby.

'He was a hoarder,' said Maggie as she took the mug of tea from Harriet. 'He bought anything and everything. It's all rubbish and needs taking to the dump, really, but I just can't seem to get the motivation to clear it. As if I'm betraying his memory somehow.' She gave a little shrug. 'Besides, I haven't got a car.'

'Well, I have a car,' said Harriet.

'So do I,' added Libby. 'We can help you.'

'Thanks.' Maggie sighed heavily. 'Isn't it awful, though? I thought I was keeping his memory alive by having all this stuff around, but your faces just then told me what I've known for a very long time. That it's all got to go.'

'That's the first step,' Harriet told her. 'Admitting what's wrong out loud.'

She stared down into the mug and realised she was offering support and advice but wasn't taking it herself. She thought back to Joe's words. Maybe now was the time to ask for help. Perhaps this was her chance to admit that she, too, was struggling.

'You're not alone,' she began tentatively. 'Sometimes saying that you need help is harder than you think. I mean, look at me!' She held out her purple-stained hands and laughed. 'I can't bear the lying any more,' she said. 'It's exhausting.'

Maggie nodded in agreement. 'I'm the same,' she said. 'The offers I've had from people to come in and have a cup of tea, and I've refused them all because, well, look at it around here. I'm lonely, really lonely. And it's all my fault.'

'Well, we can help you sort through everything if you like,' suggested Harriet. 'I'm sure Flora and Grams would give you a hand as well. Libby here is very tidy. Far more than me, in fact.'

'Won't it be embarrassing?' asked Maggie with a grimace. 'For everyone to see it?'

'There'll be no judgement,' Libby told her before looking across at Harriet. 'For anyone who needs help.'

It was then that Harriet knew she had to stop faking everything and face the future with her friends because life was better with support and friendship. It turned out that she'd always had both, if she had been brave enough to ask for them.

* * *

On the way back to Lavender Cottage, Libby looked at Harriet. 'So what if you can't make lotions and all that?' she said. 'I can't give you a decent facial, and you've seen the state of my nails when I try to paint them myself.'

'I know,' replied Harriet. 'I just thought it would be a really good use of all that lavender.'

'It would be,' said Libby. 'But perhaps you're just not the person to make them.'

'What do you mean?' asked Harriet.

'There's a lady over at Willow Tree Hall,' explained Libby. 'Eleanor's Apothecary. Now she's been really successful with her beauty products. It may be worth having a chat with her.'

Harriet nodded thoughtfully. 'Rachel said something about that a few weeks ago. You know, that's a good idea.'

'Oh, I'm full of them,' replied Libby with a grin. 'Like when I told you about your feelings for Joe.'

'I'm just meeting him later as a business associate,' said Harriet primly.

'Yeah, right,' said Libby. 'For dinner at the Black Swan Inn?'

'Well, you can't expect me to starve, can you?' replied Harriet, breaking into a grin.

27

That evening, Joe looked across the table in the restaurant at Harriet. She looked very pretty, he thought. Her long red hair was held back in a messy bun, with the V-neck top showing off her long, pale neck.

She suddenly looked up at him from the menu and smiled. 'It's really nice in here,' she told him, looking around.

He followed her gaze. The restaurant of the Black Swan Inn certainly had a romantic atmosphere with its soft lighting. Perhaps he should have chosen somewhere else, but he had really enjoyed his stays here recently, especially the food.

'I'd heard they'd renovated the place, but I hadn't had time to visit it yet,' she said.

'I've been staying in the new guest accommodation,' Joe told her. 'It's really good, and so is the food.'

Once they'd made their choices from the menu and their drinks were served, Harriet relaxed back in her chair.

'So,' Joe began. 'Did you talk to your friends?'

'About my purple hands?' she replied, laughing. 'Luckily, they've almost finally faded back to normal.' She held them up to show him. 'But, yes, I finally confessed that I'm completely useless at making potions.'

'Completely useless may be overstating things,' he told her.

But Harriet shook her head. 'It's fine. As it happens, Libby had a really good idea. So, I'm going to Willow Tree Hall tomorrow with Flora. It's a stately home near here. They've got a whole load of shops, one of which is run by a lady who makes beauty products with natural ingredients. Thought it might be worth a look and maybe even a discussion about the lavender.'

He nodded. 'I agree. Who says you need to make the products yourself?'

'That's what Libby said.'

'Well, she's right,' he told her. 'Play to your skills.'

She made a face in reply, remaining silent.

'Everyone's got skills,' he said softly. 'What did you train in? What jobs have you had?'

'Actually, I owned a beauty salon up in London,' she told him.

Joe was impressed. 'That's great.'

'Not really,' she replied with a grimace. 'The business went bust a month or so ago. Too high a rent, unfortunately.'

'That's a problem for a lot of retail businesses,' he told her. 'I'm sure your friends explained that. Or did you just hide away the hurt?'

The look on her face told him that he had guessed correctly.

She gave a little shrug of her shoulders. 'It's a hard habit to break.' She leant forward to take a sip of wine. 'That's why Cranfield is so special to me, you see. It was the only place where I ever felt worthwhile. I came here in the school holidays to stay with Aunty and Uncle, and it was like feeling whole again. Or at least until the holidays were over.'

He watched her for a moment and, seeing the sadness on her

face, had a sudden urge to take her in his arms and hold her until the hurt subsided.

'Well, you seem happy at the moment,' he finally said.

'I'm much more chilled these days,' she admitted. 'It's all this lavender. I sleep so well too.'

'Maybe I should try some,' he told her with a heavy sigh.

'Can I ask you something?' she said. 'Why did you decide to do such a tough job that you don't seem to enjoy?'

He leant back in his chair. 'Because my mum died, and I had to step up to help Dad with the family company. My dad never recovered from the loss, so I needed to take over the negotiating side of the business. I've just never stopped, and it's exhausting.'

'I'm so sorry,' she said. 'That must have been tough for you.'

'I didn't realise how burnt out I was until recently.' He looked at her, a little mesmerised by her large green eyes. 'Until I found myself missing Cranfield.'

'That's because it's so special,' she told him with a smile.

'And so are you,' he blurted out.

She looked shocked but didn't reply. Instead, a blush spread across her cheeks.

'It's true,' he carried on. 'I saw what you did here. You brought people back together with your protests and then the pruning. That's important.'

'The lavender field is important too,' she reminded him. 'Nearly everyone can see it out of one of their windows.'

'Then we need to keep the fight going, okay? With as many ideas as we can dream up.' He thought back to what she had been saying about her business. 'Play to your strengths,' he murmured to himself.

'Pardon?' she said, not quite hearing him.

'Would you say you're a good beauty therapist?' he asked.

She hesitated before nodding. 'Yes, I am.'

'And did you enjoy it? As a job, I mean?'

'Yes,' replied Harriet. 'Initially, I mean. So many people struggle with a lack of confidence. I enjoyed helping them feel better about themselves, even with something as small as a manicure.'

'Then why not expand on the lavender theme,' he said, his mind racing with ideas. 'Create a beauty salon in Cranfield using the lavender products! Surely the rent must be far cheaper than in London?'

'But what about the clientele?' she said, biting her lip. 'There's no one around here interested in all that.'

'I disagree.' He nodded at the packed restaurant they were sitting in. 'This place has been busy nearly every night I've stayed here, even on a Monday. If you have a decent product, then they'll come and spend money. Think on it.'

'I will,' she said, nodding thoughtfully to herself.

'Because if we don't do this, everything will be lost,' he carried on. 'The fields, the station, the heart of the village, and that would be a terrible thing.'

She looked at Joe for a long moment.

'What's happened to you?' she asked with a soft smile. 'You're completely different.'

'I think it must be the smell of lavender in the air,' he told her, returning the smile. 'You did say it's relaxing. Maybe it's having the same effect on me as well.'

'So maybe it's time to find out what's underneath the business suit,' she told him before she realised the double entendre and blushed furiously.

Joe laughed. 'I've got quite a respectable six-pack thanks to many hours at the gym,' he told her.

'That wasn't quite what I meant,' she said, flicking a glance at his stomach before looking away.

Joe found that he enjoyed seeing her blush. It was a hint of the passion that matched the red of her hair.

'So perhaps we can help each other,' he told her. 'I can give you my business know-how and, in return, maybe you can teach me how to relax a bit. Deal?'

He held out his hand across the table. She hesitated before moving her own hand towards his. There was a tingle up his arm as they shook.

'Deal,' she replied.

He found himself pleased that they were going to try to save Cranfield together, that encouraging her to be truthful had helped.

He just needed to do the same with his father. Perhaps when he returned to work after the weekend, he could finally be honest about his feelings.

But for now, he wanted to enjoy the evening with Harriet. He was enjoying her company more and more and could finally admit to himself that she had been the main reason that he had wanted to return to Cranfield. And why he kept wanting to return.

28

Feeling empowered after her conversation with Joe over dinner, Harriet was in a good mood as she drove Flora to Willow Tree Hall the following morning.

On the back seat of the car, she had wound the window down, and Paddington the dog had stuck his head out. The rush of air was making his silky ears flap in the breeze.

'So, Grams has organised an intervention at Maggie's house this afternoon?' asked Harriet.

Flora nodded. 'If it's as bad as it sounds,' she began.

'It is,' Harriet told her with a grim look.

'Then she's going to need all the help we can give her,' said Flora, looking out of the window as they went up the long driveway to the stately home. 'This is lovely. It feels like I haven't had a day off in ages.'

'That's because you haven't. You need to stop for a break once in a while, and I thought we deserved a better class of coffee this morning,' said Harriet, laughing.

But even she had to admit that she'd forgotten how impressive Willow Tree Hall was. It was a large, wide-fronted building, two stories high and built in a sandy-coloured stone. Like a miniature Buckingham Palace in shape, it had sixteen large sash windows spread evenly across the front. The centrepiece was a huge bright red double front door framed by large stone pillars on either side.

However, they weren't visiting the stately home, so Harriet turned the car, following the signs for the stable block and tearoom away from the large house.

Once parked up, they put Paddington on a lead and headed towards the tearoom, which was in the old dairy house.

'Okay, you win,' said Flora as they sat down at a table outside and ordered themselves two coffees and some cake. 'This really is very grown-up of us.'

Harriet glanced around the courtyard, also approving of the vintage chic of the place. Once their cakes had been served on flowered plates and the coffee pot was placed between them, Harriet chatted to her friend about the reason for their visit.

'So I thought after this, we'd visit Eleanor's Apothecary,' she said.

Flora nodded. 'It's very popular, you know. I've seen it when I come over here for the seasonal fairs. You can get all sorts here, and it's all local produce.'

'Eleanor apparently makes all her creams and soaps herself, so I thought I might be able to get a few tips from her,' said Harriet.

Flora took a sip of her tea. 'Well, she's been running her business for a year or two, so I'm sure she knows what she's doing by now.'

'Unlike me.' Harriet bit into her cake and savoured the delicious flavour. 'I guess I need to play to my strengths,' she carried on, repeating Joe's words.

'I think we all need to do that.' Flora leaned back in her chair, relishing the sunshine on her face. Harriet thought she looked a little weary.

'It's good to see you stop working once in a while,' she told her friend.

Flora hid her expression as she surreptitiously fed a piece of her cake to Paddington, who was sitting underneath the table. Once she had sat back up, she said, 'If I stop, then I'll have time to work out just how bad a state the farm is in.'

'You're doing your best,' Harriet told her.

Flora frowned. 'What if it's not good enough?'

'All you can do is your best,' said Harriet, giving her a sympathetic smile. 'That's all any of us can do.'

'You're sounding very full of confidence today,' remarked Flora, raising her eyebrows in surprise.

'I hope so,' said Harriet. 'Especially because Joe had an idea about me running a beauty salon in Cranfield. What do you think?'

'I think it's a great idea,' replied Flora, looking pleased.

'If there's any customers to be had, of course.' Harriet bit her lip. Perhaps she really was reaching for the stars with this idea, she thought.

'First of all, this means that you'll be staying for the summer,' said Flora with a smile. 'Second, I'll be first in line for any of your luxurious treatments. Especially if there's some kind of friends and family discount.'

'You get treatments free of charge,' Harriet told her with a wink.

'Thank goodness for that,' murmured Flora. 'I saw the price list for your treatments when you worked in London.'

'I'm not sure I want that kind of clientele here,' replied Harriet, frowning. 'Fair prices for local people is what I'd love to charge.'

After finishing their delicious coffee and cakes, they left the tearoom and walked the short distance to where the old stable block had been converted. It was an L-shaped block with about ten individual stables, each with green shutters and a window. They all appeared to be occupied by various businesses.

The two stables nearest the hall had a sign across that read 'Eleanor's Apothecary.' One appeared to be a workshop, whereas the other had a counter and was obviously the retail side of the business.

A pretty woman with long dark hair drawn back in a ponytail greeted them as they peered inside the shop through the open door.

'Hello,' she said. 'Come on in.'

'Thanks,' said Harriet, stepping inside. It was an Aladdin's cave, with every conceivable product filling the floor-to-ceiling shelves around the outside of the space.

'You're more than welcome to browse or just ask if you're looking for something in particular,' the woman carried on. 'I'm Eleanor, by the way.'

'Actually, I was looking for advice,' Harriet told her. 'I'm Harriet. My friend Flora is outside with my dog. We live in Cranfield.'

'Oh, I haven't been there for years, since the station closed down,' said Eleanor. 'But it was such a pretty place.'

'Right back at you,' said Harriet, laughing.

'Yes, not everyone gets to work next to a stately home, I guess,' replied Eleanor, joining in the laughter. 'Anyway, how can I help?'

Harriet hesitated to speak before Flora nodded encouragingly at her from the open doorway. 'I'm trying to keep my uncle's lavender fields open in Cranfield,' she began.

'Right,' said Eleanor, looking more serious. 'I read about the protests in the local paper. It would be such a shame to lose them.'

'Absolutely,' said Harriet. 'So, we were thinking about opening them up to the public this summer.'

'That's a great idea,' replied Eleanor, looking pleased. 'We get quite a few visitors here, so I'm sure they could combine it with a visit to Cranfield as well, especially as it's so close.'

'I'll get some flyers over to you over the coming weeks,' said Harriet, making a note on her phone.

'And vice-versa,' replied Eleanor. 'Every local business needs all the help it can get.'

'I agree,' said Harriet. 'I needed your advice, though. I have some dried lavender from a previous year's harvest. It still smells amazing, although the colour has faded a little. I thought I'd try to emulate your success, but I've pretty much had total failure so far with everything that I've tried to create.'

'It took me a long time to perfect all the different mixtures,' said Eleanor, with a sympathetic smile. 'I can always show you a few tips.'

'That would be so helpful,' replied Harriet, although she still felt everyone was overestimating her skills.

'Interesting idea though,' carried on Eleanor, tapping her chin in thought. 'I've been sourcing lavender from about twenty miles away, but if you've got some that's right on our doorstep, I'd be much happier to use yours. Is it organic?'

'Yes,' said Harriet proudly. 'My uncle tended the plants for many years, and he never used any kind of sprays or pesticides.'

'That's great,' said Eleanor, smiling. 'And so important these days. Listen, perhaps we can come to some kind of agreement. I'm happy to take the lavender off your hands and pay you the going rate when you harvest this year's crop. I would even state where the lavender came from on my website.'

'That would be amazing,' replied Harriet gratefully. She knew how popular Eleanor's products were. The trouble was that it would only work if the fields weren't sold before then.

'What were your own plans for the products?' asked Eleanor.

Harriet rolled her eyes. 'I'd thought about starting up my own beauty salon using the lavender, but the products I made were so awful that I'm not sure anyone would come!'

'A beauty salon?' asked Eleanor, nodding thoughtfully. 'I think that's a great idea.'

'The trouble is, I'm not sure there's too much call for that kind of thing around here,' Harriet carried on.

'Actually, you'd be amazed by the amount of people who suggest that I run some kind of spa here,' said Eleanor. 'But that doesn't really interest me. It's the creams, lotions and oils that are my passion, and to be honest, I'm run off my feet as it is, with the business going so well.'

'Well, it sounds to me that you've got the potential for the perfect business partnership,' said Flora, smiling at them both. 'Eleanor uses the lavender to make the products, and Harriet opens the lavender spa and uses Eleanor's products.'

'It certainly sounds like a positive outcome for us both,' said Eleanor, nodding as she looked back at Harriet. 'What do you think?'

'I have enough boxes of lavender if you think it sounds like a good idea,' replied Harriet.

'I think it sounds great,' said Eleanor, with a smile.

So, for the second time in only two days, Harriet found herself shaking on yet another deal as she promised to drop over the lavender to Eleanor as soon as possible.

At last, it felt as if she could start to feel excited about her plans. She had missed working in her very own beauty salon, despite the stress of finding the rent each month back in London. Beauty therapy had been the one thing that Harriet had found that she was good at, and it had been her dream job for a while. One small problem was where to base her lavender spa, but surely there was somewhere in Cranfield she could use which would make it her dream business once more?

As she drove Flora back home, she began to feel something she had thought lost a few weeks ago. She was starting to feel tangible hope that maybe something good could come out of opening up the lavender fields that summer.

'So, dinner with Joe was good last night?' asked Flora, breaking into Harriet's thoughts.

Harriet nodded. 'It was. I feel, I don't know, comfortable around him. We can chat about everything.'

'Everything?' asked Flora. 'Even your little crush on him?'

Harriet rolled her eyes. 'I don't think that came up in the conversation, actually.'

Flora grinned. 'Well, don't worry. Seeing as I reckon he's got a crush on you too, I think it'll come up in one of your future chats.'

'He's leaving this morning, and I don't know when he'll be back,' Harriet told her, trying to concentrate on the road. 'Although he did say it wouldn't be too long.'

And that was a good thing, thought Harriet, because she could feel herself missing him already.

But was Flora right? Was Joe starting to have feelings for her as well? She was excited to find out when he next returned to Cranfield.

29

After her successful morning at Willow Tree Hall, Harriet was in a very positive mood when she arrived to help Maggie sort through her late husband's things, which was good because Maggie was looking extremely nervous.

'We won't throw out anything without checking with you first,' Libby told her.

'Absolutely,' added Flora, nodding. 'Let's just start with one box at a time, shall we?'

They had privately agreed beforehand that slow and steady would help Maggie get over her nerves at finally facing up to the mess in her cottage.

The first box, however, was a bit of an eye-opener.

'Wow,' said Libby, pulling out a large piece of equipment that was copper plated. 'I'd be impressed if I knew what it was.'

'I know,' said Grams, coming forward to peer at the discovery. 'It's a home distillery for alcohol. My grandfather used to have something like it to make moonshine with back in the day.'

'Moonshine?' murmured Flora, with her eyebrows raised.

Grams chuckled. 'It was as rough as anything to drink, but it didn't half give you a nice warm glow on a cold winter's night.'

'And a stinking hangover afterwards, I bet,' added Libby, placing it on the floor. 'So, what do we reckon? Charity or eBay?'

Maggie shook her head. 'I just want it out of the house, to be honest, so let's give it to charity unless someone wants it.'

Everyone shook their heads. However, Harriet had an idea.

'Actually, do you mind if I have a look at it?' she asked. 'I was thinking of all things lavender, and what better than lavender gin? Unless it's disgusting, of course.'

'Ooh, I like the idea of that,' said Grams, smacking her lips together. 'Right, that's for Harriet.'

Harriet placed the copper distillery in one corner with a plan to look up how to make gin at some point. Hopefully, it wouldn't be as difficult as making soaps and hand creams!

They spent the next couple of hours brainstorming all things lavender-themed as they unpacked box after box.

'Cocktail shaker,' announced Libby, opening up the third box.

'Lavender cocktails,' said Flora, nodding her approval.

'We could open up our own bar!' suggested Grams, laughing.

Even Maggie joined in with the laughter, starting to relax as the contents of each box began to be unpacked and then either placed on the charity pile, the rubbish pile or given to one of the gang of declutterers.

'He loved every gadget,' Maggie told them as she brought out a chocolate tempering machine. 'Most of them haven't even been used.'

'Wow,' said Libby, stepping forward to stare at the machine in awe. 'I've been struggling to temper my own chocolate, but this would be great. I must give you some money.'

Maggie shook her head. 'I'm just grateful for it to be out of the house.'

When a chocolate fountain was discovered as well, Libby looked thrilled to have her own pile of chocolate-themed gadgets.

'Lavender-flavoured chocolate?' suggested Libby. 'Or is it poisonous?'

Maggie shook her head. 'No, it's a very subtle taste if used sparingly. You could always use it as a decoration on top of the chocolate.'

'That's an idea,' said Libby, nodding thoughtfully.

'And I've got a super recipe for lemon and lavender cakes that I might try out,' said Maggie.

'I have some lavender you could use,' Harriet told her. 'From my uncle's last harvest, so it's literally come from the lavender fields.

'That's great,' replied Maggie, looking delighted. 'I'd love to experiment. I love being in the kitchen.'

A foot bath was added to Harriet's pile of goodies. 'With some lavender oil, it will be a real treat for the customers,' she said.

Gradually, the front room began to be cleared and started to feel a lot neater. The magazines were put aside for recycling, and the unwanted books would be taken to the charity shops in Aldwych. Harriet's car was already piled up, ready to be taken the following morning.

When they decided it was time to finish, Maggie looked at them with a grateful expression. 'I don't know what to say,' she told them.

'We're a community,' Grams said. 'We help each other.'

This brought tears to Maggie's eyes. 'I haven't even seen the carpet properly for years. I'll need to spend the next few days cleaning as well as tidying up the rest of the house,' she told them, laughing despite the tears.

'I can spare some more time tomorrow if you'd like,' offered Harriet.

But Maggie shook her head. 'Actually, thanks to you all, I feel empowered to crack on by myself. Not that I'm not grateful. Thank you so much. And, of course, if I find anything that I think will help with the lavender or the chocolate, then I'll let you know.' She hesitated before adding, 'But I can do this now, I think.'

'Good for you,' said Grams, stepping forward to give her a hug.

'We're here if you need us,' Flora told her.

'Thanks for all the equipment,' said Libby, barely able to walk with so much to carry.

Finally, it was just Harriet and Maggie.

'Are you okay?' asked Harriet softly.

Maggie nodded. 'I really am,' she said. 'Like a huge weight has been lifted. The house feels more like a home, if you know what I mean.'

'I do,' Harriet told her.

* * *

Later that day in Lavender Cottage, Harriet thought back to what Maggie had said about her house becoming a home once more.

Feeling equally motivated, she spent the evening finally unpacking her own boxes and bags and placing her belongings around the cottage.

The front room soon had a combination of her aunt and uncle's furniture with Harriet's cushions, rug and curtains. She had cleared away a few more rickety pieces of furniture that she didn't like and were falling apart, which left a bit more space for a modern standing lamp and a white basket that she would use for the logs for the fire.

The bathroom was filled with her soaps and houseplants, and the bright blue towels brought a touch of colour to the white-washed tongue and groove around the standalone bath.

Clearing away some of the clutter that didn't have any sentimental value made Harriet feel as if she could breathe a little easier.

Bit by bit, room by room, it felt as if she were slowly taking over the cottage, keeping the heritage and her favourite pieces but also starting to make it feel like hers as well. Which was crazy because it would have to be sold soon, she reminded herself. But looking around the front room before she went up to bed, she took a deep breath and fervently hoped that her wish upon the shooting star would come true.

At the time, she had wished that nothing would change, but she now knew that time moved everything on. All she wanted to do was stay in Cranfield, but how to make that dream a reality seemed more out of reach than ever before.

But at least Lavender Cottage had finally begun to feel like home again. Except it always had been, she realised, with a soft smile.

30

'So, you've got the skills to do the treatments at your lavender spa, and now there'll be decent creams to use as well,' said Libby as she poured them all a gin and tonic later that week at Lavender Cottage.

'Yup,' said Harriet. 'Just as long as I'm not making them.'

She was truly grateful to have made a business deal with Eleanor and could relinquish all responsibility for making the beauty products. Play to your strengths, Joe had said, so she was.

Her own business was within grasp once more, if she could overcome the biggest issue of them all. 'There's just one problem. I don't have anywhere to do the treatments. I mean, it's probably only for the summer, but I didn't want people coming into my home. It's so tiny I'm not sure it would work properly anyway.'

'Oh, that's easy,' said Flora before taking a large sip of the drink that Libby had just handed her. 'I know the perfect place.'

Harriet and Libby exchanged amazed looks.

'Well, don't keep us all in suspense!' groaned Libby. 'Spill the beans!'

'What about the old summer house on the edge of the lavender field?' said Flora, looking a little smug. 'After all, your Uncle Fred built it!'

Harriet was stunned. 'You think that would work?'

'Yes, and it'll keep you dry from the rain and keep the sun off when it hopefully shines every day for the whole of summer,' Flora told her.

'It's a great idea!' said Libby. 'It's not being used for anything, and it's right in the middle of the lavender fields! You can't get better advertising than that!'

'There's even your uncle's shed next to it where you could keep all your stuff,' added Flora.

Even Paddington the dog was thumping his tail on the floor as if he too, approved of the idea.

Though Harriet couldn't deny she was buoyed by the prospect, she was a little concerned about the structure's suitability, so the following morning she headed over to look at it properly.

It was a hexagonal oak structure with a tiled roof and double glass front doors. It looked robust enough, she thought, wandering inside. Once she'd swept away all the cobwebs, there would certainly be enough space for a bed and some equipment.

The lack of privacy worried her, but she realised she could always hang up some organza curtains to pull across the glass doors. That would keep the light but also be discreet.

'This might just work,' she murmured, looking at Paddington for his approval, but he was too busy lolling in the sunshine at the open doorway.

Despite the dog's relaxed attitude, Harriet was starting to feel pretty excited about the new business. Of course, it would only work once the summer weather arrived and the place was warm enough. After all, it was just a summer house with no heating. But it was a start, wasn't it?

Stepping outside, Harriet let herself into the shed next to it. It was in the same shade of oak, so she presumed her uncle had built both. It was small, but Libby had been right, with a lock on the door, it would be secure enough to store any equipment.

She smiled as she looked at the row of garden tools lined up on their hooks along the longest wall. There was also a metal watering can, a pair of rusty secateurs and some old pots.

Harriet reached out to touch the watering can, missing her aunt and uncle at that moment so much, which was why when she walked out of the shed a short while later, she felt even more determined to make a success of the lavender fields.

* * *

Later on that week, Flora drove Harriet in her small van to London to retrieve all the salon equipment from the storage unit. After they had piled everything up inside, they began the long journey back.

'This is great,' said Harriet. 'Thank you so much.'

'I'd do anything for you,' said Flora as she frowned at the heavy traffic. 'But this is probably the worst thing ever. It's so busy here. I don't know how you coped all these years.'

'What do you mean? All the people?' asked Harriet.

Flora nodded at the outside space. 'Everyone cramped together on narrow streets. Where's the wildlife? The fields?' She shuddered. 'Definitely not for me.'

'I just kept going and dreamt of Cranfield the whole time,' confessed Harriet.

And it was true. She had soldiered on living in London, where she didn't want to be, just to try to impress her parents. But after all her hard work, had they really cared?

She made the decision there and then that perhaps it was time for her to run her own life instead of trying to emulate her successful siblings' stellar careers because that was impossible.

Whatever happened in the future, that part of her life was over. Wherever she went next, it would be on her terms. But, of course, what she wanted most of all was to stay in Cranfield.

There was lots to do as they headed back down the motorway, and Harriet began to tick off the to-do list mentally as she went through it on her phone.

The summer house needed a major clean-up inside and perhaps some prettying up on the outside too. She thought a lick of paint might help; a touch of pale purple would be in keeping. She needed some kind of signage outside so customers knew where to go. Then she needed to coordinate with Eleanor as to which products she could buy in advance to use. She had already decided on facials, manicures and pedicures, as well as scalp, shoulder, hand and feet massages.

* * *

As she stood in the middle of the summer house later that day, Harriet looked up at the oak beams crisscrossing the ceiling and decided they were the perfect place to hang a few bunches of lavender for luck and fairy lights for a touch of atmosphere.

She was excited and pleased about the beauty salon. Perhaps she might even impress Joe when she next saw him, whenever that might be. He had headed back to work after his weekend in Cranfield, and she found she missed him most days. She had a feeling that she was beginning to have serious feelings for him, but that was impossible because wherever his future lay, it most certainly wouldn't be in Cranfield.

31

Joe had spent the following weekend mooching around his flat, somewhat bored. He found that he missed the company and chat with the people of Cranfield. Especially Harriet.

Eventually, he had rung up Matt and suggested they go for a drink and dinner somewhere. Once there, he found that he couldn't stop talking about Cranfield.

Matt's eyebrows grew higher and higher as Joe chatted about the plans for the lavender fields and was equally enthralled about the train restoration.

Finally, Matt was able to get a word in edgewise. 'Did aliens come down and replace you with a better version of yourself?' he asked, laughing. 'Because this isn't the hardened businessman who only cared about profits that I've been mates with for so long.'

'I still care about profits,' Joe told him. 'Only now they're important if they help save the lavender fields.'

Matt shook his head in wonder. 'Whoever she is, she must be very pretty,' he said as he picked up his pint of beer and took a sip.

'I don't know what you're talking about.' Joe was still thinking back to his friend's criticism. 'Anyway, I like to think that I've always been a good person.'

Matt nodded. 'You know I love you like a brother and all that rubbish, but even you've got to admit that you went a bit heavy on the profit margins for the past few years.'

Joe sighed. 'I accept that, and now I want to make up for my mistakes. I want to do some good.'

'Excellent,' Matt replied. 'So, what is her name?' he pressed.

Joe took his time over a long sip of his beer before finally replying, 'Harriet.'

'Harriet who chained herself to a tree?' said Matt in surprise. 'That Harriet?'

Joe couldn't help but break into a smile. 'Yup.'

Matt grinned. 'Oh, mate, you have got it bad.'

Joe showed him a photo that he had saved from the newspaper. Harriet was smiling at the camera as she was chained against the tree.

Matt whistled. 'And I can see why.' He then gave an exaggerated shudder. 'But you wouldn't find me falling for any woman, let alone with one such a pretty face.'

'I haven't fallen for Harriet,' Joe told him quickly.

'Haven't you?' murmured Matt.

Joe swiftly changed the subject to football.

* * *

Later on the following day, thinking of his many conversations with Harriet, Joe knew that he couldn't put off talking to his dad any longer. It was time to have one of the most difficult conversations of his life.

He hesitated before putting the key in the front door lock. Then, with a deep breath, he went inside the family house.

'Hi, Dad,' he called out into the cool air of the hallway. 'It's only me.'

He heard noise from the kitchen before his father appeared, silhouetted against the sunlight of the garden behind him.

'Hey,' replied his dad, sounding extremely surprised. 'What are you doing here?'

'I figured you'd be home by now from your round of golf,' said Joe, putting his keys down on the little table and following his dad into the kitchen. 'I was just hoping that you hadn't stayed for a Sunday roast.'

'No, I thought I'd head home and watch the Masters on TV instead.'

Joe looked around the kitchen, realising, as he did every time he returned to the family home, how stark it looked without his mum's baking everywhere. He wondered if perhaps that's why he had enjoyed all the cake in Cranfield recently. It had felt like a taste of home, but home from a very long time ago.

Even at Christmas, he took his dad out for lunch at a fancy restaurant. Anything not to have to face each other at home in relative silence. But it was time to be brave.

He immediately thought of Harriet, pleased that their dinner out had catapulted her ideas into action. She had texted him recently with her plans for the lavender spa, and it was certainly all tying in together, along with the opening of the lavender fields to tourists. She was likely to have a very busy summer, which was why he had needed to come and have the conversation with his father that he had been dreading for so long.

'Beer?' asked his dad, walking towards the fridge.

'Why not?' said Joe. 'Thanks.'

Once they each had a cold bottle in their hands, as if by mutual consent, they wandered outside through the French doors and onto the large patio.

'The garden looks good,' lied Joe. It was pretty overgrown compared to a few years ago. His dad had always been a keen gardener, but all of his time was taken up with work, and any spare time was used up with golf. Joe realised at that moment that his dad obviously didn't want to be in the family home any longer than he needed to be.

'It needs a tidy-up,' replied his dad. 'I was thinking of getting someone in to give me a hand.'

'It's a pretty big area to keep on top of,' said Joe.

They sat down on the wooden bench on the patio, overlooking the garden. It was cool in the shade, a welcome relief now that they were almost at the end of May and some very warm weather had finally arrived.

'Maybe too big.'

Joe turned to look at his dad. 'What do you mean?'

His dad sighed. 'I've been thinking of maybe downsizing. I rattle around this place, and you know, it's not the same these days. You're busy, and well, you know, I'm on my own.'

'Since Mum died.' For once, Joe spoke the words that they weren't supposed to say out loud.

His dad gulped and merely nodded in reply.

'I think you need to do whatever makes you happy, Dad,' Joe told him.

'I'm not sure I'll ever be that again, son.' His dad gave him a wan smile. 'But maybe somewhere I'm not overwhelmed with memories the whole time would help.'

Joe nodded thoughtfully, amazed that they were even talking about such important matters when for far too long such subjects had lain dormant. 'Okay. Well, I'll support you no matter what you decide. Any ideas where you would want to go?'

'Not a clue.' His dad took a sip of the beer. 'Anyway, that's not why you're here, is it?'

Joe shrugged his shoulders. 'No, but at least we're talking.'

'We talk every day, at least two or three times,' said his dad.

'Not about anything important,' replied Joe in a pointed tone.

'Work is important,' his dad told him with a short laugh. 'Your work far more than mine, in fact. Your negotiation skills alone are—'

'I'm not just your negotiator. I'm your son!' snapped Joe. There followed a short silence as he dragged his hand through his hair. 'Sorry. I didn't mean to bark like that at you. It's just I've been trying to say this for a long time and, I don't know, there never seems to be a good time.'

'What is it that you're trying to say?' asked his dad.

'I don't know,' said Joe. 'It's what's missing in my life, I guess. I need more than just work. I want to feel and live. I need life in my life and people in it. I want to laugh.' And dance, he added to himself before shaking away the surprising thought.

'I see.' His dad took another sip of beer before speaking once more. 'Well, I suppose it shouldn't be a surprise. You've been talking about having a break recently. I just hoped your weekend away would have been enough.'

Joe hesitated before speaking. 'I don't think it was.'

'Right.' His dad was quiet for a moment. 'Well, there's the Manchester deal to be sorted, as well as finishing off that contract in Germany. Why don't you take a break after that?'

'I'm not sure a weekend is going to make much of a difference,' said Joe.

'Then take the summer off.'

Joe looked at his dad in amazement. 'Seriously? The whole summer?'

'You won't work as well if you're feeling that burnt out.' His dad shrugged his shoulders. 'So, take some time away and recharge the batteries if you must. The business will still be there in the autumn. I'll just put any new projects on hold until then.'

Joe nodded slowly. 'Okay. Well, thanks.'

He sipped his beer, feeling somewhat stunned. Once his current work was finished, he would have most of June, July and August to relax. Maybe feel the sun on his face for a while. Most of all, he wanted to live.

He knew exactly where he would go. He would return to Cranfield, of course. Perhaps he could do some good there to make amends for the rocky beginning. He could help with the business side of things as the lavender fields opened to the public.

He knew it would do him good to have less responsibility for a few weeks and no work. It would help him mentally to get off the treadmill of all that travel between various offices and overnight stays in hotels. He hoped to feel better and maybe even get his sleep patterns looking far healthier. Maybe he could even enjoy some more of that lemon drizzle cake. He had missed it all, the cakes and the fresh air. And seeing Harriet and Paddington most of all.

The thought of seeing Harriet again made him smile as he sat and looked across the garden. He now had a whole summer to decide what he wanted for his future. And to discover whether Harriet was part of that future as well.

32

It was the beginning of June, and the weather was growing warmer and warmer by the day.

Harriet looked across the lavender fields, marvelling at the deep blue sky that reached all the way down until it touched the green hills that surrounded the village.

The lavender was looking green too, she was pleased to see. After quite a bit of rain over recent weeks, the warm summer sun was encouraging the new growth, and the lavender was getting taller.

If the month of May had been a waiting game, then the opening date of the first of July, less than a month away, was coming up all too quickly.

All it needed were the flowers, but Harriet knew from experience that they never normally bloomed until the end of the month. But she was still peering at the plants each day to try to spot the tiny buds that would turn into flowers.

'A garden teaches you patience,' she remembered Uncle Fred telling her.

She tried to follow his guidance, be patient, and instead spent her time readying the summer house for its transformation into the lavender spa for its grand opening later that week. Harriet had decided to open the spa early, figuring she would share her time between the small amount of customers she would have along with the possibly even smaller number of visitors for the lavender fields.

'Thanks for the bunting, Del,' said Harriet as she handed it to Joe, who was on the top of a stepladder, checking the slate tiles on top of the summer house were secure.

Harriet had been thrilled when Joe had arrived back in Cranfield the previous day, telling her, to her complete amazement, that he would be staying for the whole summer. He had already negotiated a short-term rental on one of the apartments above the shops in Cranbridge, so he would only ever be a short distance away.

In addition, he had also offered his services to help get both businesses up and running. Harriet found that she couldn't stop smiling at having him back in Cranfield.

'Heard you needed it, and I've got loads of the stuff in my lock-up left over from the jubilees,' said Dodgy Del, bringing some more pastel bunting out of a carrier bag. 'Hello, pooch.'

He bent down to give Paddington a stroke. He was Harriet's constant companion these days. The foster lady had unfortunately broken her arm on her cycling holiday, so the dog was staying with Harriet for a while longer. But Harriet was discovering that she didn't mind and was actually enjoying his presence, both at home and when they walked through the rows of lavender to check on its progress each day. In return, Paddington had stopped trying to run away and seemed more than happy to be living in Cranfield with Harriet.

'Besides, I wanted to talk to Joe here about some investments,' added Del. 'I heard you're a money man like me.'

'Oh, really?' asked Joe, sounding surprised.

'Got a bit of money put aside after a blinding spring selling mountain bikes,' said Del, with a wink. 'Wanted to get your thoughts on the odds for Royal Ascot next week.'

Joe looked alarmed. 'I think you may be safer putting your hard-earned profits into a savings account,' he replied. 'Or some stocks and shares.'

Del made a face. 'Not much fun in that, though, is there? Plus, some chap at a local stables says his horse is a sure thing.'

'Not sure there's such a thing. Hang on,' said Joe, looking at the triangles of material in his hands. 'This says Happy Birthday Mum on it!'

'Oh, yeah.' Del shuffled from side to side before giving them both a half-hearted shrug. 'Turn it over. Nobody will see it.'

'They will from the inside,' said Harriet, pointing at the glazed front doors of the summer house.

Del frowned. 'Right.' He began reluctantly taking the bunting back from Joe, who had climbed back down the stepladder. 'I've got some more back at HQ. Leave it with me.'

'I can find some for myself!' said Harriet quickly.

But Dodgy Del had already walked away.

Harriet rolled her eyes. 'Honestly,' she muttered. 'What's he like?'

'Well, even without the bunting, it's looking pretty good,' said Joe, admiring the outside before following her inside.

Harriet was thrilled with the results of the makeover. The pale lilac paint had refreshed the look and feel of the place, both on the inside and outside. The white leather bed for treatments was on one side of the space. Harriet had already set it up for a photo shoot, which would go on the website that Joe was talking about creating, so the bed was already dressed with rolled-up white towels and a large sprig of lavender on top. Nearby was a wooden chair, again dressed with a white cushion decorated with a lavender pattern. There was also a matching wooden cupboard which Harriet had taken out of Lavender Cottage and given a coat of varnish.

Heading back outside, she was pleased to see it was warm and sunny, with only the occasional fluffy cloud drifting across. The summer house was going to look perfect in the photographs.

She was also pleased with the response locally. She had yet even to promote the beauty salon, apart from on *The Cranbridge Times* website, but already had a couple of people lined up for treatments.

To her surprise, Bob's wife, Rachel, had wanted a facial, apparently with a desire to look and feel younger. Bob had told her he needed a shoulder massage after all his hard work on the steam engine, and Flora had also booked herself in for a pedicure.

'Even if nobody will see it when I wear my wellies all the time,' she had said.

The products she was going to use at the lavender spa were almost ready. Harriet had taken ten of the large boxes of the harvested lavender flowers over to Eleanor's Apothecary, and the beauty products would be ready in a day or so's time. Harriet was delighted that some good use would come from her uncle's last harvest.

'Will you put bunting on your uncle's shed as well?' asked Joe, breaking into her train of thought.

Harriet wandered over to stand next to him in front of the small shed and smiled. 'Definitely,' she told him. 'I think it will look very cute.'

She opened the door to show him inside.

'All of his tools are still here,' she said with a soft sigh. 'I couldn't bear to get rid of them.'

'I don't blame you,' replied Joe, coming to stand at the entrance next to her. 'I think it's a great idea to keep his legacy alive.'

She turned to look at him. He was so close that their faces were nearly touching. 'You understand now? The importance of all this, I mean.'

'I do,' he said softly, reaching out to remove a stray strand of long red hair that had gotten caught on her lip balm. 'For the village as well as for you.'

Harriet held her breath as she stared up at him before he broke the moment by moving away.

She cleared her throat, which had become suddenly very dry. 'Any word from the council?' she asked. It was a permanent cloud hanging over her.

Joe shook his head. 'End of the summer before they make their final decision,' he said, reaching out to touch one of the garden forks hanging up. 'I think they're hoping that people have short memories and that the protests will have been long forgotten.'

'But the lavender fields won't be forgotten,' she said fiercely. 'Because it's going to be the best summer ever.'

'I agree,' he told her, spinning around to give her a wide smile, which made her heart lurch. 'By the way,' he said, 'thanks for the lavender posset. It was the best night's sleep I've had in ages last night.'

Harriet broke into a smile. 'I told you, that stuff is like magic.'

He nodded thoughtfully. 'There certainly seems to be something in the air here.'

As he wandered back outside, Harriet was left thinking how much she agreed with him. There was a feeling of calm and tranquillity all around her these days, along with excitement for what the future might hold.

She gazed across the fields. They had decided to open up the lavender fields to the public on the first day of July for a whole two months. Harriet still wasn't sure anyone would come, nor how successful the lavender spa would be. Still, she was keeping everything crossed that both businesses would flourish. And that the magic in the air would remain for the whole of the summer, she thought, stealing another glance at Joe.

33

'For a grand opening, this lavender spa is severely lacking in champagne,' said Libby, sitting down on the outside step of the summer house.

'There's cucumber water over there in a jug,' replied Harriet as she smoothed a cleanser over Maggie's face, who was lying down on the bed.

'I'm not sure we need alcohol when we're trying to improve and rejuvenate ourselves,' said Flora, who was sitting on the chair in the corner, covered in a face mask.

'Champagne improves everything,' muttered Libby, closing her eyes with a contented sigh as she leant back in the doorway. She stretched out her legs in the sunshine, letting the warmth dry her newly painted toenails. Next to her, Paddington dozed in the warm rays.

Harriet gently wiped the cleanser off Maggie's face and applied a massage oil. She had been pleased that the weather had turned so warm. Libby was right. It wasn't exactly a grand opening, but that had been Harriet's plan. She wanted to ease herself in gently. Try out the new products from Eleanor's Apothecary on her friends before any real customers arrived.

She was delighted with the look of all the products lined up on a nearby shelf. The bottles were not only made from recycled materials, but they looked crisp and professional with the smart labels.

The products themselves were also of a high quality, to her relief. Everything had a touch of lavender as one of its ingredients. It wasn't overpowering but gave the whole place a delicious and relaxing aroma.

To Harriet's surprise, the diary for the spa was already beginning to get filled up with local people who had heard about it from the small advertisement she had placed on *The Cranbridge Times* website. Perhaps Joe was right, she thought. Perhaps there was a demand in the area for a decent beauty therapist.

'I heard that Mr Baggins' cottage is going up for sale,' murmured Maggie as Harriet worked on her forehead with her fingers.

Harriet was pleased that she had managed to persuade Maggie to come along. She deserved a treat and once she had finally relaxed on the bed seemed to be thoroughly enjoying herself.

'No,' said Libby, shaking her head as she turned around to face them all.

'It's true,' Flora told her vehemently. 'Grams saw the local estate agents yesterday.'

'I mean, no, that is not the correct kind of discussion for a girls-only spa,' stated Libby. 'We need to discuss hot dates and ever hotter men.'

There was a brief silence of astonishment, and even Maggie raised her eyebrows as she looked up at Harriet with a soft smile.

'Don't look at me,' muttered Flora. 'I don't know about either.'

'Yes, we must do something about that,' said Libby, looking as if she were thinking deeply.

'No, we mustn't,' replied Flora quickly. 'Besides, I've got a field of hay to cut this month. I haven't time for dates, hot or otherwise.'

Libby rolled her eyes in reply.

'Anyway, it's not my fault all the young men left the village,' carried on Flora. 'Ryan and Ethan both left years ago.'

'Who?' asked Maggie as Harriet gently wiped the oil from her face.

'Bob and Rachel's sons,' Flora told her. 'Ryan's the eldest. A few years older than us. He's a really nice guy, but more like the big brotherly type, you know? And Ethan is—'

'The devil,' completed Libby with a scowl.

Maggie laughed. 'He's that bad, huh?' she asked.

Harriet shook her head. 'No, he's not,' she told Maggie. 'He's fun and lovely, but for some reason, he and Libby are always at each other's throats.'

Libby growled under her breath. 'He's a pain and not at all suitable for any of us,' she said shortly.

'So that just leaves Joe,' said Maggie with a wide smile as she sat up on the bed, her treatment finished.

'And he's already taken, I think,' added Flora.

All three women turned to look at Harriet with grins on their faces.

'Have you been on a date yet?' asked Maggie, looking delighted.

Harriet shook her head. 'What did you think of your facial?' she asked, swiftly changing the subject.

'It was wonderful,' replied Maggie. 'I feel so relaxed. It was an absolute treat, thank you. Normally, the closest I get to a facial is when I get a face full of steam from the dishwasher.'

'Everyone deserves a treat,' said Libby, wiggling her pink toenails. 'Great nails solve many problems, I find.'

'So, have you kissed yet?' asked Flora, seemingly not able to let the subject drop.

'I don't think I'm going to include that in the facial experience, actually,' said Harriet in a lofty tone, rearranging the bottles on the side and clearing away the used towel ready for washing.

'That's not what I meant, and you know it,' said Flora, shaking her head.

'And she means no, he hasn't kissed her,' added Libby. 'But why not? He's young and good-looking. He's got a bit of a sense of humour now he's not trying to tear the village apart. Most of all, he obviously fancies you, so go for it.'

Harriet rolled her eyes. 'He's just come back to Cranfield for the summer to give us a hand, that's all.'

'Is it?' asked Maggie softly.

Harriet hid her blushing face as she carried on tidying up. Were they right? Did he like her in that way? She couldn't deny that she was starting to have real feelings for him, and the thought of a summer romance with Joe Randall was seriously tempting. Her pulse raced whenever she saw him, and sometimes she had trouble forming a coherent sentence in his presence. Was it a crush? Something more? She didn't know. But perhaps she could take the time over the summer to find out.

Realising that her friends were suddenly quiet, she looked up to find Maggie, Libby and Flora watching her.

'Life is short,' said Maggie in a soft tone. 'So, you've got to take your chances when a shot at real happiness comes along.'

'What have you got to lose?' asked Flora.

'Just remember, we'll be ready to hear all the details,' said Libby with a wink. 'And don't worry. What happens in the spa stays in the spa!'

34

The preparation for the opening of the lavender fields to the public meant that Harriet was rushed off her feet for the next couple of weeks between the sporadic appointments at the beauty salon and arranging everything for the grand opening.

The lavender flowers now had tiny buds and were only a week or so away from blooming. The time was drawing closer.

But still, she fretted about whether there was any point in opening up the fields to visitors.

'What about the tourists?' she asked, looking around the peaceful fields late one morning.

'They'll come,' Joe told her, ever confident.

Harriet wasn't so sure, but she had to trust him. Which was strange in itself, given that she had tied herself to the large oak tree only a few months ago because she absolutely hadn't trusted him.

She blushed, thinking back to the conversation with her friends at the spa. Their gentle teasing had given her all sorts of daydreams about kissing Joe, but that was completely crazy, wasn't it?

How quickly her view of him had turned around, she thought, glancing over to where he was sitting at the old table they would use as an entrance for buying tickets. He was busy on his laptop, and she had been impressed with what he had achieved so far in terms of advertising to get the word out. He had created a website that gave directions and had even added a gallery using various photographs that she had found in Aunt May's old albums. He had also advertised their opening date the following Saturday on local pages on social media.

The only thing he kept badgering Harriet for was a decision on the ticket price.

'I'm no good at that kind of thing,' she told him.

'It needs to be enough to make a profit. I know that some of your neighbours are going to volunteer as helpers regarding car parking, but we need to cover expenses as well. That card machine is paid for monthly. Then, if the lavender spa takes off, you'll also need to offset the cost of materials as well.'

Harriet rubbed her forehead, somewhat bewildered at all the administration, which had never been her strongest skill. 'It's all just numbers,' she groaned. 'I don't understand. I never have done, to be honest.'

'Look,' he told her, turning his laptop around to show her a complicated spreadsheet. 'It's all quite easy.'

She leant forward until she realised she was so close that she could smell his woody aftershave. She then took a small step backwards as Joe rattled off a few more numbers until, finally, Harriet's mind was spinning.

'It's all gobbledygook to me,' she told him, laughing. 'Tell me about the website. Tell me sweet nothings. Anything but more numbers!'

Joe raised both his eyebrows in surprise as he stood up next to her. 'You want sweet nothings?' he asked, sounding amused as he looked down at her.

'I'd prefer them to talking about a budget, to be honest,' she muttered, somewhat embarrassed about what she had just said. But still overwhelmed by all the numbers, she just shrugged her shoulders. 'I'm useless with figures. I guess it's the dyslexia.'

The amusement on his face faded a little. 'I didn't know,' he said.

Harriet sighed. 'I'm not ashamed of it, but it certainly hasn't helped me with any kind of stellar career over the years.'

'Is that what you want?' he asked. 'A career? Because let me tell you, it's not all it's cracked up to be.'

She looked at him, surprised. 'I think all this fresh air has gone to your head because you don't sound like the Joe Randall I met all those months ago.'

He smiled. 'I don't feel like him either. But we were talking about you.'

'Oh.' She gave a sheepish grin. 'You picked up on that subtle conversation change, did you?'

He laughed. 'Oh yeah.' His face grew serious once more. 'Listen, I actually think you're very bright, but you've been led to believe that you're stupid when you're not. And I think it's that which has given you very little faith in your own abilities. That's such a shame because look at what you've achieved here.' He waved his arm around the field.

'I had help,' she reminded him.

'No, you brought everyone together, and that's incredible.' He looked down at her with such intensity that she suddenly couldn't breathe. 'Why can't you see what I can see?'

'Because I come from a family of high achievers,' she told him with a sigh. 'A couple of overbearing boyfriends later, and here I am.'

'They were obviously idiots,' he said, staring at her. 'Because I think you're amazing.'

She waited for the joke, but it never came. He was entirely serious. Blushing, she muttered, 'Thank you,' if only to brush off the compliment, as she always did.

To hide her blushing cheeks, she bent down to pick up the picnic hamper she had brought with them.

'Now, I may not know much about figures, but I can sure pack a decent picnic,' she told him.

'For all three of us, I hope,' said Joe in a pointed tone. He looked at Paddington as he settled down next to them. 'Because you're not getting any of my lunch, sir.'

Paddington panted and smiled, comfortable in the knowledge that he had already watched Harriet pack him his favourite cheese and sausage snack earlier that day.

They all sat on the rug Harriet had brought and ate their lunch in companionable silence. It was the peace that always struck her about Cranfield. On a glorious sunny day, the only noise came from the birds and the breeze gently brushing over the plants. It was so still and quiet that you could hear the lavender plants rustling in the air.

'This is great,' said Joe suddenly. 'I can't remember the last picnic I had.' He paused as he looked at the sandwich he was holding. 'Actually, maybe I can. We used to go to the seaside in the summer holidays, and Mum would always pack a picnic lunch for the beach. Me and Charlotte would race up the sand, bolt down our sandwiches and crisps before racing back to the sea once more.'

Harriet watched as he sighed a sad smile in memory. Automatically, she reached out and squeezed his other hand. She knew all about grief and wanted him to know that he wasn't alone.

To her surprise, he turned his hand over and squeezed hers in thanks before letting go. Harriet was pleased that he was opening up to her. It felt as if she were getting to know the real Joe, not just the businessman.

After lunch, he thanked her for the picnic and helped Harriet get back to her feet. He seemed to hesitate before finally letting go of her hands.

'Time to get back to my exciting spreadsheet,' he told her, breaking into a wide grin that lit up his face.

She smiled back at him. 'Rather you than me,' she said. 'But I don't want you to think I don't appreciate all this help. I'm pretty certain I couldn't have gotten this far without you. In fact, I may even still be lying on the ground if it wasn't for you.'

He smiled in memory. 'I'm sure Paddington would have saved you.'

'I'm not so sure about that!' she joked before looking up at him as he stood in front of her. 'You know what?' she said. 'I'm starting to think you might just be a good guy.'

'Don't,' he replied, surprising her by shaking his head.

She laughed. 'Why not?'

He took another step forward until their bodies were almost touching and leant his head down towards her. 'Because the thoughts I'm having right now are not ones that good guys normally have,' he told her before dropping his head down quickly and brushing his lips against hers.

They kissed until Harriet began to lose all coherent thought, whereupon Joe lifted his head and lips away from hers.

'Sorry,' he said with a grin. 'As you said. Must be all this fresh air.'

Then he wandered away, leaving Harriet to touch her lips in wonder. Had that just happened? Her bruised lips told her that it had.

Her friends had been right. He definitely had feelings for her; that, at least, had just been proven. And she was left wishing that their first kiss wouldn't be the only one that they would ever share.

35

After only a month in Cranfield full-time, Joe felt as if he had been transformed. No, he thought, looking out across the lavender fields. It was more the feeling that he had been brought back to life. As if he had been living the past two years since his mother died in a kind of fog, and now it had lifted, and he could see all the colours once more. The blue of the sky. The purple of the lavender that had just burst into flower only a day before. And the deep red of Harriet's hair.

He must have caught a touch of sunstroke when he had kissed her on the lips two days ago because he hadn't thought of anything else since then.

He still couldn't quite believe that he had kissed her. Not that he hadn't kissed any women before, of course. But ever since his mother passed away, he had pretty much concentrated on work and had left dating to an absolute minimum.

Now that particular work had taken a back seat, he had a few ideas, but he needed to run them through with his dad. He just hoped they could come to some kind of agreement regarding the future of the business when he finally returned to work after the summer. Still, for the time being, he was enjoying being in blissful, however temporary, limbo.

Harriet had organised a midsummer party on the eve of the grand opening of the lavender fields to the public. Joe had invited his dad along in the hope that maybe they might have a moment to talk. He was also keen for his dad to see and talk to the locals, with a view to perhaps also changing his perception of their current business policy.

The party wasn't a grand affair. Nothing in Cranfield was. But he was beginning to realise that it didn't matter, that it was really about companionship, friends and family.

So, a hastily arranged gathering occurred at the last minute. There were a couple of tables that had been carried across the bridge, as well as some camping chairs. A great spread of food was laid out, much to the delight of Paddington, who was having a marvellous time going from person to person for a little taster. Soft music played in the background, but the main noise was conversation and laughter.

As the evening wore on, old jam jars were filled with flickering candles inside to bring about a fairy-like glow. Nobody was keen on leaving, it seemed, so everyone who had come stayed on as the warm sun set late into the evening. Laughter filled the air, and so did conversation. People were starting to come out of themselves and perhaps leave their loneliness behind too, including Joe. His dad was at the centre of the party, chatting to Grams about life in Cranfield.

'Such a shame about the railway line,' he was saying.

'Definitely,' replied Grams. 'Especially as the bus into Aldwych goes only twice a week. Not that I get much chance to do anything but work on the farm these days.'

His dad nodded thoughtfully. 'At least work fills a gap for us widowers, don't you find?'

Joe thought it ironic that his dad could talk about these things with Grams but not with his own son.

His dad carried on. 'But I should think a place like this leaves you quite isolated.'

'Oh no,' Grams told him. 'I have Flora, my granddaughter. Family is so important, wouldn't you agree? Anyway, Cranbridge is only a mile away, so I can walk there if I need a bit of excitement. They've got a corner shop and a pub and everything.'

'I'm staying with Joe for a couple of nights in a flat in Cranbridge,' said his dad. 'The food is tremendous at the Black Swan Inn.'

'That's because my great-nephew, Brad, is the head chef,' said Eddie, who had been standing nearby. His voice held a proud tone. 'The lad has built himself up from nothing.'

'Has he really?' replied Joe's dad. 'How proud you must be.'

He caught his son's eye and excused himself.

'I must say,' his dad began as they walked away from the group. 'When you said I was invited to a party, this wasn't quite what I had in mind.'

'I know,' said Joe, starting to make his excuses. 'It's just that I mentioned you were staying with me, and Grams, in particular, is very hard to say no to when she gets a bee in her bonnet.'

'I can imagine! But that's not what I meant,' said his dad quickly. 'I mean, it's nice. They seem like decent people. And you're spoken of in quite high terms, you know.'

'Now I know that's definitely not true,' replied Joe, laughing.

His dad frowned. 'What do you mean? They all seem friendly.'

'Yes, but when I arrived, I was the enemy.' Joe sighed and sat down on the wooden bench now placed under the oak tree. Remembering when Harriet tied herself to the tree, he smiled to himself.

His dad sat down next to him. 'Come on, lad. Tell me what's going on.'

Joe hesitated. 'It's just that we don't build anything,' he began. 'We seem to destroy it and move on, leaving who knows what behind for the local people to deal with. I know it's the nature of the business, but it doesn't sit comfortably with me any more.'

His dad looked out across the field in deep thought. 'I see,' he said, finally.

'I'm grateful for the family business and all that it's taught me,' Joe said quickly. 'It's just—'

'I understand.' To Joe's surprise, his dad smiled as he turned to look at him. 'It's not entirely breaking news, to be honest.' He looked at the fields around them. 'I mean, how can two lavender fields take up so much of your time?'

Joe shuffled in his seat. 'Well, they needed some business advice.'

'They did?' asked his dad. 'Or did a certain redheaded beauty need more personal attention, perhaps?'

Joe was surprised by how perceptive his dad could be.

'I can see how distracting she could be,' his dad told him. 'Pretty, kind, funny and apparently very hard-working, according to the other villagers. She reminds me a bit of your mother.'

'She does?' Joe was amazed by this sudden insight.

'That same zest for life.' His dad sighed. 'When I lost her, that excitement for everything went with her. I know that you were burdened with much of the pressure of the business, for which I'm grateful, son.' He lay a hand on Joe's shoulder and gave it a squeeze. 'Thank you.'

'You don't have to thank me,' said Joe, his throat feeling a bit thick with emotion. 'I'm your son, and I would have done anything to keep the business afloat.'

'And you did.' His dad nodded. 'But perhaps it's time for me to move on as well after the summer.'

'What do you mean?' asked Joe, worried. 'Where would you go?'

'Oh, not too far, never you fear,' said his dad, giving him a teary smile. 'But I thought perhaps my golf would give me a bit of structure, and heaven knows I certainly could do with some more practice! It would give me a bit of company as well, to be honest. Not all of us are lucky enough to live in a place like Cranfield.'

Joe nodded. 'I agree.'

'Nothing to stop you enjoying your time here for a while longer, though,' said his dad. 'And whilst you're here over the summer, perhaps you'll come up with a new business plan for us. I have faith in you, son.' He stood up and smiled down at Joe. 'Or perhaps Harriet could help you find a new purpose in life.'

His dad walked away before Joe had time to reply.

Joe remained sitting on the bench for a while longer, watching his dad before turning his gaze across the gathering to where Harriet was sitting on a picnic rug chatting with her friends.

Should he stay on beyond the summer? Did he miss the endless hotels? No. Not even the job, if he was honest. He had an expensive flat in London, but it was pretty soulless, really just a bed to sleep on. It wasn't a home, messy and warm, filled with home cooking. And Harriet. She would make a home. Look at what she'd done with Lavender Cottage already.

He wanted to be a part of Cranfield, to make a difference in people's lives, this time for the better. But, most of all, he wanted to see Harriet each and every day, if not every hour. He could feel himself falling for her and, to his surprise, found that he had absolutely no need to run away from his feelings any more. If anything, he wanted to run towards them and her.

He got up from the bench smiling, hoping to have the opportunity sometime in the near future to share the strength of his feelings. And perhaps another one of those delicious kisses as well.

36

The sun slowly began to sink on the midsummer celebrations in the lavender field.

Harriet was so pleased with how well the evening had gone. Nearly everyone in the village had come, and all the villagers were getting very excited about the opening of the lavender fields to the public.

Harriet was equally excited but was also a bag of nerves. What if nobody turned up? What if they weren't that impressed?

Although that second point was pretty ropey, she had to concede because in the soft glow of the setting sun, the rows of lavender looked stunning. They were just bursting into their full colour, and any second now, that blaze of purple would appear all across the fields.

She had been pleased to meet Joe's dad, who seemed very nice. Grams had taken him under her wing and was ferrying him around a never-ending queue of villagers, who were all dedicated to showing him just how magical Cranfield could be on a summer's evening.

Libby had brought her Bluetooth speakers, and there was soft music coming from them, adding to the fairytale-like quality of the evening.

Harriet couldn't help but smile as she saw Joe walking back from the bench under the oak tree, having had a quiet conversation with his dad. Perhaps there might even be time to follow up on that kiss they had enjoyed, albeit all too briefly, a few days ago.

She couldn't stop herself from heading over to greet him.

'Hey,' he said as she grew closer to him.

'Hey yourself,' she replied. 'Are you having a good time?'

'Actually, yes, I am,' he said, sounding surprised before laughing. 'I was just having a chat with dad over there.'

'I saw. He seems to be enjoying the party,' she said.

Joe nodded. 'He is. It's good to see him out and about, to be honest.'

Harriet couldn't help but smile at the irony. 'Maybe he thinks the same thing about you,' she told him.

Joe raised his eyebrows before slowly nodding. 'You may be right about that,' he replied. 'I don't think I've stopped and taken some time for myself for ages.'

'Since you lost your mum,' said Harriet softly.

Joe nodded. 'I had to pick up the business and see it through for Dad. But I can see now that it was for me as well. A way of burying our grief. Or at least trying to. But now...' His voice trailed off as he frowned, trying to find the right words. 'I'm changing, I think.'

'Is that a bad thing?' asked Harriet.

He smiled. 'I don't think that it is,' he replied.

'So, what happens next? Are you heading back to the city soon?' The thought of him leaving filled her with dismay, although she kept her tone light.

He turned to look at her. 'I thought I'd stay on for a while. See if that business plan I've worked out for the lavender fields does the right job.'

'Oh. Well, that's great.' She looked at him. 'I'm pretty nervous, to be honest. What if it fails?'

He reached out to take her hand and squeezed it. 'You're the strongest person I know. You've got this. We've got this.'

'We make a good team,' she found herself saying.

'Yes. We do.'

Something caught her eye in the sky, and she glanced up. 'Look,' she said, pointing. 'A pair of swifts. Summer is definitely here.'

He leaned in close to follow her hand to where she was pointing, and suddenly she could smell the woody aftershave on his skin. Slowly, she turned her head and their eyes locked, just inches from each other. The sun had almost set, dusting everything with a golden hue, including Joe in his tight T-shirt.

'So, the sunset is pretty magical,' she said, anything to fill the silence as he stared down at her.

He nodded. 'I'd like to enjoy many more with you this summer.'

She smiled. 'Well, if the last couple of years have taught us anything, it's that life is precious, so you should do whatever makes you happy.'

He raised an eyebrow, a smile playing at the corner of his lips.

'What?' she asked, puzzled.

'The only thing I can think of at this exact moment to make me really happy would be to kiss you again,' he told her, his eyes fixed on his lips. 'But if that makes you uncomfortable...'

She shook her head and smiled gently at him. 'Go for it,' she murmured. 'I mean, what have you got to lose?'

He leant forward, and finally, their lips met. It wasn't like the previous kiss. It wasn't a gentle brush on the lips. It was electricity, a spark that lit something deep inside her and made her move her arms around his shoulders to pull him in for an even deeper kiss.

She really had no idea how long it had been when he pulled away slightly.

'Happy now?' she couldn't help but ask.

His face lit up into a wicked grin. 'Absolutely,' he replied.

He took her by the hand and led her back around from the oak tree and towards the party. As they grew nearer, Harriet realised that Libby had changed the music to a more upbeat tempo and was dancing somewhat drunkenly with Flora to the music.

Harriet laughed and kicked off her flip-flops.

'Dance with me?' she said, turning to look at Joe with an expectant grin on her face.

But, to her surprise, he suddenly looked terribly serious and shook his head. 'Er, no. Thanks. I don't dance,' he told her in a stilted tone. 'And I should probably check on my dad. Excuse me.'

He swiftly dropped her hand and walked away, leaving Harriet stunned. Where was the warmth that he had just shown her? That incredible kiss? It was as if something had switched inside him.

'Come on!' urged Libby.

Harriet joined her friends and danced as if she hadn't a care in the world. But all the time, she wondered what on earth had happened to make him shut down like that. And whether she had read more into their relationship from the kiss than he had.

37

The day of the grand opening of the lavender fields to the public dawned overcast and grey.

Harriet tried to remain optimistic but was filled with dread and doom until the clouds suddenly cleared and the sun began to shine.

'Told you so,' said Libby, giving her a nudge with her elbow.

'Yes, yes,' replied Harriet, rolling her eyes. 'You are the weather guru. All-seeing and all-powerful.'

'You'd better believe it, babe.'

They were helping Joe put up a gazebo next to the main entrance, which would act as a kiosk for the visitors. *If any came*, thought Harriet.

'Is it to keep the rain off or the sun?' asked Joe as he raised the final corner.

'Sun, hopefully,' said Harriet, giving another nervous glance up to the heavens, but there was now far more blue sky than grey overhead.

'Here's hoping,' said Joe, tying the gazebo into place on its stand.

He certainly seemed to be okay, thought Harriet. His mood had abruptly changed so quickly the previous evening, and yet she didn't know why. All she knew was that one minute they were passionately kissing, and the next, she had asked him to dance, causing him to move away swiftly. She desperately wanted to ask him what had happened.

But there wasn't time to worry about that now, she decided, securing a piece of tarpaulin to the stand. Hopefully, there wouldn't be time to dwell on anything if they were rushed off their feet with customers later. She hoped, mentally crossing all her fingers and toes.

Libby wandered off to answer her phone, leaving Harriet alone with Joe.

'Don't look so worried,' he told her. 'It'll be okay.'

She took a deep breath and could smell the sweet aroma of lavender in the air. It instantly calmed her down, so she smiled and nodded at Joe in reply.

Inwardly, though, she knew her nerves wouldn't settle until they had their first visitor. Surely someone wanted to visit a place as gorgeous as this?

Then, with everything ready and in place, they waited.

Harriet had remembered to put on some suntan lotion, so she sat out in the sun for a while on one of the camping fold-up chairs they had brought with them, joined by Joe.

Now that the clouds had cleared, the sky was a brilliant blue. There was a carpet of bright purple lavender stretched out as far as the horizon, only interspersed here and there with touches of green and the large oak tree outlined up the small hill.

Harriet was just wondering whether, despite the beauty of the place, she had completely and utterly failed in her notion of opening it to the public when she heard the noise of a car engine.

She looked across the field and squinted in the sunshine. Was it someone from the village? She couldn't make it out at first as the car parked up along the no-through road alongside the field.

Then she saw a family clamber out and head over to the summer house.

It was their very first customers, and she couldn't stop herself from beaming at them in relief as she leapt up from her chair.

'Hello and welcome to Cranfield Lavender Fields!' she said.

'I read about it on the local newspaper website,' replied the woman, looking over her shoulder at the field beyond. 'We had no idea this was even here! It's absolutely beautiful!'

'Thank you. We're very pleased to have you here,' said Harriet as they paid their entrance fee.

As the family walked into the lavender field, taking photographs on their phones, Harriet stole a glance at Joe, who was also beaming.

'Told you so,' he said with a wink.

She grinned in response and nodded gratefully. She did, however, give a nervous glance at the nearly empty road and wondered how many more customers would actually come.

The entrance was set up right next to the oak tree, and she reached out to run her hands across her aunt and uncle's initials for good luck, sending up a silent prayer that more customers would come and that the road would look much busier in time.

But after a couple of hours, Harriet was wondering whether her prayers had been answered all too eagerly instead because suddenly there were far too many customers to cope with. The lane alongside the entrance to the lavender fields had become as busy as the M25 on a Monday morning. There were cars beeping their horns and frustrated drivers squaring up to each other over parking spaces.

Meanwhile, those people that could get parked were growing impatient with the long queues to get in as Joe tried to explain that the credit card machine wasn't working due to the intermittent signal and that they could only take cash payments. Children were becoming bored and hot in the heat of the sunny day, and parents were asking for refreshments, which Harriet hadn't even considered providing. The unhappy children became upset, and there were quite a few tears. By the end of the day, Harriet knew how they felt.

The photographer from *The Cranbridge Times* had turned up to document the grand opening. Harriet felt sick to her stomach in case he decided to concentrate on the car parking nightmare and the lack of facilities.

Just after the last customer had left before 5 p.m., Harriet slumped into the chair alongside Joe. She didn't care that she was hot and dusty. All she cared about was that it had been an unmitigated disaster.

'What a mess,' she said, realising that that was even more truth in that statement as she tried to run her hand through her tangled hair.

'Well, it could have been worse,' Joe told her, but he too looked unhappy and grim-faced.

'How could it have been any worse?' said Harriet with a sigh.

'You might never have opened up the fields in the first place,' replied Joe, leaning forward to peer into the cash box. 'We've made some money.'

'But we could have made a lot more if not for the fact that people left because they couldn't pay with their cards. The reviews are going to be awful!' cried Harriet.

'Let's go and get a drink,' said Joe, standing up. 'There's no point worrying about today. Let's concentrate on tomorrow instead.'

Harriet nodded, but as she walked over to the railway bridge with Joe, she was left wondering whether the lavender fields would be closed for business after being open for just one day.

38

After the somewhat unhappy grand opening day of the lavender fields, Libby and Flora had persuaded Harriet and Joe to join them in the back garden of Lavender Cottage. Harriet assumed it would be less of a celebration and more a case of drowning their sorrows.

Libby poured everyone a drink of cold white wine as they sat on the patio, watching the evening sun begin to sink towards the horizon.

'Thanks. I can't deny I didn't need this,' said Joe, taking a grateful sip. 'What a day.'

Harriet merely took a large gulp of the chilled wine before leaning back against the bench she was sitting on.

What a day indeed, she thought. Their grand plans to open up the lavender fields to the public had been an unmitigated disaster.

'It's all my fault,' she muttered.

Joe turned his head to look at her. 'Of course it wasn't,' he told her. 'This is all on me.'

'How?' asked Harriet. 'It was my responsibility to open up the fields to try to save them.'

'And it was my idea that I just didn't think through properly,' said Joe. 'I should have foreseen all the problems. I do it all the time in my own line of work. I was just distracted by...' He didn't finish the sentence, leaving Harriet wondering what on earth had distracted him.

'Anyway,' she said, taking another large gulp of wine. 'I should never have started with all of this.'

'What are you talking about?' asked Joe, frowning.

'Yes, what are you talking about?' said Libby, rolling her eyes. 'Of course you needed to try to save the lavender fields. Why on earth wouldn't you?'

'But the problem was that I didn't plan properly,' groaned Harriet. 'I'm useless at business stuff. I mean, look at the failures on my CV if you want proof.'

'Rubbish,' scoffed Joe. 'Who could have realised what would have happened today? I mean, we were too popular from day one! Who could have predicted that?'

'Exactly,' said Flora, nodding vehemently. 'So, let's list all the problems and work our way through them to a solution.'

Joe smiled at her. 'That sounds like a plan.'

'A business plan,' remarked Libby, laughing. 'Okay, so what's the worst problem?'

'The parking,' said Harriet and Joe at exactly the same time.

Libby and Flora looked at each other with raised eyebrows.

'Great minds,' muttered Joe.

'Not that great if we can't find anywhere for everyone to park,' replied Harriet with a heavy sigh. Although, she couldn't deny feeling a little pleased that they were on the same wavelength, despite their vast difference in business knowledge.

'The lane isn't big enough,' remarked Libby, shaking her head. 'That's the real problem.'

'But there isn't anywhere else in the village big enough for a proper car park,' said Harriet. 'It's either tiny lanes or fields.'

'You can park on my field if you like,' suggested Flora in a thoughtful tone. 'The one on the other side of the path. That's close enough, and it seems as if the whole crop has failed anyway.'

Harriet had seen the rolls of hay on the other fields all cut and ready for the autumn. However, that nearest field hadn't seemed to have grown much that spring.

Harriet gave Flora a sympathetic look. 'Maybe the whole crop hasn't failed,' she said, trying to remain positive for her friend.

'Grams and I checked it this morning. The grain won't yield any wheat whatsoever. It's just rotted away after being flooded out for so long over winter. The crop's barely above ankle height.'

'Is that true?' asked Joe, frowning.

'Yup,' said Flora, giving him a small smile before taking a large sip of her wine.

'I'm sorry to hear that,' said Joe, nodding thoughtfully. 'But maybe it might work.'

'Not a chance,' replied Flora with another short laugh.

'I meant about the car park instead?' said Joe, looking at her. 'We need somewhere for people to park, and you need an income from that field. If it's not going to yield any crop and be left fallow for the rest of the summer, then why don't you take a percentage of the entrance fee, and you can still have some income that way.'

'I don't know,' said Flora, looking at her friends. 'Would that work?'

'Absolutely,' said Libby. 'We can put up signs at the other end of the village instead. They can head down your lane to the farm and park on that first field. Then they only need to walk across the path to the lavender fields. That frees up the other lane and gives everyone far more space to park, so no more fisticuffs.'

'All we'll have to do is move the gazebo and the entrance to the other side of the lavender field next to the path,' said Harriet, finally catching up on the idea and becoming more excited and relieved at the same time.

'Excellent,' said Joe, looking delighted. 'And it's a heatwave, so nobody will get stuck in the mud.'

'I've always got my tractor if they do,' noted Flora, beaming. 'Not that there's any rain in the forecast for the weeks ahead.'

'Then let's go for it.' Joe looked at Harriet. 'What do you say, partner?'

She nodded.

Partner had a nice ring to it, she thought, as she sipped her wine. Business partner, but perhaps there was something more there as well?

'What other issues are there to sort out?' asked Libby.

'I'm going to get the credit card machine fixed tonight,' Joe told her. 'I think it's a Wi-Fi issue, so that should get rid of that problem in a day or two. I guess the only other problem was the lack of refreshments. It was so hot, and the children needed something.'

Harriet glanced across the back gardens of the other cottages on Railway Lane and smiled to herself. 'Actually, I have the perfect answer for that particular problem,' she told them, beaming.

And she hoped that her idea wouldn't just help the customers but her new friend as well.

39

By the following morning, the revised plan for the lavender fields was coming together, and Harriet was feeling far more hopeful.

Joe had spent the evening making sure that the road signs were now sending any visitors through the village and onto the lane that led to Flora's farm. In the meantime, Flora had opened up the gate and ensured that the field was ready to be used as a car park. Thankfully, the failed crop was only a few centimetres high, so parking on top of it wouldn't be a problem.

Joe and Harriet had moved the gazebo all the way across the field and placed it near the summer house and shed.

'We might even get some passing trade from over there as well,' said Joe, looking at the long path that led all the way to the village of Cranbridge.

On the opposite side, Harriet could see Flora pinning up some bunting along the edge of the wooden fence on the perimeter of the field so that it was in keeping with the theme.

It was a team effort, and she was so grateful for everyone's help and enthusiasm. Thanks to everyone's hard work, the lavender fields were set for any new visitors.

This just left the problem of the lack of refreshments, so just before opening time, she headed over to the railway cottages and knocked on one of her neighbour's front doors.

'Good morning!' she said to Maggie when she opened the door.

'Hello,' said Maggie, looking surprised. 'Are you all set for another busy day? It looked amazing from my upstairs window yesterday afternoon.'

'Actually, that's where you come in,' Harriet told her. 'If you have the time.'

Maggie's eyebrows shot up. 'I have nothing but time these days. What do you need?'

'Lemon drizzle cake,' said Harriet, with a smile.

It had been a light-bulb moment when she had been sitting with Joe and her friends the previous evening. Drinks could be bought at the cash and carry in Aldwych, and Libby had been dispatched earlier to deal with that, but Harriet felt that the lavender field needed something food-wise.

'And what better than your delicious cake,' said Harriet as she told Maggie her plans.

'Well, I don't know,' replied Maggie, looking unsure. 'I've never charged anyone for anything that I've baked. I just make it for friends and neighbours.'

'Well, you should have charged us,' Harriet told her, 'because your cakes are fantastic.'

'Really?' Maggie bit her lip.

Harriet decided that a bit of gamesmanship was needed to break the deadlock. 'Listen, we can always get something in for tomorrow, but if you have anything spare for today, that would really help us out,' she said. 'We're desperate. People were really moaning yesterday, and I'd hate for that to happen again today. We need this plan to work to keep the lavender fields.'

Maggie nodded. 'Of course,' she said. 'Of course,' she repeated, this time a little more vehemently. 'Give me an hour and I'll bring a few bakes over for you.'

'You're a superstar,' Harriet told her. 'I've set up a couple of spare tables by the summer house for the refreshments.'

'I'll be there,' said Maggie.

Harriet left with a smile on her face.

* * *

Once opening time had arrived, the day went far more smoothly than the previous one. The new car park worked a treat, and people were excited by the rural feeling of parking in a field. The till was busier than ever, and Joe had even worked out the problems with the credit card machine. As it happened, moving the front kiosk to the new location meant a better Wi-Fi connection, so payments worked properly that day.

The first visitors were smiling as they entered through the gates, and Harriet watched and listened.

'It's so beautiful,' said one lady as they walked past. 'Is it a new meadow?'

Harriet shook her head. 'Apparently, lavender was grown here in the 1960s by my grandfather, but the field remained dormant for a number of years until my uncle planted new lavender plants over a decade ago.'

'How wonderful,' said the lady, nodding her approval. 'It feels like it belongs here, if you know what I mean.'

'I do,' replied Harriet.

'I'm thirsty,' piped up her little boy.

'Actually, we have some drinks over by the summer house,' said Harriet, pointing them in the right direction. 'Thought we'd better have something to offer, with the weather being so warm, and there's some lovely homemade cakes as well.'

Maggie had already turned up bearing both a wide smile and piles of Tupperware boxes, all filled with her delicious cakes. Having made her delivery, she had announced that she was heading home to try out some more recipes.

'It's going to get even hotter in the coming weeks, they say,' remarked the man. 'A heatwave, apparently.'

'Gosh,' said Harriet. 'We'd better get some more drinks in.'

She was smiling as she walked over to where Joe was holding the fort at the entrance.

'What we really need is an ice cream van,' said Joe.

Harriet laughed. 'I'm not so sure that'll be so easy,' she told him. 'But Maggie's cakes certainly seem to be going down a storm.'

It was true. The homemade cupcakes and biscuits were being bought almost in the same quantities as the drinks, and Joe's credit card machine was in constant use.

More visitors arrived in the afternoon, and by the end of the day, they had had almost fifty paying customers through the front gates.

'Not a bad start,' said Joe. 'Hopefully, more will come tomorrow.'

Actually, Harriet was quite grateful for the gentle beginning, numbers wise. Although she knew that time was of the essence and they needed to max out their profits as quickly as possible to keep the field open, time was required for everyone to get their rhythm and make sure that they didn't run out of anything.

'I'd better cook some more biscuits tonight,' said Maggie later on. 'And maybe a few more cakes as well.'

'Will you have time?' asked Harriet, although she was delighted that Maggie wanted to be more involved after being so reluctant before

'Oh yes,' replied Maggie, beaming. 'Happy to stay busy.'

She wasn't the only helper smiling by the end of the day.

'Everyone loved parking in the field,' said Flora, laughing. 'And I loved bossing them about, telling them where to park!'

'And we've had a few people wander over to look at the train as well,' said Eddie, nodding his approval. 'A couple of gentlemen said they will come back and give us a hand with the couplings.'

'That's great,' said Harriet.

As the villagers chatted excitedly about what the day had achieved, Harriet was filled with hope. She had set out to save the lavender field in memory of Aunt May and Uncle Fred, but now she realised that everyone else needed it saving as well. Perhaps just as much as Harriet did.

40

The following day dawned sunny and bright once more. It seemed as if the prediction of a forthcoming heatwave was to be right.

The sunshine brought even more visitors to the lavender fields, and Maggie had to restock the cake stand twice over to accommodate all the requests. They had also borrowed another gazebo to keep both the refreshments and Maggie shaded in the warm sunshine.

Harriet made a mental note to discuss with Joe about ensuring that Maggie wasn't out of pocket for her baking materials and would hopefully make a small profit as well.

But hers wasn't the only business gaining the interest of the visitors. Harriet had many enquiries about the lavender spa and soon had a number of appointments booked into the diary for the following days. There were also customers who wanted their treatments on the day they were visiting, so Bob had been drafted in to help with all the visitors whilst Harriet was rushed off her feet.

'This is wonderful,' said one lady as Harriet gave her a shoulder massage in the lavender spa. 'It feels very luxurious. Almost like I'm on holiday.'

'The setting helps,' Harriet told her, glancing out through the organza curtains to the lavender beyond. The fields were a stunning shade of purple now, and with the sky turning a deep blue up above, nearly everyone walking up and down the rows were taking photographs in every direction.

Between appointments in the lavender spa, Harriet rushed backwards and forwards to make sure that everything was running smoothly. Tom, the editor from *The Cranbridge Times*, turned to take some photographs. Harriet was pleased that it was fairly busy with visitors and so looked as if it were a popular destination for tourists. Best of all was the smashing picture of a very happy-looking Paddington trotting down one of the rows of lavender.

'We'll get it up on the website,' said Tom. 'It's absolutely stunning, so should definitely bring in some more visitors.'

He was right. The heatwave continued, and with the heat came the crowds.

By the end of the first week, word had begun to spread. Each weekday brought more visitors, mainly mums and toddlers, as well as retirees, but there were some after-school arrivals too, so they kept the gates open until 5 p.m.

Harriet was thrilled with the positive reactions to the lavender fields and that so many people were getting so much enjoyment from them. However, she enjoyed the fields best first thing in the morning and last thing in the evening when there was nobody else around but her and Paddington. Out in the fields, with the bees buzzing around and the butterflies flitting among the flowers, it felt like her very own patch of purple heaven. It was like a soothing balm after the craziness each day.

Word had certainly spread about the beauty of the lavender, and everyone appeared to be taking photographs of themselves for social media, which, in turn, created more visitors.

Thankfully, the villagers didn't seem to mind.

'I think it's grand,' said Eddie, beaming. 'Brings a bit of life to the place.'

'About bloody time,' muttered Rachel. She seemed to be the only one not enthused or offering to help out. She was always too busy, she told them.

In contrast, Maggie was rushed off her feet with the cake and drinks stand and even had to drag in some help on the busier days from Eddie. She seemed happy to be out of the house, thought Harriet as a delighted Maggie told her all about her new flavour of lavender-decorated lemon and honey biscuits which had been going down a storm with the visitors.

The gates were manned by Joe and Harriet, plus Grams, Flora and Libby when they could spare the time. Plus, Paddington the dog was always a draw for any children and seemed to delight in the attention, as well as having his photograph taken now that he had a brand-new purple collar.

Of course, there was the small matter of what Harriet would do when the lavender fields faded and the visitors stopped coming in the autumn. Would the council then decide that it had all been for nothing? Whilst they were finally making a healthy profit and showing that it was a proper business, it was only a few short months of high income and then nothing at all. She wondered how on earth the business could continue into the winter months until the lavender bloomed the following summer, if they were given that much time by the council.

Hopefully, she would think of something, she told herself, trying to stay positive.

* * *

After another successful but long day, she caught up with Maggie as they headed over the railway bridge on their way home, Paddington racing along ahead of them.

The weather really was turning out to be fantastic that summer, she thought. The lavender would look pretty whatever the weather, but with the deep blue of the sunlit sky it looked truly sensational.

As they walked along the platform, Harriet saw that there were new posters stating that the lavender field was 'this way!' She smiled to herself. It must have been one of the villagers. She liked that the community had become closer these past few months. It pleased her that more people were coming out of their houses and beginning to mix with each other.

'I must buy some more lemons for the elderflower cordial,' said Maggie, deep in thought.

'And we must sort out some kind of compensation for all the ingredients and your hard work,' Harriet told her.

'Really?' asked Maggie, looking delighted.

'Of course!' said Harriet. 'We'll all take a profit from the sale too. Is that okay, or am I being far too cheeky?'

Maggie laughed, her attractive face lighting up. 'That sounds good. If you think they'll keep selling.'

'Of course they will,' said Harriet. 'Your cakes and biscuits are a huge hit! Let me talk numbers with Joe, and we'll arrange something, okay?'

'Are you sure that's what you really want to be talking to Joe about?' said Maggie softly, throwing her a knowing glance.

Harriet blushed. 'Yes, yes, I know. I'm an open book.'

'I think it's lovely,' remarked Maggie. 'He's such a nice man.'

'Yes, he really is,' said Harriet. 'But he's leaving at the end of the summer, so I'm not sure how much future there is in it for us both.'

She was trying not to think about it, or how each day she looked forward to the moments she got to spend with Joe.

'Why don't you ask him and find out?'

Harriet shook her head. 'I guess I'm too scared to know the answer in case it's not the one I want to hear.'

'I understand,' Maggie told her, reaching out to give Harriet's arm a squeeze.

The truth was that she was still a little upset about his reaction to her inviting him to dance on the eve of the grand opening. He was still chatty and charming each and every day, and yet she couldn't help but wonder what had caused him to be so short with her at the time. It had made her question everything about their relationship. After all, they had only shared a couple of kisses. The trouble was that she would dearly love to have many more with him.

Perhaps she needed to protect her heart no matter how strongly she felt for him. And it wasn't as if they had even had a date yet. He was still talking about finding a new project for the autumn, too. Harriet tried to make the best of it, but she knew she would be heartbroken when he left.

41

As July continued, the visitor numbers to the lavender fields grew and grew. Each and every day, Harriet watched as many people wandered up and down the rows of flowers, enjoying the lavender perfume that filled the air with its scent.

Equally busy was the lavender spa, which continued to be very popular with both advanced bookings and the impromptu ones by the day visitors.

She found that she felt confident in her abilities at last and could finally cope with a business and be happy. It had been a light-bulb moment. She knew her strengths and the previous failures didn't matter any more. The belief that she wasn't good enough was finally put behind her, and she could look forward to whatever the future held.

With the increasing amount of visitors, Maggie had upped the number of cakes and biscuits she was baking, so much so that Harriet had made sure that they were priced accordingly so that Maggie wasn't out of pocket. In fact, she was even making a small profit on each sale.

'And I know exactly what I'm going to do with the money,' said

Maggie, her eyes gleaming with excitement as she counted the profits at the end of Thursday. 'I'm going to treat myself to a Mason Cash mixing bowl. I've always wanted one.'

'Good for you,' said Harriet, pleased for her.

As the cans and plastic bottles weren't quite in keeping with the image of an environmentally friendly field, they gradually changed the drinks menu as well. Homemade lemonade and elderflower cordial were held in jugs and kept in cool bags until required. They had invested in some bamboo cups that could be washed and reused, so it was a win-win for the environment as well. They also had to invest in a couple of bins, two of which were recyclable, by the entrance.

Unfortunately, far less environmentally friendly was the ice cream van that Dodgy Del drove into the car park one afternoon.

'Lovely cold ice cream! This is what's needed, I reckon!' he declared from the open driver's window.

Harriet stared at it in horror. It was filthy, old and accompanied by a faint smell of smoke as it wheezed to a halt.

'Oi! Del!' called out Flora, marching across the car park towards him, looking aghast. 'What is that smelly old thing doing in my field?'

'It's not old,' replied Del. 'It's vintage!'

Flora rolled her eyes. 'It looks like a health hazard. Get it out of here.'

But when he turned the key in the engine, it failed to start.

'Del,' began Flora with a warning note in her voice.

'I'll get it fixed,' he told her.

But two days later, the dilapidated ice cream van was still sitting there, much to Harriet and Flora's despair.

Thankfully, Libby's brainwave had garnered a far more positive reaction and was more in keeping with Harriet's vision for the fields. She had been on visitor duty when there had been a lot of questions about the type of lavender grown as well as the wildlife that it attracted, so Harriet was hard at work on some posters that she was going to place around the field with information and facts.

'That's a great idea,' said Joe when he came to find her after the last of the visitors had left for the day.

He joined Harriet, who was sitting on the wooden bench under the shade of the old oak tree, drafting up various ideas for posters on her phone. Paddington was nearby, sprawled out in the shade, fast asleep, after a busy day having his photograph taken with many of the visitors.

'Biodiversity,' he murmured, leaning in to read over her shoulder. 'That's good. Maybe a few questions and answers for the children as well.'

'Great idea,' she replied.

She tried to remain calm but could feel her pulse racing at sitting so close to him. He still hadn't mentioned the kiss they had shared nor his reaction to her asking him for a dance, so neither had she, but it felt as if a wall had come up between them.

'Well, I'd better make sure everything's sorted,' she said, feeling awkward and going to get up.

But he gently put a hand on her knee. 'Stay,' he said softly. 'It's all done. Everyone's closed up properly.'

Harriet smiled and tried to relax back against the bench. Now it was just them and the lavender to enjoy. As it was so quiet, she could hear the gentle buzzing of the bees as they flitted from flower to flower in search of pollen. A breeze drifted across the plants, rustling the leaves, but it was welcome as the air was becoming so warm.

But there was no denying that there was still a slight atmosphere between them, and Harriet felt uncomfortable.

'Listen,' she suddenly heard him say and turned her head to

look at him, 'I need to apologise for what happened at the party. I'd like to explain it to you.'

Harriet went to reply, but suddenly her stomach rumbled extremely loudly, making her feel embarrassed.

But Joe just laughed. 'How about we get some food first?' he said.

'I should have brought a picnic,' she told him as her stomach continued to squeal in protest at the lack of food. She had only had a piece of cake for lunch as it had been so busy.

'Then why don't we?' he replied. 'We could have some cold food out here together.'

She turned to look at Joe. 'Really?'

He nodded.

'I've got some French bread, cheese, cold quiche and salad,' she said, feeling pleased.

'Then I'll bring the wine and glasses. See you in half an hour.'

* * *

Harriet had thought about putting on some more make-up but in the end figured it would look too obvious. Joe had seen her in all sorts of trouble, so there was no point putting on an act now, and she didn't want to. She didn't want to pretend. Not when her feelings were becoming so much stronger day by day.

They sat on the rug that Joe had placed in the shade of the oak tree and enjoyed the early-evening sunshine. It was just them, the birds singing and the bees buzzing.

It was magical, she thought.

'So, about that night,' he began when they had finished eating.

Harriet shook her head. 'It's such a nice evening,' she remarked. 'Let's not spoil it.'

The truth was, she didn't want to hear his excuse as to why he had rejected her.

'Hopefully, it won't,' he carried on. 'But I'd like to explain.'

Harriet took a deep breath and nodded somewhat nervously.

'You see, I don't dance,' he told her.

Harriet was stunned. 'At all? Never?' she asked, her mind racing.

'I have my reasons,' he replied. 'But, as you said, it's such a nice evening, so we'll talk about them at some other time.' He leaned forward to pour them both another glass of chilled white wine. 'I haven't thought about work once this week.'

Harriet caught the swift change of subject and so let the thought that Joe never danced slip for the time being.

'That's good,' she said before hesitating. 'Isn't it?'

'I think so,' he told her before taking a sip of wine. 'It was all I ever thought about, the next project, the next big deal. Now I want to talk to people. Find out what's going on with them. Not just on a surface level.'

'You sound like me,' she said.

Joe laughed. 'Unfortunately, you've definitely rubbed off on me,' he replied.

'Sorry,' she told him with a sheepish grin.

He put down his wine glass and reached out to tuck a long lock of red hair behind her ear, but he left his hand on her hair afterwards.

'Don't be,' he said, suddenly all serious as he stared into her eyes. 'I feel like a whole new person, a better one. And it's because of you.'

'You were always a good person,' she told him. 'You just got a bit lost with having to take over the business. You didn't know what you really wanted.'

'And now I do.' The look of desire on his face made her stomach leap. 'I know I shouldn't have kissed you,' he said, his hand moving to stroke her cheek. 'I felt as if I took advantage of you.'

Harriet smiled as she leaned forward so that their lips were almost touching. 'Then let me take advantage of you instead,' she told him, finally closing the gap between them to kiss him.

As his arms drew around her and the kiss became more passionate and deep, Harriet thought that she never wanted the summer or the kiss to end. It wasn't the romantic setting, although that was pretty special. It wasn't the spectacular sunsets or the endless sky. Nor even the hum of the bees still busy and the flutter of butterfly wings. It was Joe. She was falling in love with him.

She had just drawn away from him to look up at him with starry eyes when she saw Paddington suddenly stand up next to them.

Joe's expression rapidly changed as he looked around, and suddenly he was frowning. Was the kiss not as good for him? she wondered.

But as Paddington started to bark, Harriet began to worry as she too realised what he had sensed. It was the smell of smoke.

She looked around in a panic and saw flames on the opposite field. One of Flora's fields was on fire.

42

At the sight of the fire in Flora's field, Joe jumped up, the romance of the picnic and kissing Harriet in his arms all but forgotten.

'It's that bloomin' ice cream van!' he shouted, bringing out his phone as he ran towards the fire. He dialled 999 and asked for the fire brigade.

Whilst he went through the details, he could hear Harriet on the phone as well.

'They're on their way,' he said once he'd finished the call, but now that they were closer to the fire, he was totally overwhelmed by the sight in front of them.

The ice cream van was fully alight, but even worse, the sparks from the fire had leapt onto the straw-like grass nearby. Suddenly, there were flames all around in the field that Flora had been using as a car park.

Joe ran towards the fire, very aware of the hard ground underneath his feet. It had been weeks since there had been any rainfall and the soil was tinder dry. It would have only taken one spark for the fire to start. He was just hoping that it didn't jump across the path and spread to the lavender field as well.

'I've rung Flora and Bob,' said Harriet as she stood next to him, biting her lip and trying not to cry. 'They're going to call Del. But by the time he gets here...' Her voice ran off as she looked at Joe with horror on her face.

He gave her a quick hug. 'We'll do what we can,' he said.

But what could be done? He glanced around him, scratching his head. There was no water or anything nearby that could be used to put the fire out.

Harriet had suddenly spun around with a frantic look before shouting, 'Paddington! Stay there! Sit! Good boy!'

They both watched as the golden retriever automatically sat on the ground on the other side of the path, next to the summer house, out of harm's way for the time being.

At the sound of a battered 4x4 arriving, Joe looked up to see Flora and Grams racing across the next field in Flora's pickup. The van lurched to an abrupt halt, and Flora leapt out, looking around her in despair, but underneath there was also fierce determination.

'Bloody Del!' she shouted.

'We've got sand for the grass fire,' said Grams, getting out of the car. 'Let's try to contain it until the fire engine gets here.'

Joe lifted out the sandbags that had been flung into the back of the vehicle in extreme haste.

'They were used for the flooding,' explained Flora as she tore one open with a knife. 'Never thought I'd need them for a drought, to be honest.'

She poured the contents on a small circle of flames, which was immediately extinguished. Joe copied her and did the same on the next row of flames, but the fire was catching hold quite quickly and had already spread to the far side of the field nearest to the path.

'There's too much of it,' said Grams, sounding terrified. 'The whole farm could go up.'

At that moment, Joe watched in horror as a spark jumped across the path, and suddenly the summer house was on fire as well. Paddington leapt up and went off in the opposite direction, safely out of range of the fire.

'Oh no!' cried Harriet, jumping forward as if to run into the fire.

But Joe took her hand and held her back, shaking his head. 'It's too dangerous,' he told her. 'You'll get hurt.'

He could understand her despair. The lavender spa was now in flames, and it would only take one stray spark for it to set light to the nearby row of lavender.

Just then, Joe heard someone shouting across the railway line from the station. It was Bob, who was standing next to Eddie, both waving their arms around to get their attention.

'What's he saying?' said Joe, straining to hear.

'Something about water,' said Harriet, sounding equally confused.

They watched as the two men began to move the large pipe stack that was next to the train workshop. It was then that Joe understood.

'It's the water pipe that they use to fill up the train engine,' he said, remembering when Bob had shown him around the old train and how it worked. 'We can use it to help put out the fire if it'll reach across from the track.'

He rushed over just as the pipe swung around in the opposite direction to where it normally faced. He knew from Bob's tour that the tank held a lot of water for the engine to be filled up. He just hoped it was enough to extinguish the flames in the field and the lavender spa as well.

Flora had already jumped into her van and had followed Joe across the field, so when the pipe began to get nearer, Joe was able to clamber onto the roof of the van and pull it the remaining way so that the opening was over the edge of the field.

'It's on!' shouted Bob from the other side of the fence.

Joe hopped off the van, and Flora quickly moved it out of the way just as the water began to gush out of the pipe.

The pressure caused a small wave to rush across the parched field, quickly extinguishing many of the flames on the grass. The remaining ones were put out using the sand. They then rushed across the path and used a line of sand around the lavender spa, which was still alight, to stop it spreading to Uncle Fred's shed and the lavender.

'I think it's contained,' said Joe, watching nervously and glancing around the lavender plants. *For the moment*, he added to himself, not wanting to upset Harriet further.

That just left the ice cream van, which was now fully on fire and in danger of sparking more flames onto the field.

'What about getting a hose pipe and using the water on it?' asked Harriet.

'You can't!' replied Grams, looking anguished. 'It's too dangerous to use water on a vehicle fire. You need the proper type of fire extinguisher.'

At that point, Joe realised what Bob and Eddie were carrying between them as they rushed across the pedestrian bridge. He ran over to take one of the red fire extinguisher canisters from Eddie and quickly ran back to the ice cream van, pulling the release on the safety valve as he went. Then he pointed the extinguisher hose at the van's engine and pulled the trigger, sending up a small prayer as he did so.

The extinguisher made a difference, but not quite enough, even when Bob joined in with his own extinguisher. The fire had taken complete hold of the vehicle.

Thankfully, the sound of a siren nearby made Joe give a sigh of relief. Professional help was on its way. The fire engine roared up next to the farmhouse, and the firefighters quickly assessed the situation and swung into action.

The fire on the ice cream van was swiftly brought to a stop, as well as the summer house. Any remaining small pockets of flames around the field were also doused, and sand was used to ensure that the heat from the fire didn't spread over the coming hours and cause any breakout flames.

Soon, the danger was past, and everyone breathed a sigh of relief as the flames slowly ebbed away.

Nearby, Flora was suddenly taken over with shock, and Joe watched in dismay as she burst into tears. Harriet and Grams held her close, the three of them in a huddle.

'It's okay,' he could hear Grams murmur, 'the danger's past now. We're okay.'

Harriet looked over Flora's shoulder at Joe, and he nodded at her. Yes, the danger of the fire had passed. The lavender fields were safe, and so was Flora's farm, but the lavender spa had been lost.

He slumped against Flora's car, knowing just how close it had come to wiping out everything that he held so dear. In that moment, he knew that he would fight tooth and nail to prevent the council from taking over the lavender fields. They meant so much to him now. Almost as much as Harriet herself did, he realised.

43

Harriet was tearily relieved that the danger of the fire had passed. Although now she could see just how upset Flora truly was.

'I thought the whole place was going to go up in smoke,' she sobbed into Harriet's shoulder before pulling back with a sniff. 'We can't lose it. Not the farm. Not after everything else.'

'I know,' Harriet told her, pulling her in for another hug.

Harriet herself was trying not to cry and be strong for her friend, but as she looked across Flora's shoulder, all she could see was the smouldering remains of the lavender spa that she had spent the summer building into a successful business.

'We'll be just fine,' Grams told them both in a shaky voice. 'All that matters is that nobody got hurt.'

'What on earth happened?' said Libby, running across the field, still wearing her navy flight attendant uniform. 'I've just passed a fire engine in the lane.'

'The ice cream van set itself on fire,' Joe told her. 'And then it spread to the car park field and Harriet's lavender spa.'

Libby took in the burned remains of the lavender spa before

rolling her eyes in exasperation. 'Bloody Del!' she snapped. 'Where is he?'

'On his way, apparently,' said Harriet, stepping back from her group hug.

Libby came across and wrapped her arms around Flora and Grams in her place.

'Is everyone okay?' she asked. 'Nobody's hurt?'

Grams shook her head. 'Everyone's fine. Joe called the fire brigade straight away, thank goodness.'

Libby nodded and let go of her friends to head over to where Joe was still standing. He seemed to be a little stunned at the turn of events. Then he looked even more shocked as Libby swept him into one of her giant hugs.

'Thank you,' Harriet heard Libby say to him. 'Thank goodness you were here.'

He smiled and nodded in response as Libby stepped back.

Harriet found her feet moving towards him.

'You can't get rid of me that fast,' he said, attempting a smile. He searched Harriet's face with his eyes. 'Are you okay?'

She nodded, although the tears springing into her eyes betrayed her. Joe quickly drew her into a hug, and for a moment, she relished the strength coming from him. She stayed in his arms until she had her emotions under control.

Nearby, Bob and Eddie had sat down on the ground after their mad dash with the water pipe and the fire extinguishers.

'Bob and Eddie were the true heroes of the day,' Joe carried on, still holding Harriet close to him with his arms wrapped around her. 'As well as the firefighters, obviously.'

'Couldn't have the whole place going up,' said Eddie, still clutching his chest and breathing heavily. 'It's our home. Not the station, I mean. This land. All of it. Cranfield.'

'Quite right,' agreed Grams, still sounding a little shaky. 'But we owe you both a large drink.'

'I think we need it,' said Bob, still breathless.

'Me too,' said Grams with a wan smile.

Flora went up to Bob and Eddie and gave them both a kiss on the cheek.

'Thank you,' she told them.

'You're welcome, love,' said Bob, reaching up to give her a hug. 'I'm just so sorry that it happened.'

'It's not your fault,' Flora told him.

'Too bloody right, it's not,' snapped Libby, pointing in a completely different direction. 'It's his!'

They all turned to watch Dodgy Del walk over the railway bridge, frowning at the blackened grass and the smouldering remains of his ice cream van.

'Well, well,' he said, nodding thoughtfully as he arrived. 'This is a surprise, ain't it, Uncle Bob?'

'Not where you're concerned, Del, no it's not,' said Bob, rolling his eyes.

'People could have been hurt, you idiot,' added Eddie.

'Everyone's okay, aren't they?' asked Del, looking around in panic.

'We're all right,' Harriet told him.

'Apart from being apocalyptically angry with you,' added Flora, glaring at him.

'I don't know what happened,' said Del, looking at the charred remains of his van. 'That was a quality vehicle.'

'About fifty years ago, maybe,' remarked Joe, looking at him in disbelief. 'The firefighters reckoned that it was some kind of electrical fault that caused the circuit to short and set fire to itself.'

Del frowned. 'Can't think of any kind of fault, to be honest. I mean, the windows have been going up and down by themselves, and the windscreen wipers have a mind of their own as well, but other than that, it was in tip-top condition.'

Joe looked at the others with raised eyebrows. Harriet knew that trouble followed Del around with an alarming frequency.

Rachel suddenly appeared.

'Where have you been?' asked Bob, frowning at his wife. 'You've missed all the excitement.'

'Doesn't matter,' said Rachel, with a shrug.

Harriet felt that she looked a little shifty as she leant against the fence, although right now, that was the least of her worries.

'So, what happens now?' asked Harriet.

'The fire chief said to wait and get the vehicle towed away tomorrow,' Joe told her. 'And just to keep an eye out, especially if the hot weather continues.'

Everyone nodded thoughtfully.

'Be a shame to see the old girl go,' said Del, looking sadly across at what was left of his ice cream van.

'Some of us will be extremely glad to see the back of it,' snapped Grams.

'Yeah.' Del gave her a sheepish smile. 'Sorry about, you know, almost burning down your farm and all that.'

'Oh, Del,' sighed Flora in despair. 'I don't know whether to kiss you or kill you.'

Del's smile grew wider. 'A kiss sounds better,' he replied.

'You'll be lucky,' said Flora with a grim look.

Del's smile faded. 'Yeah, I know. I truly am sorry. But, hey, look on the bright side. Maybe we could have one of those new outside pizza ovens instead, eh?'

His laughter was quickly drowned out by Grams heading over to clout him around the ear with her hand.

44

The following day, and despite the faint touch of smoke still in the air, the popularity of the lavender field continued, as did the sunshine.

However, the charred remains of Harriet's lavender spa remained to remind everyone to be vigilant in the hot weather.

The fire appeared to have had a surprising effect on Dodgy Del, who had designated himself Chief Fire Officer and spent the day telling people, 'No cigarettes or rubbish to be left behind.'

In the end, Harriet had to send Del off to make some fire hazard posters as he was putting a few of the customers off their enjoyment of the scenery.

Harriet tried to stay positive, despite the unhappy task of clearing what remained of her lavender spa. At least her uncle's shed was untouched, she thought with a teary smile. As well as the lavender fields, for which she was eternally grateful.

As Harriet closed the gate on the end of yet another busy day full of visitors, she smiled to herself. It had worked. It was a success. The decision by the council still hovered over them, but for now, it was a start and a pretty good one at that, despite the fire.

She looked across the landscape. The colour of the flower heads remained strong. She could certainly understand why so many people spent most of their time taking photographs.

The school holidays had arrived, and she sensed that the fields would be busier than ever. She just hoped it would be enough to save them now that the lavender spa had had to close.

And then what? It was a question that worried her, but for now, she was trying to take each day as it came.

'At least the ice cream van has finally been towed away,' said Joe, coming over. 'Phew. It's hot today.'

Harriet nodded. 'I know. Poor old Paddington is struggling a bit in the heat, so I'm going to take him for a walk to cool off.'

She glanced over to where the dog had been lying down on the grass, seemingly asleep, before instantly waking up upon hearing that magic word of 'walk'.

'I think I'll join you if that's okay,' said Joe. 'But I'm not sure how much cooling off we'll find in this temperature. It's got to be at least thirty degrees.'

She looked at him and smiled. 'Then you've obviously never been to the far corner of this field.'

Joe gave her a puzzled look but stayed quiet as they began to walk along one of the long rows of lavender towards the back end of the field.

Harriet was thrilled to hear the buzz of the many bees as they went. Although less thrilled with the oppressive heat.

'Yuck,' she thought, trying to pull her T-shirt away from her sweaty body without Joe seeing, although he looked a bit pink in the face as well. However, Paddington was bouncing up the field, excited by what lay ahead.

At the end of the field was a small wood marking the boundary. However, there was an old gate, almost hidden by a large holly bush, which they were able to use.

'Where are we going?' asked Joe.

'You'll see,' Harriet told him.

They walked through the woods, relishing the cooler air in the shade of the trees. Then, finally, Harriet could see the glistening of water through the large trunks of the trees. They made their way to the riverbank, where she turned to look at Joe, who had a surprised expression on his face.

'It's a small tributary of the river Ley that runs through Cranbridge,' said Harriet. 'Isn't it lovely?'

'It's beautiful,' replied Joe with a smile.

He was right. The sun could be seen through the leafy branches of the trees all around as birdsong filled the air, butterflies fluttered along the riverbanks, and a kingfisher looking for minnows darted across the water.

A soft breeze cooled the temperature, but it wasn't enough for Paddington, who headed straight into the shallow clear water for a paddle.

It was so warm that Harriet was seriously tempted to follow him. She turned to say as much to Joe, but he was kicking off his trainers and wading into the water after the dog. He and Paddington then had a playful tussle, which resulted in Joe being absolutely showered from head to toe with water.

Harriet laughed at the sight of him dripping. It was a far cry from the man in the designer business suit that she had met all those weeks ago.

Joe turned to look at her. 'Are you coming in?' he asked.

She stared down at her denim shorts. 'Maybe.'

'Come on,' he urged. 'I thought you were a country girl! Anyway, you look really hot and bothered.'

'Perhaps I'll just put my feet in,' she told him.

She slipped off her flip-flops and tiptoed in. 'Aaaah,' she sighed as the cool water went over her feet. 'That's so nice.' But she was still only up to her ankles in the water.

'That's no good,' said Joe, striding towards her. 'You've got to go deeper than that if you want to cool off.'

Before she realised what was happening, he had swept her up into his arms. She was suddenly aware of lying against his wet chest, his face very close to hers.

'Joe!' she warned him. 'Don't you dare!'

He laughed and held her closer. Then she shrieked as he began to wade deeper into the water so that it was up to his knees.

He smiled at her, his face close to hers. 'You know that I'm not really going to dunk you in, don't you?' he said.

'How do I know I can trust you?' she asked.

'After all we've been through, do you still need to ask me?' he said, laughing.

But as he went to lower her down onto her feet, a very excited Paddington charged up to them and sprang up in excitement at Joe's legs. Suddenly losing his footing, Joe staggered backwards, and they both went into the water.

Harriet struggled up to a sitting position in the water, spluttering. She was completely soaked. She was going to pretend to be cross, but Joe began to laugh. The sound was so infectious that she couldn't help but join in.

Then a huge water fight broke out, with Paddington splashing about happily between the two of them.

Finally, they staggered out of the water and sank onto a sunny patch of grass to dry off, leaving Paddington to have a nose around the shallow edges near the riverbank.

After a few moments, Harriet went to sit up, but, to her surprise, Joe pulled her back down to lie next to him once more.

'Unless the field's on fire again, leave it for now,' he told her. 'Just relax for once.'

She smiled to herself, pleased to hear uptight Joe Randall telling her to relax!

It was nice to let go of her worries and just enjoy the sun, but where she had moved, their arms were now touching. She tried to inch hers away subtly but found every time she made a minute shuffle to the right, his followed suit.

In the end, he reached down and took her hand in his. Lifting it up, he held it in front of his face. 'Must be all the lavender,' he told her, giving her hand a kiss. 'I don't think I've ever been this relaxed.' He put it back down but kept it held within his.

Harriet watched as he closed his eyes, and he probably would have drifted off to sleep under the warm sun, but suddenly, Paddington wandered out of the water to stand next to them. Harriet knew what was coming before it even happened, but it was too late. He shook himself violently, the water flying out of his fur, and they were drenched once more.

Thankfully, they were too busy laughing to care, and he joined them for a sleepy doze in the late-afternoon sun.

At that moment, Harriet wished that the day would never end and that, somehow, all three of them could remain in Cranfield forever.

45

After the fire, Harriet had been more upset over the loss of the lavender spa than she had let on.

She knew it was a hard habit to break, but there was already so much for everyone to worry about, and she just didn't want to add to their burdens.

But the truth was that she had enjoyed interacting with local people, as well as the day visitors to the lavender fields. In fact, she had actually started to gather quite a few repeat customers, as well as requests for more and more treatments. In addition, Eleanor from the apothecary at Willow Tree Hall had been pleased with the extra sales, so it had been a win-win situation for them both. It felt as if she had failed again, even though Harriet knew it wasn't her fault.

In a way, it had been the most enjoyable job she had known. People had gone away feeling refreshed and armed with more creams, which had encouraged further sales. It had been a link to the lavender, which had added a more personal dimension to her business. Mostly, it had felt as if it were her own business for once, without the pressure from her parents. Something that she had been able to set up mostly on her own too.

However, without a place to carry out her treatments, she was stuck. She wondered about setting up under the shade of the oak tree, but that would ruin people's photographs and views, plus it was just too exposed.

'What about your cottage?' asked Libby, who had joined Harriet and Flora for a coffee one morning.

Harriet shook her head. 'It just doesn't feel right in there. I'd only have the front room and, I don't know, I'm not sure Aunty and Uncle would approve.'

Libby shook her head. 'They loved you and wanted you to be happy,' she told her.

'I know.' Harriet gave a heavy sigh. 'But there's nowhere else empty, apart from Uncle Fred's old shed, and only one person can stand in there at the same time.'

'Actually, that's not true,' said Flora, tapping her chin in thought. She had been silent until that moment.

Harriet looked at her friend. 'It really is,' she replied. 'Between Uncle Fred's workbench and the tools—'

'That's not what I was talking about,' said Flora. 'I mean, it's not the only place around here that's empty. What about the old post room at the station?'

Harriet and Libby exchanged a surprised look.

'It could work,' said Libby, nodding her head.

Harriet, however, was thinking hard. 'How long since it's been used?' she asked.

Flora gave a little shrug. 'Since the station closed down, I guess.'

Harriet grimaced. 'So, twenty years' worth of grime? What if it's not even habitable?'

'There's only one way to find out,' said Flora.

* * *

As it turned out, Flora's optimism paid off.

Later that day, Harriet went to see Bob to tentatively ask about renting the old post room.

Bob was delighted and, along with Rachel, quickly walked her down the platform to show her the room.

It was quite a large single-story building with high beams, giving it an airy feel. It had a small window at the front, but other than that, it was a great space, thought Harriet, somewhat amazed.

'It should be watertight,' said Bob, following her gaze to the vaulted ceiling. 'The station is sweet as a nut, building wise.'

Standing next to him, Rachel rolled her eyes. 'It's just a shame it's such a mess, like everywhere else in this place. No wonder I've given up trying to tidy up.'

'It's homely,' he countered with a soft smile.

But it wasn't returned. Rachel had already turned to look at Harriet. 'So, what kind of treatments are you talking about? The same as before?'

'I could actually have more choice of treatments in here,' said Harriet, beginning to get excited at the prospect of all the additional opportunities the post room would give the business. 'As it would be more private, I could do full body massages, leg waxing. Anything really.'

'Could you make me look twenty years younger,' joked Bob.

Rachel sighed. 'Don't think anyone's skills would be up to that,' she snapped. 'But I'll have a manicure when you're up and running in here.' She glanced at her nails. 'I feel like a treat. God knows I don't get any others around here.'

She stalked out, leaving Bob and Harriet to the uncomfortable silence.

'Sorry,' said Bob. 'You know what she's like these days.'

'It's fine,' said Harriet, reaching out to squeeze his arm. 'Look, we need to talk about how much you'll want for rent.'

'Oh, I don't want any money, love,' Bob told her.

Harriet was stunned. 'But I'm using the space,' she protested. 'Don't you think I should pay you something?'

Bob shook his head. 'It'll be great just to have it used. A bit of life in the old place, eh? Besides, I still owe your Uncle Fred a favour or two, and I reckon that'll be my debt paid.'

Harriet stepped forward to give him a hug. 'Thank you so much,' she told him, touched at his generosity.

'They'd be so proud of you,' said Bob, giving her a warm smile, but he frowned as he looked at the various boxes piled up everywhere. 'I'll make sure it's cleared out for you. Think it's mainly old stuff from the station, which I could put in our attic room.'

'I can do all the cleaning,' said Harriet quickly, excited to get started.

'Then let's get going,' he told her, smiling.

Harriet was amazed at the ease with which she had found a new location for the lavender spa, as well as being mightily relieved. The rent had been so extortionate in London, so to have none to worry about was a huge weight off her mind. Perhaps it might really work.

Of course, there was an awful lot of dust and cobwebs to clear, but it would do for the summer. Harriet felt as if hope had returned. She was just going to keep everything crossed that the customers did as well.

46

Joe was pleased to see Harriet looking so excited when she bounded up to him the following morning and dragged him over to view the old post room in the station.

'So, what do you think?' she asked, her green eyes gleaming. 'Isn't it great?'

'It is,' he replied, trying to concentrate on business and not her eyes. 'It's a great space.'

'I may need your business savvy to sort out all the financial gobbledygook, though,' said Harriet, laughing.

'Haven't you worked out the figures and profits yet?' he asked with a smile.

She shook her head. 'Nope. I'm too afraid to look, just in case it's not enough.'

'Let me deal with the accounts,' he replied. 'But let's have a breakdown of your costs first, based on the business you did in the first lavender spa.'

'I have a confession,' said Harriet, looking a little downcast. 'About my past.'

Joe was shocked. Was this going to be an old boyfriend who she was still in love with? He found that he was holding his breath.

'I have some debts from my previous business,' she said.

'Oh. Right.' Joe found himself immensely relieved that it was nothing personal. 'Well, let's have a look at all the accounts and see how we're doing.'

They spent the next hour poring over the costs of the creams, as well as the other items needed for the treatments. Harriet also showed him the paperwork of her business debt from her London beauty salon.

But Joe found it hard to concentrate when they were sitting so close. Her sweet perfume was making his senses reel. In addition, on that hot day, she had her hair swept up into a ponytail, and the sight of her pale, soft skin at the back of his neck was all too tempting for him to place his lips on.

He had to give himself a mental shake. He was, after all, a professional businessman, but Harriet had an effect on him like no one he had ever known. They'd shared three kisses so far, each as enjoyable as the last. The trouble was that he found himself wanting more with each passing day.

A bump against his legs brought him to his senses as Paddington came and sat on his feet under the table.

'You know,' said Joe, concentrating on the figures once more. 'If the appointments continue to be booked as often as they have been so far, there's no reason why you couldn't continue with them over the autumn and winter in here.'

'Really?' Harriet looked around the space once more. 'I hadn't thought that far into the future, to be honest.'

'This place is weatherproof, so it will absolutely carry you into autumn and beyond,' carried on Joe. 'I reckon that unless you book yourself a fancy holiday in the Caribbean, you could have those debts paid off by the end of winter.'

'I could?' Harriet sat back in her chair for a moment. 'So that means...' Her voice trailed off, and, to Joe's horror, he watched her reaction as she suddenly burst into tears.

'What's the matter?' he asked, aghast. He put his arm around her. 'Do you need a holiday that badly?'

But Harriet carried on crying until Paddington sat up under the table, banging his head as he did so. Then he placed his shaggy, furry head on her lap.

'It's okay,' she told him, wiping her face and giving the dog a stroke of his silky ear before looking at Joe. 'Neither of you need to worry about me.'

'Of course we're worried,' said Joe softly. 'We care about you, and you're crying. Now, tell me what's wrong.'

'Nothing.' To his surprise, Harriet laughed despite her tears.

'I'm not sure I understand.' Joe had a feeling that perhaps he had bumped his head on the table instead of the dog.

'It's just that I've been sorting out the cottage to sell because of the debts that needed repaying,' she told him, her voice still a little tremulous. 'And that was breaking my heart because it's the only place that's ever felt like home.'

Joe nodded but didn't want to interrupt her, so he merely squeezed her shoulders as he held her close.

'And now you're telling me that if I can keep the lavender spa business going, then there's a chance that I can pay off the debts so I can keep the cottage as well?' She smiled, her cheeks still shiny with tears. 'Which is exactly what Aunt May and Uncle Fred wanted for me all along. And what I wanted for me too. Cranfield is home for me.'

Finally, Joe understood. They were happy tears.

'I'll double-check my figures, but I'm pretty certain you can do this,' he told her.

Harriet gave a sigh of relief. 'I can't believe it,' she said. 'All these months of worry, and now I might just be able to stay here.' But a frown appeared on her forehead. 'Of course, I might own a cottage that overlooks a giant industrial warehouse if the council have their way.'

Joe shook his head. 'We're going to keep appealing any decisions and fight that every step of the way. Anyway, with the sheer amount of visitors we're now receiving on a daily basis, that's really helping to build our case.'

'Is it?' Harriet's face lit up.

'I think you should remain optimistic but realistic,' said Joe, trying not to shatter her dreams.

'Oh, real life is too scary,' said Harriet, laughing. 'I'm a dreamer, or haven't you figured that out already?'

Joe nodded. 'I've definitely worked that out, thanks.'

They shared soft laughter, and Joe liked how his pulse raced a little as he looked at her and she smiled back at him.

Harriet wiped the tears from her face. 'There's just one problem, though,' she told him.

'What's that?' he asked.

'I can't be in two places at once,' she replied. 'And if the lavender spa is going to be a success, then I'm going to need to make the best of it, but how do I manage the visitors over at the lavender fields when I'm here at the station?'

He was relieved. 'Oh, that's easy,' he told her. 'I can take over managing the fields.'

The surprise showed on her face.

'Well, I'm probably no good at manicures and pedicures,' he said, laughing.

She joined in with his laughter. 'No, I guess not.' Her smile faded a little. 'By the way, sorry to be all emotional on you like that earlier.'

'I don't mind,' Joe told her, gently withdrawing his arm from around her shoulders, despite the emptiness the action made him feel. He tried to concentrate on the business side of matters. 'I guess we might need some extra help, though, with the fields.'

'I'm sure Maggie would help if she were asked,' replied Harriet.

Harriet was right because when Joe asked Maggie the following morning, she was delighted and began work straight away at the entrance.

When there was a slight pause in between arriving visitors, Maggie looked at Joe. 'You've certainly changed since that first protest all those months ago,' she told him.

'I guess all this fresh air has gone to my head or something,' he replied with a smile.

'Or someone,' she added with a soft smile.

'Maybe that too,' he replied after a short pause.

'You know, both you and Harriet have been working so hard,' carried on Maggie. 'I see both of you out of my bedroom window some evenings when it's gone seven o'clock. I'm sure you could both do with a decent meal. There's a brand-new summer menu over at the Black Swan Inn.'

He laughed. 'You're a born matchmaker, if not a very subtle one, Maggie,' he told her.

She laughed. 'Sorry. That really was a bit obvious, wasn't it?'

'A bit. But perhaps it was a good idea,' he conceded.

'Harriet's lovely,' said Maggie. 'She's got such a kind heart. It would be good to see her take an evening off and enjoy herself.'

Her words played on his mind for the rest of the day.

So, as they closed up, he asked Harriet what plans she had for that evening.

'None,' she replied, sounding a little surprised.

'Good,' he told her. 'We're going out to eat.'

She looked confused. 'Like a business meal?' she asked.

'No. Like a date,' he replied. 'You're always telling me that I take life too seriously, so I thought I'd be spontaneous for a change.'

She gave him a soft smile. 'Careful,' she told him, 'you might get to like it.' She went to turn away before looking back at him. 'And dinner sounds lovely,' she added. 'Thank you.'

Joe smiled as he watched her walk away. It was strange, he thought, how quickly the heart could outweigh the mind and completely take over rational thought. He had been longing to take Harriet into his arms and kiss her again. He felt loose, a little wild, a little out of control. Free, at last. And he wasn't sure that he didn't like the feeling.

47

Early that evening, Harriet was still tearily overjoyed that she could stay in Lavender Cottage and not have to put it up for sale now that she had a plan to pay off her business debts. If the new lavender spa was successful, of course, it would mean a lot of hard work and a lot more luck, but there was hope for the first time in many months.

The icing on the cake had been when Joe had unexpectedly asked her to dinner.

'Why do you think that is?' said Flora, giving her a wink as she handed over the wedge heels that Harriet had asked to borrow.

'It's not like that,' said Harriet, sitting on the sofa and putting on the shoes.

'I thought he'd asked you out on a date?' asked Flora. 'And he's kissed you a couple of times. Isn't that a bit of a clue as to how he feels about you?'

'Because whatever happens with the lavender fields, he's leaving after the summer break,' replied Harriet.

'Perhaps you could try living in the moment,' suggested Flora. 'Just enjoy the summer romance.'

Harriet stood up. 'What do you think?' she asked.

'You look great,' Flora told her.

Harriet glanced down at the white cotton skirt, pretty T-shirt and wedge heels. Smart casual but still a little dressier than her normal shorts and trainers.

'And Paddington's staying with me this evening,' carried on Flora with a wink. 'Just in case you're a bit, er, late home.'

Harriet blushed but couldn't help but smile at her friend. 'Well, you never know,' she said with a soft laugh.

* * *

'I thought we might be going for a picnic,' she told Joe when she met him outside the Black Swan Inn later.

He shook his head, smiling. 'Last time we tried to have a picnic, the whole of Cranfield nearly went up in flames. I thought this would be safer.'

He led the way around the side of the inn and into the pub garden at the back. It was very pretty, thought Harriet. It was mainly laid to lawn with a white picket fence running along one side. On the other side of the fence, she could see the river through the gaps as the evening sun dappled on the crystal-clear water. The garden was also filled with many beautiful hanging baskets and pots of overflowing colourful flowers.

Joe gestured for her to sit down at a table for two that had a reserved sign. The chairs were generous and comfortable, with soft cushions and a matching umbrella that had fairy lights wound around the inside.

Along with the fairy lights entwined amongst the picket fence, as the sun began to sink into the sky, it gave the whole place a magical atmosphere.

And a romantic one as well, thought Harriet.

'It's certainly very popular,' she said, looking around. The garden was almost full, and the sound of lively conversation and laughter filled the warm evening air.

'It's great, isn't it?' he replied. 'I ordered us a bottle of white wine in advance, but if you'd prefer something else, I can get you that instead.'

Harriet shook her head. 'Sounds perfect,' she replied.

He picked up the bottle that had been chilling in an ice bucket on the table and poured her out a large glass.

'Cheers,' she said before taking a sip. 'That's lovely. And much needed. What a day!'

'How's the spa looking?' he asked.

'After much elbow grease and some last-minute deliveries of the replacement beauty products from Eleanor, I think we're all ready for the big reopening tomorrow,' she replied.

After a couple of long hard days, the new lavender spa was looking great. Thankfully, the insurance had taken care of the cost of replacing the equipment that had been lost in the fire, but it had still taken some late hours to get it all ready in time. 'And how were the visitor numbers today?' she asked.

'Good,' he told her before leaning back in his chair. 'But it's too nice an evening to talk about work.'

She nodded. 'I agree.'

They spent a lovely couple of hours chatting about anything and everything else.

For once, though, the discussion went a little deeper. Over the main course, Harriet found herself chatting about Aunt May and Uncle Fred quite a bit. How they had taken care of her and how her friendship with Flora and Libby had continued over the years.

In return, over dessert, Joe opened up for the first time about losing his mother. It had obviously been a tough time and had impacted his decision to take the summer off.

'And then what will you do?' asked Harriet.

'I'm not sure,' he told her. 'For once, I don't seem to have a plan for the future.'

'Sounds exciting,' she replied.

'And nerve-wracking too,' he said. 'I mean, I have some ideas about the direction I'd like to take my business in, but I'm not sure how my dad's going to feel about it.'

Harriet wanted to ask more, but they were interrupted by the arrival of a band on the makeshift stage at the end of the garden. She hadn't noticed it until then, but a couple of guys with acoustic guitars and a keyboard suddenly struck up a mellow tune. One of them was Pete, the owner of the Black Swan Inn.

It was now twilight, and the soft music and fairy lights added to the romance of the evening. Harriet found herself beaming at Joe, and he was smiling back at her. Conversation would be hard above the music, but she didn't mind. They didn't need to talk. His eyes told her everything and mirrored her own. There was tenderness there, flirtation too, as well as desire.

She found herself reaching across the table, and his hand automatically found hers.

She was temporarily distracted by a few people getting up to dance to the music as the tempo picked up a little.

Harriet never needed an excuse to dance and delightedly leapt up to join in. She knew that Joe had told her that he never danced but surely he hadn't meant it? She was certain that he would break his silly rule for her.

Feeling full of passion and confidence, she held out her hand to Joe. 'Shall we?' she asked.

His tender expression immediately faded, and in its place was almost something akin to a frown.

She began to feel foolish as she stood there with her hand held out. Quite a few people were watching them.

Quickly, she withdrew her hand, wishing she hadn't gotten up at all.

'Look,' began Joe.

But Harriet was too upset by his rejection, too humiliated by the thought of the audience that was still watching them both, to listen to what he had to say. So, feeling angry and embarrassed, she snatched up her handbag and quickly walked out of the garden without looking back.

48

Joe scrambled to gather his thoughts as he watched in disbelief as Harriet walked out of the garden at the Black Swan Inn. What on earth had just happened?

Of course, he knew. He should have made the effort before now to explain his personal reasons for not dancing any more, but he had never talked about it with anyone. Ever. But keeping those feelings locked deep inside might just have ruined the promise of the most important relationship he would ever have.

He stood up, wanting to dash after her and explain, but he needed to settle the bill for their meal first.

Finally, after what felt like ages waiting for the credit card machine, he raced out of the garden, across the river that ran down the middle of Cranbridge and headed towards the small church where the path to Cranfield began.

The sun had set a while ago, and there was only a light glow of dusk to guide him as he headed down the stony path in the semi-darkness. He was jogging now, desperate to catch up with Harriet. Finally, in the distance, he could just about make out her lone figure walking quite quickly down the path. By stepping up his pace to a full-out sprint, he was able to draw closer to her.

'Harriet! Wait!' he shouted.

Harriet came to an abrupt halt and turned around, a scowl on her face as he crashed to a halt in front of her.

He took a moment to catch his breath. 'Look,' he began, 'I know what you're thinking.'

'Do you?' she snapped. 'Because what I'm really thinking is that I wish I'd worn my flip-flops because then I could have walked an awful lot faster and got away from you!'

She spun around as if to start walking away once more, but Joe grabbed her arm and held her back.

'I need to explain,' he told her.

Harriet still had her back to him. 'No need,' he heard her say. 'I get it. You've been having fun with me all summer, flirting and kissing, but it meant nothing to you. You're just the cold-hearted businessman you were all those months ago. Nothing's changed.'

'Everything's changed!' he told her, stepping around to stand in front of her. 'This summer has meant more to me than anything has for the past fifteen years!' He let go of her arm, sighing heavily. 'I don't blame you for thinking the worst about me. I've stuffed up by keeping it back from you, but it's time to tell the truth.'

Harriet's reaction was to raise a cynical eyebrow at him, but she remained silent.

He dragged a hand through his hair, trying to find the words that he had struggled to say for so long. 'I need to tell you about Charlotte,' he finally said.

Harriet gave a start at the swift change of subject. 'Your sister?' she said, sounding stunned.

Joe nodded and took a deep breath. He hadn't admitted this to anyone, not even his mum and dad, but it was time. 'I can't dance,' he told her.

'So what?' Harriet still looked cross with him. 'A lot of people can't do certain things.'

'I don't mean it like that.' Joe reached out and took her hand in his. 'Charlotte loved to dance growing up. There was always music blaring away somewhere in the house, and she often dragged me up to practise with her. She wanted to be a ballroom dancer, you see. I could probably still do a mean foxtrot if...' his voice trailed off before he took a shaky breath, 'if I wasn't so overwhelmed with the grief of missing her every time I've tried to get up to dance since the car accident. It just hurts too much. I tried a couple of times in the early years after we lost her, but it was just too painful. So, I don't try any more.'

His words stopped abruptly as Harriet suddenly stepped forward to draw him into a hug. He dropped his head onto her shoulder and drew strength from her warmth and kindness as she comforted him.

'Why didn't you say?' she said, her words muffled by his neck as she held him close.

'Because I've never admitted it to anyone,' he replied.

She didn't say anything more for a while, just stood there in the darkness holding him.

Finally, Joe lifted his head and looked into her face. Her green eyes were filled with kindness and concern as she stared up at him.

'I'm sorry,' he told her.

Harriet shook her head. 'It's okay,' she murmured, reaching up to hold his cheek with her hand.

Then she drew his head down towards her, and once their lips met, Joe forgot about everything but Harriet.

Sometime later, when he drew back but still held her in his arms, she spoke again.

'Come on,' she said, taking his hand in hers and starting to walk towards Cranfield.

'Where are we going?' he asked.

'Home,' she told him as she led him towards Lavender Cottage.

In the darkness of the bedroom, Joe took her in his arms once more. He felt more at peace than he had done for years. He realised that by sharing his darkest secret, he felt lighter. He wondered how much time he had wasted and lost by keeping everything locked inside. But as her lips touched his, his thoughts were of nothing but Harriet.

49

It was the summer bank holiday, and Harriet was grateful to see blue skies and sunshine on the very last day that the lavender fields would be open to the public later that morning.

As Paddington rushed ahead of her, she stood at the corner of the field and looked across the landscape. The purple of the flower heads had faded a little now that the end of August was approaching, the intensity of the early weeks diminished, but there was still a blur of colour spreading out up to the brow of the hill and beyond. The grass in between each of the plants was faded and brown. After a couple of weeks without rain, the sun had baked the grass and the flower heads as well.

Time and summer were moving on quickly. Rain was forecast later on in the week, and the daylight hours were beginning to shorten already. There were still the occasional hot sticky days, but it was now dark by nine o'clock in the evening, and there was a real sense of the year jumping onwards to the next season.

At least with autumn just around the corner, she had a semi-successful business with regards to the beauty salon. People were coming in for treatments all the time, specifically with the use of the lavender products, and her diary was almost full for the next couple of weeks.

It was hard work, and Harriet didn't think she had ever felt so tired in all of her life, but it was strangely satisfying as well. It was less a beauty salon, despite the name, and more a place to chat and catch up as well. It was still quite basic inside the old station post room and most definitely not the upper-class salon that she had owned previously, but it had a much nicer feel, and people often popped in just to say hello.

She felt much more confident these days and had even begun to send her family the occasional text with photos of both the lavender fields and the lavender spa. The response from her parents and siblings had been muted praise, but Harriet was happy to take any kind of compliment from them.

She continued to walk through the rows of lavender, noting their fading flowers. Maggie and the other helpers had made a huge difference in manning the kiosk and car parks over the previous weeks, as well as providing delicious refreshments. Libby had even had success creating some lavender-topped chocolate truffles, which had proved popular as well.

And then there was Joe. Harriet gave out a little sigh as she stopped to watch a bumble bee make its progress from flower to flower on a nearby row of lavender

These had been the best weeks of her life but also the worst as well. The thought of Joe and his sweet kisses made her smile to herself. Each night was spent in the bliss of his arms, but the days were running into each other so quickly, and the end of summer had suddenly arrived.

She knew that he had nothing to keep him in Cranfield but her, and surely she wasn't enough when he had his career on the line? The old doubts over her own worth had resurfaced, and with it, her old habit of hiding her true feelings had rushed forward once more to the forefront. So, she smiled and kissed him, falling more and more in love with Joe each and every day whilst expecting him to leave at any moment.

With another sigh, she turned around, and Paddington swept past her, hoping that maybe they would have an early breakfast instead of a dip in the river.

The dog had been a huge comfort to her these past few weeks, and when the foster lady had rung Harriet the previous night to say that her broken arm was mended and that she could take him off her hands, Harriet had found herself offering to keep him instead.

'How wonderful!' the woman had told her. 'He's got a home at last. And in Cranfield. It was obviously meant to be!'

Harriet had felt a little teary, but it was most definitely the right thing to do. Paddington belonged on Railway Lane, and so did she. Lavender Cottage was hers if the lavender spa continued to succeed, and Paddington would be alongside her every day too. On the verge of losing Joe, she couldn't bear the thought of losing the dog as well.

* * *

The last day rushed past in another busy blur of visitors, all desperate to visit the lavender fields one last time before it closed.

'We'll be back next year,' they all said as they left.

'Let's hope so,' she had replied each time.

Harriet was still keeping everything crossed that they had done enough to persuade the council not to get rid of the fields, that they had an actual viable business here to be cherished. But now it was at an end, and as she locked up the gate, she wondered if it was for the very last time. Was all the hard work for nothing? She just didn't know.

All the other helpers seemed to have left early, leaving somewhat of an anticlimax to the whole summer. Even Joe had gone on without her.

Harriet felt a little despondent as she walked across the path towards the pedestrian bridge, with Paddington rushing ahead of her. Was this the end of Joe? Of the lavender fields? She felt a little teary as she began a slow descent up and over the bridge.

She stopped and briefly looked back at the view. It really was glorious as the sun began to sink down behind the large oak tree. What a summer it had been. Trying to save the lavender field, reconnecting with her best friends once more, and Joe. He had been the biggest revelation of all.

She turned away from the view she knew so well and walked down the steps to the other side, deep in thought. She was so lost in her thoughts that she had almost reached the bottom step when she realised that there was a small crowd on the platform looking up at her expectantly.

'Hello,' she said, automatically fixing a smile on her face at the small gathering of her friends from the village. 'What's all this?'

There were some exchanged glances before Eddie burst into song, 'For she's a jolly good fellow.' And everyone else joined in.

Harriet felt emotional as they came to a somewhat ragged end of the song and blushed as they all clapped.

'We just wanted to say thank you from the bottom of our hearts,' said Maggie. 'You've worked so hard, and it's given us all a chance to fight for the lavender fields as well and feel like we've contributed to something special. You've made a huge difference, and we're so grateful. So, three cheers for Harriet.'

As they hip-hip-hoorayed, Harriet hung her head and tried not to cry. How could she tell them that it might not be enough? That she might have failed despite everyone's best efforts and hard work.

'Hey, don't cry,' said Libby, marching up to smother Harriet with a hug.

'You've done your best,' added Flora, embracing them both. 'That's all anyone can ask.'

'Where's Rachel?' said Bob, looking around. 'Thought she'd be here by now. Anyway, we've got a bottle of champagne somewhere gathering dust. Let me go grab it, and we'll have a proper toast.'

There was much excited conversation as everyone gathered around Harriet. She smiled and nodded as they all chatted away to her, her eyes searching the crowd until she found Joe's. He was watching her and smiling softly.

'Where's that champagne?' said Grams. 'I'm that parched. I'll have to go and get a bottle of gin from home if Bob doesn't hurry up.'

'Here he comes,' said Flora.

But Harriet immediately noticed that Bob wasn't holding a bottle of champagne but an envelope instead. He was looking extremely distraught.

'Whatever's the matter?' asked Harriet, rushing towards him. He appeared to be very upset.

'It's Rachel,' he stammered, holding out the letter in front of him. 'I think she's left me.'

50

The villagers gathered around Bob in shocked silence as he stood on the platform holding a letter in his shaking hand. Joe felt equally stunned as he looked at Bob, who appeared utterly devastated. Had Rachel really just walked out on the marriage like that?

Finally, somebody spoke.

'Where's she gone?' asked Maggie.

'Spain, according to the note,' whispered Libby, who had taken the note from Bob to read.

Joe watched as Harriet stepped forward to give Bob a hug.

'I'm sorry,' Bob told her. 'This should be a happy night to celebrate the end of the summer.'

'It's fine,' she told him, giving him a gentle hug. 'You're all that matters right now. Have you rung your boys?'

He nodded. 'They're both trying to get flights home. Ryan's working in Rome, and Ethan's been in Dubai.'

'Good,' she said. 'You need your family around you at times like this.'

Her words struck a nerve with Joe. Harriet had lost the two members of her family who had been her rock during the worst of times. He was lucky that he still had his dad, and they were starting to talk a little more these days, although they still needed to have a conversation about Joe's future with regard to the business. He had continued to put off that most difficult of talks, but he knew that the blissful last few weeks couldn't carry on for much longer. Now that the summer was over and the lavender fields closed for business, there was no excuse to stay any longer. But that would mean leaving Cranfield and, worst of all, Harriet.

The days and nights he had spent with her over the past weeks had been the happiest he had ever known. He hadn't told her that he loved her, nor had she said the same to him. Perhaps that was for the best, he thought. Despite how he really felt about her. Wasn't his plan to move away now that the summer was over? Wasn't it best that he didn't get too close, no matter how he longed to kiss her and hold her in his arms forever more?

Even now, standing near her on the platform, he could see the freckles on her nose and the shine on that luscious red hair.

He took a step backwards and found himself stepping on someone's foot.

'Sorry,' he said, spinning around.

He came face to face with Dodgy Del.

'All right?' said Del with a nod. 'Poor old Uncle Bob, eh? This is why I keep my girlfriends at a one-month maximum.'

Nearby, Eddie rolled his eyes. 'My great-nephew, the Cranfield Valentino,' he said. 'Anyway, seeing as how your last girlfriend threw you out and that you're now squatting on my sofa, I wouldn't be bragging about your romantic entanglements if I were you.'

Joe gave a start, his mind suddenly racing in an unexpected direction. 'What did you say?' he asked.

But as Eddie started to reply, Joe wasn't listening. Instead, he was staring across the railway track at the lavender fields beyond.

An idea was forming, and he was trying to make sense of what it meant.

'Excuse me,' he said to Eddie and Del before rushing over to where Harriet was talking with Libby and Flora in hushed tones.

'Come with me,' he said, taking her hand and leading her to the edge of the platform, where he turned to face her. 'How long did you say your uncle had been tending the plants here?' he asked.

Harriet looked a bit shocked at his question. 'I don't know,' replied Harriet.

'I do,' said Bob, who was standing nearby, still looking shell-shocked. 'It was probably just over twenty years ago.'

'And when did he put up that shed?' asked Joe, starting to feel excited.

'I'm not sure.' Bob turned to ask his father, but Eddie had already come over to join them.

'What's going on?' asked Eddie.

'Joe wants to know when Fred put up that shed in the lavender field,' Bob told him.

Joe held his breath as he waited for the answer.

Eddie thought for a moment. 'Same time as when he built the summer house. It was sixteen years ago,' said Eddie finally. 'I remember giving him a hand. It was the last winter before the station closed.'

Joe stood still for a moment before bursting into laughter.

Harriet looked up at him in stunned amazement, as if wondering what all this was about.

'Squatters' rights!' said Joe, feeling a massive grin spread across his face.

'What?' said Harriet, still confused. 'I don't understand.'

But Eddie interrupted. 'I do!' he said, beaming as he clapped a hand on Joe's shoulder. 'That's it, lad. You've done it!'

'Done what?' asked Harriet, bemused.

'He's saved the lavender fields!' said Eddie, rushing off to tell everyone else.

That left Joe standing alone with Harriet.

Joe took her by the shoulders and tried to explain. 'A long-term squatter can become the registered owner of any property or land that they've occupied without the owner's permission,' he told her.

'But we don't know who the owner of the lavender fields is,' Harriet told him, looking confused.

'That doesn't matter,' Joe replied, smiling at her as if to reassure Harriet that this was good news. 'By building a shed and tending the fields for over ten years, it became your uncle's rightful land. And, as your uncle's successor, you can apply to the government to take ownership of the land. It's called squatters' rights. It's all legal and above board.'

Harriet was silent for a moment. 'Which means...?' she began to say.

'Which means that you will legally own the lavender fields and that the council can't do anything about it!' finished Joe, laughing. 'I can't believe I've been so stupid! I should have thought of squatters' rights ages ago!'

Harriet stared up at him as the gasp went up around the platform whilst Eddie explained Joe's idea.

Joe looked down at her with a soft smile. 'It means that the lavender fields will be safe for generations to come.'

A huge cheer went up, and suddenly everyone on the platform was hugging and shouting.

Harriet appeared to be in shock, unable to take it all in.

Joe and Harriet still stared at each other. He nodded his head. It's true, he told her with his eyes.

Suddenly, she burst into tears of happiness and leapt into Joe's arms. He could feel her shaking as he held her tight, wrapping his arms around her.

'It's okay,' he murmured against her hair. 'It's all going to be okay from now on.'

She pulled back from his shoulder and looked up at him. 'I can't believe it,' she said, trying to blink away the tears that were still pouring from her eyes.

He pulled up his hand and brushed her cheek with his thumb, trying to help wipe the tears away.

She gave him a teary smile before heading over to see her friends and celebrate the saving of the lavender fields. Joe watched her for a moment, already missing having her in his arms. Whatever happened in the future, he had helped to save the lavender fields at long last. Cranfield was saved too, and so was the small community that lived there.

However, he had only thought of Harriet. He had done it for her, because he loved her. But he had to leave Cranfield, didn't he?

Joe was left hoping that perhaps if he could do something as amazing as save the lavender fields, then maybe he could just find a future for himself and Harriet as well.

51

Everyone seemed happy to help out with the pruning of the lavender fields for the second time that year.

'And we won't have to do it in spring now that we've done it at the proper time for harvesting,' Harriet told the group that had offered to help.

The lavender fields were saved. The council had admitted defeat, and there was nothing but huge relief as the stress of the recent months disappeared into nothing. Harriet could live in Lavender Cottage and look out over the lavender fields for many years to come.

Thrilled that the future was now secure in Cranfield, she had even plucked up the courage to send a text message to her dad. To her amazement, she had received a phone call in response. He told her that he was pleased, even proud of her.

'I guess we're not all alike,' he had said. 'Fred and I were never close, and it's a shame that it's the same for you and your brother and sister. But I'm glad that the lavender fields are safe. For the family and for you.'

And she had felt her heart heal a little because of it.

But, for some reason, she wasn't fully happy. She knew it was because she was still counting down to when Joe would leave. She tried to make the most of it, knowing that every kiss might be the last one, every night could be the final one they spent together.

She looked around at the people that were helping with the lavender harvest. She was thankful to have Libby and Flora, as well as Maggie, there. Bob and Eddie had also joined in. At least Bob seemed happy to be keeping busy and had come out of the station for the first time since his wife Rachel had walked out a few days earlier.

'It's a terrible thing,' Eddie had told Harriet quietly when they couldn't be overheard. 'But Rachel has been unhappy for so long. Sometimes it's better to be happy apart than miserable together.'

Their eldest son, Ryan, had arrived to stay with his dad and had offered to help with the harvest. Harriet and Libby managed to have a quiet chat with him when his dad was up the other end of the field.

'How's your dad doing?' asked Libby.

Ryan blew out a long sigh. 'Not good,' he told them.

Libby and Flora had gone to school with the Connolly brothers, Ryan and Ethan, and so they knew each other pretty well throughout childhood. After sixth form, the brothers had spread their wings a bit and ended up on opposite sides of the world. Libby had always had an acrimonious relationship with the younger brother Ethan in particular.

'When's that brat of a brother of yours coming home?' she asked with a snarl.

'He's on his way.' Ryan grinned. 'Absence hasn't made the heart grow fonder yet, Libs?' he asked.

She snorted a note of derision. 'Not absent for long enough, as far as I'm concerned.'

Harriet rolled her eyes. 'You're still harbouring a grudge after all these years?' she asked.

'He ruined my prom, and I'll never forgive him,' said Libby, sticking her chin out in stubborn disapproval. 'However, I am willing to put up with him being in the same village as me for a few days if he's coming home to comfort his dad.'

Ryan's smile dropped. 'I'm not sure anything's going to comfort Dad,' he said sadly. 'He's still in shock, I reckon.'

'What about your mum?' asked Harriet.

'She's living the high life in Spain and tells us she's never been happier,' said Ryan, running a hand through his hair. 'What a mess.'

'What will you do?' asked Harriet.

'I don't know,' replied Ryan with a shrug. 'I'm between jobs, so I thought I'd stick around for a while and keep an eye on him. The whole place is in chaos, and it wasn't exactly tidy to begin with.'

Harriet looked across the field to the station, which was looking particularly forlorn and abandoned in the bright sunshine. The blue of the sky and the green of the fields made the station appear even more faded and derelict. She decided to hang up a few of the lavender bunches under the eaves of the platform roof to give it a bit of cheer, but it was going to need a lot more work than that for it to get into a decent-looking condition. Quite a few of the lavender field customers had enquired about the closed station but seemed put off by the run-down state of the place. Perhaps a spruce-up would help, especially if the upstairs apartment where Bob and his family lived was in that bad a state.

Of course, Harriet didn't have the kind of time on her hands to offer to help. Each day she was flat out with beauty treatments in the old post room. So much so that she had had to block out a whole weekend for the pruning. Otherwise, she wouldn't have had the time.

At the end of the first day, she glanced over at the huge sacks of lavender flowers that were beginning to be piled up nearby. They all needed to be checked and properly sorted before she could send them over to Eleanor's Apothecary to start to turn them into various creams and treatments. Thankfully, the weather was dry and sunny, perfect for harvesting.

'What a lovely day,' said Maggie. 'And tomorrow's weather looks good as well.'

'Let's have a celebration,' said Joe, who had been standing nearby. 'I think we could all do with blowing off a bit of steam after all our hard work this summer. And there's lots to celebrate too.'

He smiled at Harriet, causing her heart to flutter as she smiled back at him.

She loved him, that much she knew.

He had stayed on to help with the harvesting of the lavender, but she knew in her heart that their time together had come to an end. They had just one more day before he had to leave, and her heart would break forever.

52

The harvest festival was a great celebration, thought Joe, and good timing as well. The pruning of the lavender was complete, and it felt as if the summer was coming to an end.

He was pleased that he had made a hasty phone call to his dad to join them for the party, but he was feeling nervous at the conversation that he knew had to take place that evening.

He suggested they take in the view and wandered over to sit on the bench under the old oak tree. It was a favourite spot of Joe's, where he often spent time with Harriet, so it was strange, but not unsettling, to be sitting there with his dad instead.

'This is lovely,' said his dad, looking across the landscape and across to the station.

They both watched as Harriet laughed and chatted away with Ryan and Bob at the nearby celebration.

'She's a lovely girl,' said his dad in an approving tone.

'She is.'

Joe watched how Harriet's red hair glinted in the setting sun and itched to run his hands through it. It was like an irresistible force that kept pulling him towards her.

'So how did the lavender field business go in the end?' asked his dad, interrupting Joe's thoughts. 'Is it viable?'

Joe nodded. 'I think it will be, going forward into next summer. Visitor numbers should increase year on year.'

'I see.'

His dad had taken the news that the fields weren't up for sale any more remarkably calmly, Joe thought.

'So, what's your plan?' asked his dad.

Joe turned to look at him. 'Why do you assume I always have a plan?'

'Because that's how you've coped so well with everything in the past,' his dad told him. 'But I suppose my main concern is, are you happy?'

It was a question that startled him. 'I think so,' said Joe slowly after a long pause. 'Or at least I'm beginning to find out what makes me happy.' He found his eyes drawn to Harriet once more as she carried on chatting with Bob.

'It's not the family business that I've built up though, is it?' said his dad.

Joe was surprised. 'What do you mean?' he asked.

'I've watched you, son. Your heart isn't in it any more,' said his dad.

Joe wanted to shake his head, but he couldn't deny his feelings any more. 'I don't think it is, Dad,' he blurted out. 'I'm sorry. I know that you wanted me to take over eventually.'

'Don't be,' said his dad. 'It was my business to start, and you've coped admirably whilst I've been, er, well, recovering from losing your mother.'

Joe took a deep breath. His dad hardly ever mentioned his mum these days.

'So, what's wrong?' asked his dad.

Joe finally said the words that he had carried within himself for so long, the frustration spilling out as he spoke. 'I just want to care about the businesses that I deal with,' he began. 'Help them in some way. I don't know. I feel different suddenly, or at least I finally feel something, and I like it.'

His dad nodded but didn't speak.

'We don't help anyone, by which I mean the little people,' carried on Joe. 'The small companies get lost somehow. We just help to set up more and more multinational businesses. It's not right, nor is it fair on the communities that are impacted.'

Joe finally stopped and waited for his dad to speak.

'I agree.'

Joe was stunned and spun around to look at his dad. 'You do?' he asked.

His dad nodded. 'Yes. I think times have changed, and perhaps we both have as well after a tough few years.' He looked at his son. 'So, what are you going to do about it?'

'Me?' Joe smiled. 'It's your business, Dad.'

But his dad shook his head. 'It's time for me to retire and for you to take over. Of course, you've already done that these past few years.'

'That would mean I could take the business in a new direction,' said Joe slowly, trying to get his head around the changes. 'I want to invest in local companies. Rural ones, I mean. Give them a decent business plan and help them to strategise for the future. It would be a new eco-focused business, with people and community at the heart of decisions that affect them.'

His dad nodded. 'It sounds like you're all set then.'

Joe was grateful for his dad's support and encouragement. He could feel the excitement building inside of him. He could help people properly and make a real difference at last. The future was looking much brighter suddenly.

It was also going to be a business where he could work

anywhere and not necessarily be based in his soulless flat in London.

'I'm proud of you, son.' It was said so quietly that Joe almost missed it.

'Thanks, Dad.'

'And your mum would have been as well.'

Joe gulped back the emotion that was making his throat thick with tears, so he just nodded and smiled at his dad, grateful that they could finally begin to talk about his mum again, that perhaps time had started to heal their shared grief.

'And whilst you do that, I might make a few changes myself. Even retire out here in the countryside.'

'And leave your clubs in London?' asked Joe, laughing.

'Turns out folks are more friendly here,' said his dad. 'And the chance to dabble with an old steam train is too good an opportunity to miss, to be honest. Of course, if you lived here, I could visit fairly often. So, there's a few decisions to be made for us both, I reckon.'

Joe nodded. As he looked across the fields, his gaze went from the train workshop, past the station, to the railway cottages, where he found himself breaking into a smile.

'Well, you did always have the best ideas, Dad,' he said, the future spreading out in front of him. And he knew exactly the person he wanted to share that future with.

53

After the conversation with his dad, Joe wandered around the party with a beer in his hand, feeling far more relaxed now that the future of the business was decided.

He smiled and chatted away with the villagers. It was incredible to him how many people he had gotten to know over the summer. They were becoming – dare he even think it? – friends.

His dad had certainly made friends. He was now chatting with Bob and Eddie. Joe didn't need to eavesdrop to know that it was almost certainly about the steam engine. There were some abandoned carriages on the old track as well, but it was the actual steam locomotive that had drawn his dad's interest.

'Are they still talking about trains?'

Joe turned to see Ryan, Bob's eldest son, standing next to him. 'I would put money on it,' he replied.

They had spoken briefly, and Joe thought that it might be nice to have another male of a similar age around. He found Ryan funny, with a dry sense of humour. Although not perhaps quite as much as his younger brother Ethan, who had just arrived and was currently the centre of attention as he told an outlandish story of various exploits he had endured in Dubai.

'And you should have seen the camel!' he said as the adoring crowd roared with laughter.

Ryan rolled his eyes. 'My baby brother, the serious businessman.'

'Maybe it's not a bad thing to be not so serious,' said Joe out loud before catching Ryan's enquiring look. He smiled. 'I used to be too serious myself, according to quite a few people around here.'

'That's because they don't have so much going on in their lives,' said Ryan. 'Or maybe they do these days, thanks to the lavender fields that apparently you helped save. Quite the success.' He grimaced. 'Wish someone would do the same with the station for my dad. It's in a right mess.'

'You could always roll up your sleeves and get stuck in yourself,' said a voice behind them.

They both turned around to see Libby heading towards them.

'Pass me the duster and I'll be there,' said Ryan, taking a sip of his beer.

'Are you and your despicable brother sticking around for a while?' As ever, Libby was straight to the point.

Ryan smiled. 'Can't speak for Ethan. He'll be off on another adventure very soon, no doubt, but I'll be here for a while.'

'Good,' said Libby. 'You're far more responsible than he ever was anyway. Now, push off, will you? I need to speak to Joe here.'

'You know, just because you're older now doesn't mean you can get away with being rude,' said Ryan with a grin.

'Rubbish,' replied Libby, laughing. 'I was always rude.'

'Yes, you were,' said Ryan, joining in with her laughter. 'In which case, I'll go grab another beer.'

When he had gone away, Joe looked at Libby expectantly. 'Am I about to get a telling-off as well?' he asked.

'Absolutely,' she said, suddenly looking stern, to his surprise.

'What have I done to possibly upset you?' he asked. 'Aren't you pleased about the lavender fields being saved?'

'Ecstatic,' she replied, looking a little more cheerful. 'It feels like a weight has been lifted from everyone's shoulders. Thank you.'

Joe was confused. 'So, what's the matter?'

'Nothing whatsoever with me, you great idiot. I'm talking about Harriet,' she replied.

'Harriet?' Joe was astounded. 'Is she upset?'

'Not that she would tell you anyway.'

Joe's mind was racing. 'What have I done?' he asked.

'It's what you're going to do that's upsetting her,' replied Libby. 'So, when do you leave to go back to the big bad world of profit margins and all that rubbish?'

'Actually, I'm starting a new business venture,' Joe told her.

Libby frowned. 'Which is what exactly?'

'It's something I've been thinking about for a while now,' Joe told her. 'I'm going to change my dad's business with regard to what kind of projects will be taken on. I've decided to use our resources to invest in local businesses at the heart of rural communities to try to get them on their feet when they need help.'

'Heart of rural communities,' repeated Libby. 'Hard to do when you're about to leave to go live in London, I'd say.'

'I don't think that I've said anything about leaving,' remarked Joe, frowning.

'And yet you haven't said anything about staying either,' said Libby in a pointed tone. 'So, what's a girl to think? That you just kiss her and take off into the sunset.'

Joe was aghast. 'I see.' He surprised them both by kissing her on the cheek. 'Thank you,' he told her softly.

'Go,' she urged him. 'Go find our girl and tell her how you feel. I've just seen her heading towards the bridge.'

But just as he was crossing the field to catch up with Harriet, his path was blocked by Grams of all people.

'Dance with us, young man,' she said, taking his hand and dragging him towards where both Flora and Maggie were also dancing to the music coming out of a Bluetooth speaker.

Joe tried to shake his head, but there was no choice when Grams made her mind up about things. So, under her extreme urging, he began to sway to the music and in time to the beat.

At first, he was tense, fully expecting the bad memories to come rushing back. But they didn't, and he found himself actually relaxing as he moved. Fifteen years was a long time to live without music in his life. He had always enjoyed dancing. It was too long to live without love as well. And he had found the right girl, he suddenly thought. Hidden away in the tiny village of Cranfield, he had found love and a life as well.

It was as if the fog of the past few years had lifted. He could see again and feel again too. And it was all Harriet.

The world had shifted. His world was now a shared world with Harriet. One he didn't want to lose.

He was reminded of the first time they had met, her wild hair flying. She was full of life. So much had happened since then. So much had changed. And now he knew what it was like to kiss her and hold her in his arms, and he wanted that to last forever.

He laughed to himself. It was so obvious to him now. It was time to live and to love.

He abruptly stopped moving and turned around to leave.

'Where are you going?' asked Grams.

Joe smiled at her. 'To find my dance partner,' he replied before heading off towards the bridge.

54

Harriet had been enjoying the party right up until the moment when she had been crossing the bridge and looked back to see Joe dancing with Grams, Flora and Maggie.

At which point, her heart broke into a million pieces. So it wasn't that he didn't dance. He just didn't dance with her. He didn't care. He didn't love her. He didn't feel the same way about her at all.

She bit her lip to stop herself from crying and turned away to rush down the other side of the bridge and into the darkness of the platform. She had been heading home to get some more snacks for the party, but now she just wanted to stay there in the shadows and hide away forever more. She couldn't believe what she had seen. She kept trying to tell herself to stop being so stupid, but she couldn't help herself. She was heartbroken.

But amongst the heartbreak, she was also grateful as she listened to the sound of laughter drifting across from the party. Wasn't it remarkable, she thought, how two lavender fields could bring about such positive changes for so many people? Even now, with Bob being upset, helping out with the pruning had given him a sense of purpose for the past couple of days. Maggie had completely come out of her shell, and even Grams seemed more full of life than ever.

But what about me? Harriet leant against one of the lamposts on the platform and wondered. Well, she had brought about great change in her own life as well. She had a new salon which she loved, and a dog which she adored. Her neighbours had become her friends, and she could live in Cranfield, right next to her best friends, not just for holidays but forever more if she wanted. Nearly all her dreams had come true.

Harriet looked across the fields and felt a little teary. The purple flower heads were gone for another year, but left in their place was the fresh green, and in the spring, the new growth would start all over again, with hopefully another glorious display of the purple colours next summer. And the business would survive for her to see it. But now she knew that Joe wouldn't be there alongside her to enjoy the success as well. She wasn't important enough to him.

She turned away from the party and stared down the railway track, where it disappeared into the inky black night beyond the engine workshop.

She could hear the laughter and merriment of the party over the other side of the line and was happy for everyone. Joy had returned to the village, but there was none for her that evening. If ever again, she thought before laughing at herself for being so melodramatic.

'Well, that's a good sign.'

Harriet spun around and found Joe walking towards her.

'I thought you looked upset, but if you're laughing...' But his voice trailed off as he looked at her stricken face. 'You are upset! What's the matter? What's happened?'

'Nothing,' she said, quickly turning away. 'I'm fine.'

She heard him sigh with impatience. 'Please don't lie to me,' he said, coming to stand in front of her. 'I thought we'd moved past all that.'

He reached out to take her hand, but she held it back from him. 'When I was crossing the bridge, I saw you dancing,' she told him.

'Grams wouldn't take no for an answer.' He sighed. 'There's quite clearly something the matter. Tell me.'

She hesitated, thinking it would sound ridiculous, but she finally spoke. 'Well, it's great that you dance now. It really is, but...'

'But what?' he prompted.

'You danced with them and not me.'

There, she had said it out loud. She rolled her eyes inwardly at herself. She could even feel her bottom lip jutting out like a petulant child.

'This is all your fault,' she told him. 'You told me to be honest with everyone, and now look at me! Anyway, I thought you didn't dance.'

She tempted a glance up at his face and saw that he was smiling at her.

'I'm thinking it might have hidden advantages,' he told her.

'Like what?' she said, unable to look away from his eyes, which were full of desire.

'Such as it gives me the perfect excuse to hold you close,' he said, taking a step forward. 'Yes, I danced with the other ladies tonight. And yes, it was the first time in a very long time that I've danced with anyone and not been overwhelmed with grief. But now that I've found my feet and can dance again, I realised that I only want to dance with you.'

Harriet blinked as she took in his words and stared up at him. His eyes told her that he was telling her the truth.

'And I know that as soon as I take you into my arms to dance,' he carried on, 'there's a very real danger that I might never let you go again.'

The silence stretched out as they looked at each other.

'Personally, I think we should take that chance,' she finally said with a soft smile.

He laughed and reached out to pull her against him. He wrapped his arms around her and began to sway in time to the distant beat of the music being played in the lavender field.

'Well, don't say I didn't warn you,' he told her before leaning his head down to kiss her.

It was a kiss unlike the others that had come before. It felt real, definitive and permanent.

When they finally drew apart, he spoke once more.

'I thought I was numb,' he told her. 'That the world held nothing for me and that I couldn't feel anything, but this, right here, right now, I can finally feel something. I feel you. Only you.'

He kissed her once more with a passion that almost took her breath away.

'I love you,' he carried on when he finally lifted his head. He looked a little concerned. 'But you're actually silent for once, so forgive me if I'm starting to panic, but—'

'Oh, Joe!' said Harriet, pulling him to her to shower his face in kisses. 'I love you too. It's always been you.'

'Thank God,' he murmured before pulling her close and kissing her properly once more.

Sometime later, they drew apart.

'But what about your work? Aren't you leaving?' she asked, staring up at him in wonder. Was this really happening? Was this real? She was pretty certain it was and still couldn't believe how happy she felt.

'I've decided to work from home,' he replied.

'Oh.' That brought her up short. Was he going back to his fancy flat after all?

'And Cranfield is my home,' he told her with a gentle smile. 'Or wherever you are, in fact.'

Her shoulders sank in relief.

'I need to be near you,' he carried on. 'We're a team, aren't we? Facing everything together.'

'Absolutely,' she told him, stroking his face with her hand. 'But actually, it's more than that. I feel like I can do anything when I'm with you.'

'You can,' he replied. 'You can save a lavender field. Mend a broken village. You can do anything.'

'As long as you're with me,' she told him.

'Always,' he replied. 'That's how long you're stuck with me for.'

The passionate kiss he then gave her confirmed his promise. It was only when they finally drew apart that Harriet realised that they weren't alone. Paddington had rushed up to them to lean against their legs, making sure that he was included in their future plans.

But that wasn't all.

Over her shoulder, Joe stared into the darkness before bursting into laughter. Harriet turned around and saw that the party had now moved to the top of the bridge whilst they had been kissing. Everyone was looking down at them, clapping and cheering.

'Told you so!' she heard Libby shout.

Harriet turned back to look at the love of her life. 'Well, I guess you're not my secret love any more,' she said.

'No,' he told her. 'I'm your forever love.'

'Yes, you are,' she replied, just as their lips met once more.

55

One month later, Joe walked back from his evening stroll, with Paddington racing through the rows of lavender plants ahead of him.

Autumn had arrived now, and there was a chill in the air. Not that he minded the changing of the seasons. In fact, because he was out in the countryside so often these days, it was a pleasure to watch as nature began its spectacular display. The trees along the boundary of the field had changed to a kaleidoscope of yellows, oranges and reds. The lavender plants all looked healthy as well, shaped into perfect spheres by the recent pruning.

The cut lavender was drying everywhere. Bunches were hung up in the eaves of the station platform, in Uncle Fred's shed and especially all around Lavender Cottage. It was the scent of home to him.

He thought back to a year ago, wondering where he was at that time. It would probably have been in some bland hotel or meeting room. What a difference to the colourful world he now found himself in each and every day.

He was relaxed and, more importantly, enjoying his work. He

had already begun to build up a portfolio of local businesses that he was trying to help. Rural communities needed investment and advice, all of which he was starting to gain knowledge of. In fact, he was already being approached by further businesses through word of mouth. He could apply the knowledge that he had built up over the years, but this time, he felt as if it was doing some good and making a difference to people's lives.

His best friend, Matt, had been helping advise on the rural businesses.

'Maybe you're a good guy after all,' he had joked the previous day on the phone.

Joe's dad had also been impressed when Joe had shown him some of his recent work. They were much closer these days. He had spent the past few weeks carefully nurturing a closer relationship with his dad. With Harriet's encouragement, his dad had been invited to Lavender Cottage for Sunday lunch that weekend, which he had eagerly accepted. Joe was grateful that they were both so close and that his dad always turned up with a couple of treats in his pocket for Paddington.

The short-term rental of the apartment in Cranbridge had finished, and both Joe and Harriet had been keen for him to move into Lavender Cottage full-time. Together with the dog, it made for a very happy home. One where music was often playing in the kitchen where he worked at the table. Music had returned to his life, and he felt all the better for it.

As he walked past one of the large oak trees, he glanced up at the initials of Harriet's aunt and uncle. He hoped that they would have approved of him. Harriet had assured him of as much.

At least the lavender fields were saved. That gave Joe great pride that they could be enjoyed for generations to come. The council had reluctantly agreed that Harriet's uncle had indeed secured squatters' rights, and therefore the land rightly came under her inheritance. They had been named Cranfield Lavender Fields because, as Harriet had told him, 'They belong to everyone here.'

For Joe, they were the beginning and the heart of the relationship between him and Harriet. He glanced over at the other oak tree, where only the past weekend, he and Harriet had carved their own initials into the bark. It was a promise of a shared love for the long future ahead. He was certain now it would be forever.

As he and Paddington headed back over the bridge, he saw that the light was still on in the old post room. Harriet was obviously still working in the lavender spa, which had become such a success. It was a bright spot amongst the derelict railway station, although Ethan, Bob's youngest son, had told him that he had an idea about how to change the place. It certainly needed it, thought Joe.

As he reached the platform, he saw Ryan at the other end.

'Beer? Tomorrow night?' shouted Ryan down the platform.

'Sounds good!' called out Joe in reply.

Ryan had stayed on after their mum had walked out to keep an eye on Bob. He and Joe had started to become close friends, enjoying a mutual interest in football and rural businesses.

Paddington had already rushed ahead up to the door to the salon, and as he passed the front window, Joe glanced in and smiled to himself, as he always did when he saw Harriet. His life had been transformed ever since that first day when he saw her dancing in the middle of the lane. He counted his blessings each and every day that she was in his life.

Cranfield was his home, but it was Harriet that made it feel that way. He was so grateful to have her as his partner and forever love.

He pushed the door and headed inside.

56

Harriet had switched the radio on after her last client had left. The post room was looking cosier now that she had added a few finishing touches, such as soft lighting and some shelves.

Of course, the best feature was the aroma of lavender that came from the products that she used. Eleanor had already come up with some exciting new product ranges using the lavender that had been recently pruned, and Harriet couldn't wait to start using them.

The lavender spa business was going well. Joe had already created a brand new, even better website with photographs from that summer of the lavender fields in full bloom. In addition, he was planning to list the lavender beauty products online for more sales.

The reviews they had received so far were very positive, and Harriet woke up every morning excited about what the day would bring.

Next summer, the lavender would bloom again, hopefully bringing even more visitors. For her, summer would always be a special time, filled with memories of her aunt and uncle and now with falling in love with Joe as well.

The magic of the lavender had healed and restored her, and it could be enjoyed for many generations to come.

The lavender also seemed to have had a knock-on effect on the villagers of Cranfield as well. Flora was thinking about diversifying the business on the farm and had begun to talk tentatively about a hopeful future for both her and Grams. Libby had well and truly caught the chocolate bug and had started experimenting with all sorts of flavours in her spare time. Maggie was still baking and talking about spending the winter trying out new recipes.

Harriet had kept a couple of boxes of lavender back for herself, but there was still plenty left over from the harvest for everyone to use. Although, Dodgy Del had come up with the idea to make lavender beer, which everyone was desperately trying to avoid tasting.

After work, she would head home to Lavender Cottage, which was warm and lived in once more. It was a measured mix of old and new, much like herself, she felt. She would always carry the sweet memories and happy times with her aunt and uncle with her, but she also now had the confidence that they had tried to instil in her from an early age. She could do anything, she felt. With the love and support of a good man, she added to herself, smiling.

Harriet allowed herself a happy sigh. Life had changed so much over the summer but having Joe by her side was the biggest and happiest change of all. He supported her, listened to her and, most of all, loved her. And she loved him right back.

'Dancing Queen' came onto the radio, and Harriet laughed to herself. All those months ago, she had thought Joe a cold fish, someone who only cared about himself and business. She now knew that had been totally untrue. He was warm and funny, generous and loving. She loved every minute she spent with him, and together with Paddington, they had turned the cottage back into a warm and happy home.

She glanced over at the framed photograph on one of the new shelves. It was a picture of Aunt May and Uncle Fred in the middle of the lavender fields many summers ago. She blew them a kiss, grateful that the lavender plants would remain in place for many years to come, their legacy both to her and to the people of Cranfield.

She suddenly remembered Aunt May's advice about dancing in the rain. Well, it had been sunny albeit cold that day, but there was always time for dancing, wasn't there?

She had just begun to move and spin around when the front door to the salon opened, and Paddington rushed inside ahead of Joe.

'Hello,' she said, bending down to give the dog a cuddle before looking up at Joe. 'How was your walk?'

'It's definitely turning colder out there,' he told her. 'We thought we might pick you up on the way home before lighting a fire and getting cosy.'

'I was just finishing up,' she replied.

Joe put his head on one side as he listened to the song. 'Harriet Colgan,' he said in a mock stern voice. 'Have you been dancing without me again?'

To her delighted surprise, he shrugged off his coat and moved forward to take her in his arms.

Harriet giggled and relished having him so close to her. She didn't think that thrill would ever fade.

As they began to move together from side to side, Harriet glanced over and saw Paddington settle down on the rug and close his eyes in contentment, happy to sneak in a pre-dinner snooze as long as there would be food at the end of it.

'Why, Mr Randall,' said Harriet, as she moved her hands up to the back of his neck to press her body against his, 'you wouldn't be dancing, would you? And in a public place too?'

Joe's eyes gleamed with love as he drew her even closer. 'Some dance partners are worth waiting for,' he said as he brought his head down to kiss her.

ACKNOWLEDGMENTS

A huge thank you to my lovely editor Caroline Ridding for her continuing support and encouragement as we embark on our third series together!

Thank you to everyone at Boldwood Books for all their hard work, especially Jade Craddock for her wonderful work yet again on the copy edits.

Thank you also to all the support and cheer from all my lovely fellow Team Boldwood authors.

Thank you to all the readers and bloggers for their enthusiasm and reviews, which are so important to so many authors, myself included.

Thank you to all my friends, especially Jo Botelle, for being just as encouraging with this, my 12th book, as she was with the very first one all those years ago.

Huge thanks to my wonderful family for all their continued support, especially Gill, Simon, Louise, Ross, Lee, Cara and Sian.

Special thanks once more to Dave for first discovering the lavender field for me and for his tireless support when I needed to test out a cream tea on the Bluebell Railway line! As always, this book could have never been written without your love and support.

MORE FROM ALISON SHERLOCK

We hope you enjoyed reading *Heading Home to Lavender Cottage*. If you did, please leave a review.

If you'd like to gift a copy, this book is also available as an ebook, digital audio download and audiobook CD.

Sign up to Alison Sherlock's mailing list for news, competitions and updates on future books.

https://bit.ly/AlisonSherlockNewsletter

Explore more feel-good novels from Alison Sherlock.

ABOUT THE AUTHOR

Alison Sherlock is the author of the bestselling *Willow Tree Hall* books. Alison enjoyed reading and writing stories from an early age and gave up office life to follow her dream.

Follow Alison on social media:

- facebook.com/alison.sherlock.73
- twitter.com/AlisonSherlock
- bookbub.com/authors/alison-sherlock

Boldwœd

Boldwood Books is an award-winning fiction publishing company seeking out the best stories from around the world.

Find out more at www.boldwoodbooks.com

Join our reader community for brilliant books, competitions and offers!

Follow us
@BoldwoodBooks
@BookandTonic

Sign up to our weekly deals newsletter

https://bit.ly/BoldwoodBNewsletter

Milton Keynes UK
Ingram Content Group UK Ltd.
UKHW040756040124
435437UK00004B/228

9 781804 264348